Being
Livi Starling

The **Livi Starling** series

Being Livi Starling

Karen Rosario Ingerslev

PURE&FIRE

Being Livi Starling
First published in the UK by Pure & Fire in 2016
Pure & Fire, England
www.pureandfire.com

ISBN: 978-0-9934327-2-9
eBook ISBN: 978-0-9934327-3-6

'Before I formed you in the womb I knew you...'
— Jeremiah 1:5

~ 1 ~

Being sensible and responsible

The easiest way to get rid of an unwanted Christmas present is to leave it outside the house with a sign that says, *'For sale.'* My sister Jill did this with a garden gnome from our aunt and within twenty minutes someone had nicked it.

When Aunt Claudia gave us the three-foot gnome she did so with the full knowledge that we don't have a garden. However, she likes to treat people as they *'ought'* to be, instead of as they are.

"Nobody in their right minds would live in a house without a garden," she scoffed when we moved in last summer.

"It's all we could afford," Jill tried to explain.

Our aunt just tutted and said, "Don't be daft."

She seems to think that us renting a tiny house in Leeds is a momentary blip on our path to a proper life. To some extent Jill lives up to this by pretending to be a businesswoman and buying *'Horse and Home'* magazine.

The gnome, who I'd named Basil, was terribly miserable-looking. He wore an ugly sneer and carried a rifle. We had used him as a hat rack for a few weeks but, after mistaking him for a miniature burglar for the third morning in a row, Jill declared he had to go. So she tied a *Waitrose* carrier bag to his gun and priced him at £50 which no doubt contributed to his swift removal.

The day of Basil's eviction ought to have been a happy occasion. For months I had been begging Jill to let us redecorate the house[1] and that morning she had finally conceded.

"We'll do it next weekend," she announced over lunch.

---

[1] I imagine that the old man who lived here before us had a passion for the circus; most of the peeling walls are covered with grey bears and the door knobs are shaped like clowns.

I nearly fell out of my chair with excitement, not least because Jill, who is usually rather uptight and unreasonable, even granted me the honour of deciding what colour to paint the hallway.

"You're getting older now, Livi," she said, handing me a recent edition of 'Horse and Home.' It was open on a double-page spread: 'Painting the Townhouse Red: French Puce is the New Black.'

"I am."

"I need to take you seriously."

"You do," I agreed, grateful for an opportunity to prove my maturity. I considered the magazine article and assured her she was doing the right thing.

But, that evening, I went on to prove her wrong by almost setting fire to my head.

Despite the fact that this was the coldest winter we had ever known, Jill was determined to save as much money as possible by keeping the heating off. Today had been particularly icy and I was shivering at the kitchen table as I attempted to do my homework in mittens. I was supposed to be drawing a self portrait for Art but was shaking so much that my picture looked more like a depiction of a crazed monkey. The mittens didn't help and, as I reached clumsily for an eraser, I dropped my pen on the floor. I growled and bent down to retrieve it. Suddenly, a gentle warmth caressed my face. I looked across in surprise. The oven was on. Jill had left it to pre-heat before putting a pie in for dinner. I slipped off my chair and crawled over to the oven, sighing with joy as I leant my frozen head against the door.

"That's so nice!" I murmured.

I took my mittens off and pressed my hands against the oven. Then, without really thinking, I carefully opened the door and leant in, turning from side to side as the glorious heat embraced me.

"Livi!" Jill's sudden shriek made me jump.

"Ow!" I exclaimed as I whacked my head on the oven.

"What are you doing?" My sister yanked me out by the arm.

"I was cold."

"What?" Jill looked at me as though I was mad.

"I was just warming up my hair."

She didn't reply.

I forced a smile. "It's warm enough to put the pie in now."

"This isn't funny," Jill warned.

"It was just a mistake..."

"A stupid mistake!" Jill exploded. "You could have really hurt yourself."

"Well, I didn't," I said with a sniff. "You don't have to keep banging on about it."

But she *did* keep banging on about it. For a full twenty minutes. And then she phoned Aunt Claudia and got her to bang on about it too.

"You must show some sense, Livi," my aunt squawked down the line. "Don't upset your darling sister!"

I had half a mind to tell her what my darling sister had done to Basil the gnome. Instead I grunted and assured her I was trying.

"Very trying," Jill muttered beside me.

Later that evening, feeling slightly unnerved following what Jill had called my *'most idiotic act to date,'* I decided to seek some wisdom from the Bible. I was pretty sure Jesus had never put his head in an oven and I needed a quick burst of maturity in case Jill reconsidered her decision to let me help pick the paints. I sat in the lounge, curled up on the sofa, pondering where to begin.

"Show me what to do..." I whispered, running a hopeful finger across the soft pink edges.

I flicked through the pages, trying to find something useful, but kept getting distracted by the melodrama of a tacky soap opera. I glared at the television and debated turning it off but we always keep it on at the weekend and I didn't want to do anything out of the ordinary because Jill still didn't know about my decision to follow Jesus. I was pretty sure she would disapprove because the only Christians we know are our neighbours, the Ricos, and they are rather weird— apart from Ruby who is my best friend.[2]

After I had tentatively broken the news to Ruby's family that I was *'sort of a Christian now,'* her mother, Belinda, had let out a squeal, hugged me senseless, and rushed out to buy me a brand new Bible. It was bright pink and emblazoned with sequins and white flowers— incredibly beautiful but far too conspicuous. On this particular occasion I had hidden it inside a copy of *'Hot Gossip'* in the hopes that Jill wouldn't notice me reading it and be alarmed.

I felt nervous as I thumbed through the delicate book. It had only been three weeks since my hasty conversion and I still wasn't sure what to expect. I didn't even know if I had done things right. All I'd done was concede that God was probably real and that I believed Jesus had died for me and that I needed his help to live right. I didn't really feel any different after I'd done it and it had

---

[2] Well, my *only* friend, but whatever.

seemed that everybody else was more excited than me. Ruby's younger brother, Oscar, had broken into raucous singing,[3] and her older sister, Violet, had grabbed me with both hands and screamed, "I hear you've met Jesus!"

I pulled away and said awkwardly, "I didn't actually *meet* him. I just prayed a prayer with Ruby."

She laughed and said, "Oh Livi!" which I took to mean that something exciting was about to happen because Violet hardly ever laughs.

So, that evening, I put on my best dress and tidied my bedroom in anticipation of Jesus arriving. All through dinner I could barely contain my excitement.

Jill kept looking at me strangely and asking what was so funny.

"Nothing," I said smugly, thinking how shocked she would be when Jesus turned up.

"Why are you wearing your nice dress?"

"Just because... Can we save some sausages?"

"What for?"

"You'll see..."

But Jesus didn't come and, when I asked Ruby about it the next day, she giggled and said, "Violet didn't mean meeting him like *that*. She just meant you had asked him into your life."

My heart sunk. "Oh."

"Don't worry. You'll know him more deeply as time goes on."

"How?"

"By talking to him and spending time with him. And by reading the Bible." Ruby indicated my Bible which, at that time, was concealed in a school newsletter about nits.

"Right then," I said resolutely. "I'll read the Bible."

Originally, I had determined to read the whole book from beginning to end in the hopes that Jesus would appear when I finished it. But, despite my best efforts, I was struggling to make it through Genesis. The beginning was interesting; about how God made the world and all the business with the snake, and how Adam and Eve got banished from the garden in Eden and what happened when they had to go it alone without God. But, after the flood, it got a bit boring. Instead, I had taken to flicking through it sporadically in the hopes that this constituted a Bible study.

---

[3] *"Boom boom boom, I hear the heartbeat of my Lord! Boom boom BOOM! Let the lion ROAR!"*

On this occasion, my study (which I had titled *'Being Sensible and Responsible'*) was particularly unproductive, what with the distraction of the television and the awkwardness of my mittens.

After about half an hour Jill came in and I hastily raised the front of the magazine so that the Bible was definitely out of sight.

"Hi," I said cheerily.

Jill glanced over at the magazine and gave an approving nod. "Anything interesting?"

In actual fact, I had just stumbled upon a story about a donkey speaking, but I wasn't sure this was the hot gossip she was expecting. I carefully folded over the page in the Bible and turned quickly to the magazine. "There's a new series of *'Sing for Survival'*[4] coming soon," I said nonchalantly.

Jill snorted. "What's that about?" She pointed to a story on the cover: *'My traitor budgie spied on me.'*

I shrugged. "Dunno."

"Read it out."

"I don't want to." I shuffled the Bible uncomfortably as Jill tried to peer over my shoulder.

"Let me have a look then."

"No!" I slammed the magazine shut and shoved the whole thing under my jumper. "It's *my* magazine."

Jill looked at me in surprise. "Come on, Livi. Don't be selfish."

I felt my cheeks grow hot as I gave a growl. "You can read it later," I snapped, running for the door.

"It's just a magazine!" Jill yelled as I stormed up the stairs.

"You don't understand!"

"What's there to understand? You've been acting weird all day. Just when I thought I could trust you to be sensible."

I ran to my room and thrust the Bible under my bed. So much for expanding my wisdom; now I looked even stupider than ever! I sighed and vowed that from now on I would only read it at night.

I pulled off my mittens and went to the window. A figure in a dark coat was shuffling across the street and, for the briefest moment, I thought it might be Jesus, coming to save the day.

But it wasn't Jesus. It was the thief who'd taken Basil. I watched in astonishment as he placed Basil in front of our house and lined up a further three gnomes beside him. He left a note too: *'Please accept my apologies. I don't know what I was thinking.'*

---

[4] A reality TV show where contestants are placed on a desert island and have to impress the public with their singing to be rescued.

Ms Sorenson's tin of truth

In the end I decided on *Electric Lime* for the hallway. I saw Jill wrinkle up her nose as I added a pot to our shopping trolley. It looked especially garish beside her stack of *Average Magnolia* for the rest of the house.

"Can I get some for my room as well?" I asked eagerly.

"No. Your room is fine the way it is."

"It's brown!"

Jill sighed and did some sums on her fingers. "This will have to do for now. Wait till I've earned a bit more."

"Okay," I muttered. I knew better than to push any further. Jill is always getting stressed about money and comments like, *'But money is paper so it does grow on trees!'* tend to irritate her.

I called Ruby when we got home and asked if she wanted to help us paint the house.

"Seriously?" Ruby shrieked down the phone. "I'd love to!"

If it were the other way round I'm not sure I'd be quite so enthusiastic, but Ruby is dependable like that. She arrived in a shower cap and a bright green tunic.

"What are you wearing?" I asked in confusion.

"My painting outfit. Mum said I should cover up so I don't get paint on myself."

"That's great, Ruby," Jill said dryly. "You'll match the hallway."

I'm not sure this was a compliment, but Ruby grinned and said, "Thanks!"

I held up the tin of *Electric Lime*. "Jill let me choose it," I told her proudly.

Ruby nodded in approval and grabbed a brush.

My sister gave a curt smile and disappeared into the lounge.

"The rest of the house is going to be really boring," I continued in a whisper to Ruby. "So we'd better make this look good."

"Alright..." She dipped her brush in the paint.

"Try it out," I said as I loaded up my roller.

Ruby gave another solemn nod and carefully slapped a stripe of neon green onto the middle of the wall.

We stood back to inspect it.

"Yeah," I said. "That will look good."

We worked in silence for a while, careful not to let any of the paint drip down the skirting boards. Jill had cleared the hallway of any clutter and covered the floor with newspaper but, even so, I was determined to make a neater job of the hallway than she would of the living room.

"What are they?" Ruby asked suddenly, pointing to a pile of bodies on the stairs.

"Oh, those are our gnomes. The one with the gun is Basil. I haven't named the others yet."

Ruby raised her eyebrows.

"We didn't buy them," I added. "But Jill's scared that if we throw them away we'll end up with even more."

Ruby gave a confused giggle.

"You can name one if you want."

"Really?" Ruby put her brush down and went over to the gnomes. "I like this one!" She patted a stout little fellow with enormous feet and a faint moustache. "Can we call it Molly?"

"You mean after Molly Masterson?" I asked with a guffaw.[5]

"No! I meant after my Great Aunt Molly. She had a moustache."

I gave a little splutter. "Seriously?"

"Well, it was actually a scar. But it looked a bit like that." She ran a finger across the gnome's ugly face. "Oh, hang on... Is it meant to be a man?"

"Yes!"

"Oh!" Ruby put a hand to her mouth. "Not Molly then. I'll think of something else."

"It's alright," I said. "I think Molly suits it." I would certainly enjoy giving it a kick every time I went down the stairs.

An hour or so later we finished the hallway and tried to look sensible as Jill came out of the lounge to inspect our work. I saw her grimace at how bright the walls were but she didn't complain.

---

[5] Molly Masterson is one of my least favourite people in the world. Her best friend, Kitty Warrington, is the coolest girl at school. We were sort of friends for a day but it didn't last.

"There's still some paint left," I said hopefully. "Can I use it for my room?"

Jill nodded and went back into the lounge.

I grinned at Ruby and we ran up the stairs, pausing briefly to add a spot of paint to the gnomes' cheeks.

"I might call them Molly, Kitty, Melody and Annie after their whole gang!" I declared. "The one with its bottom out can be Kitty."

"That's not very nice."

"I'm only joking!"

"No you're not."

I rolled my eyes. "So what? They're horrible people."

She didn't reply.

"Don't you remember what Kitty said in Science the other day?" I reminded her. "She said your face looked like an exploded pumpkin."

Ruby shot me a wounded look. "I *know*. But that doesn't mean I should be nasty back."

I peered at her. Ruby is rarely mean about anybody. It must be boring to always be so nice. "Are you scared in case God tells you off?" I challenged.

Ruby laughed. "No, Livi. I'm not afraid of that."

I gave a careless sniff. "Well, me neither. Anyway, let's paint." I forced a grin and stomped up to my bedroom.

Ruby adjusted her shower cap and followed me up.

We didn't speak much after that. I was too lazy to remove the furniture from my room so it required quite a lot of concentration to paint around everything. Unfortunately, we ran out of paint halfway through so I ended up with two lime walls and two brown ones. It looks a bit like a kiwi.

~*~

I started this school term with a brand new pencil case which I had resolved to keep as neat as possible. But, less than a month in, it is covered in splodges of *Electric Lime* paint, animal doodles[6] and a short ode to Audrey Sorenson, my favourite teacher.

---

[6] Documenting all the animal noises I am determined to perfect this year, including *Worried Whale*, *Presumptuous Duck* and *Mild-Mannered Grizzly Bear*.

'Her name is Audrey
She is never tawdry
But always groovy.'

Ms Sorenson teaches Personal and Social Development, potentially the most crucial class in the curriculum. Last term, Ruby and I did a project on dinosaurs, offering carefully considered proof that they never died out. And, for the first couple of weeks after the Christmas break, we examined the many wonderful differences between males and females where a particular highlight was Ms Sorenson drawing everyone's attention to my painting of an Adam's apple,[7] so it was with great anticipation that we headed to her lesson the following Monday.

The chairs had been arranged into a circle. The class broke into hushed whispers. Something exciting was about to happen.

Ms Sorenson was sitting behind her desk, writing in her filofax. "Come in and sit down," she said, indicating the circle.

We ran to the chairs like a group of small children in a party game, desperate not to be left without a seat. Kitty Warrington and her gang were squealing inanely as they secured the seats nearest the window and then proceeded to vet those interested in sitting beside them. The boys took the opportunity to engage in a spot of wrestling and Wayne Purdy ended up face down on the floor. Ruby and I tried to look nonchalant as we joined the rumpus but, in truth, we were desperate to sit as close as possible to where Ms Sorenson had parked her register.

I lunged across the coveted seats just before Connie Harper who shot me a cold look and said, "I was going to sit there."

I tried to be polite. "Well, it doesn't really matter, does it? It's just a seat."

Connie was about to reply but Ms Sorenson suddenly got our attention by slamming something heavy down on her desk. "If you've quite finished!" she yelled.

The class immediately fell silent and those who were on the floor shuffled sheepishly into a seat. Ruby sunk into the chair

---

[7] We had also watched a rather bizarre sex education video which featured aliens from outer space warbling, "How do they make babies on *your* planet?" Halfway through, Ms Sorenson had branded it *'a load of nonsense'* and switched it off. Her straight-talking lecture was certainly a lot more informative although I was a little disappointed that we never found out how the aliens do it.

beside me and shot Connie a timid smile. Connie scowled and went to sit on the other side of the circle.

Ms Sorenson strode towards us holding the heavy thing that she had slammed on the table. It was a tin of beans.

I looked at Ruby in confusion. Were we going to learn how to cook? I supposed that was a vital part of Personal and Social Development. It just might tread slightly on the toes of Miss Day, our Food Technology teacher.

The rest of the class looked equally bemused. I saw Kitty nudge Molly and snigger.

To my disappointment, Ms Sorenson didn't take the seat beside me. Instead, she took another empty seat on the other side of the circle— which happened to be next to Connie Harper.

"If you want to speak," Ms Sorenson said. "You must wait until the tin is passed to you." She waved the beans at us. "If you don't want to speak, simply pass the tin on." She gave a thin smile and handed the tin to Connie.

Connie gulped before hurriedly passing the tin to Fran Gorman, who was beside her. Fran smirked and gave it to Freddie Singh. Freddie sniffed the tin and handed it to Wayne Purdy. Wayne frantically gave it to Ritchie Jones as though it were a ticking bomb.

We went on in this manner, with the whole class keeping mute as they passed the tin on. A few people paused, as though they were considering saying something, but most people sent it on as hastily as possible. Molly passed it so fast that it landed on Annie Button's foot and Ms Sorenson made her pick it up and do it again.

When the tin got to me, I gave it to Ruby as carefully as possible, feeling my cheeks grow hot as I did so.

The tin arrived back in Ms Sorenson's lap without anyone uttering a word. I thought she might tell us off for not having the guts to speak. Or at least make some sarcastic comment like, *'Oh now you're all silent.'* But she didn't. She just smiled and said, "Well done. Let's go round again. This time, and only if you *want* to speak, I would like you to tell us something you did over the Christmas break." She paused before adding, "I caught up with some old school friends in Dublin."

She gave the tin to Connie who thought for a moment before saying, "We played lots of games."

Fran took the tin and said, "I made an igloo with my brother."

As the tin went round and my classmates shared their tales of family fun and festivity, a deep ache bubbled inside me. My

Christmas had been awful. It had begun with the surprise revelation that my father had once been Jill's fiancé and that I was no more than the unexpected product of a hideous affair between him and our mother. In other words, I was a total mistake. After this bombshell he disappeared and I've not heard from him since. We had then spent a boring week at Aunt Claudia's eating endless plates of lamb, the highlight of Christmas day being visiting my mother's grave and wondering what life was really all about.

Although... I inhaled sharply. The *end* of the holidays hadn't been so bad. That's when I'd decided to give God a go and say yes to the whole Christian thing. I know it had been hasty and it still didn't feel like anything had changed... but still, I was fairly sure it had been a good decision. I just wasn't sure why yet.

I chewed the inside of my cheek as I considered what I could say. '*I became a Christian...*' Too geeky. '*I found God...*' Too whimsical. '*I gave my life to Jesus...*' Too freaky. I sighed. No matter how it's said, it isn't exactly the sort of thing any sane person would share in front of a class.

Kitty Warrington had the tin. "Over Christmas, I saw Leeds from the sky. In my dad's helicopter."

"An *actual* helicopter?" Wayne asked in shock, clasping a hand to his mouth for breaking the '*no-speaking-without-the-tin*' rule.

Kitty turned her nose up at him. "Obviously."

My classmates exchanged astonished glances. I felt my stomach knot even tighter.

Suddenly it was my turn. I took the tin from Aaron Tang who was beside me and held it clumsily on my lap. It was cold and heavy. I sucked in my breath as I felt the hungry gaze of my classmates upon me. I debated sending it on without speaking but everybody else had said something so I'd look like a weirdo if I didn't. Plus, people might think I'd had a dreadful Christmas or something.

"Erm..." I began helplessly. I looked up and caught Ms Sorenson's eye.

She gave a kind smile and I quickly looked away.

"Well..." I stuttered. "I, erm..." I bit my lip.

Across from me, I saw Kitty and Molly exchanging smirks.

I was about to say that I'd acquired an ugly collection of gnomes but, without thinking, I blurted out, "I went to Los Angeles with my dad."

A few of my classmates looked impressed.

"The *actual* Los Angeles?" asked Wayne.

"Yeah," I said coolly. "He's sort of an actor so he gets to travel round the world and sometimes he lets me come. He was... making a film."

The class gaped at me and started asking questions.

"What's the film called?"

"When is it on?"

"Is he famous?"

I blushed and cleared my throat but, to my relief, Ms Sorenson silenced the questioning. "No speaking unless you are holding the tin!"

My classmates continued to gawp earnestly (apart from Ruby, of course, but I deliberately avoided her gaze). I opened my mouth to add some wild twist, perhaps that I had been given a part as an extra. But the words wouldn't come. I gave a coy shrug and passed the tin on.

When everybody had finished Ms Sorenson sent the tin round once more and asked us to name our favourite meal. Again, I felt at a loss at what to say. Jill's cooking is rather unadventurous to say the least and a typical dinner for us is a microwave meal or a takeaway. Would 'Macaroni cheese' really be a fitting answer for the daughter of a film star? In the end, I said I liked pizza. I figured this was ambiguous enough because you can put almost anything on a pizza so it's not necessarily just for poor people. For example, on my favourite TV show, 'Freaky Human,' they recently showed footage of a pizza covered with lobster and flakes of gold.

The tin went round another three times and each time I felt increasingly more anxious. I didn't want to describe my favourite possession, or what I would do to make the world a better place, or my dream holiday.[8] I kept stealing glances at Ms Sorenson and wondering whether we were getting marked on our answers. I didn't want her to think I was stupid.

Finally, the lesson came to an end. I gave a relieved sigh and picked up my bag. We had finished the exercise with the only question I had felt safe enough to answer truthfully: my favourite colour.[9]

---

[8] What I said: My locket with my name on; Plant fruit trees across Africa to feed the poor; A safari adventure with my father. The *truth:* My teddy, Sausage-Legs; Give each young person a pet of their choice; *Anywhere* with my mother.

[9] Yellow.

As she dismissed us, Ms Sorenson waved the tin in the air and said, "Thank you all for your honesty." This made me feel truly awful.

On our way out of the classroom Annie Button said loudly, "I didn't know Livi's dad was an actor."

"So what?" Kitty sneered. "My uncle was the Lord Mayor of Leeds."

"Do you live in a mansion?" Annie asked me.

"Of course she doesn't," Melody Vickers piped up. "She lives in a council house in Wormley."

"It's not a council house," I said fiercely. "We have a landlord called Mr Bentley."

"Do you have a maid?" Annie continued.

"He can't be a very *good* actor," Molly interrupted. "Otherwise we'd have heard of him."

A few of our classmates turned and looked at me.

"Well, he is," I muttered, rushing away before anyone else could join in.

I felt terrible for the rest of the day. Ms Sorenson's lesson went round and round in my head and I wished I could go back in time and change my answers.

'This Christmas, I saw a deer in the snow,' I would say. That was true and perfectly valid. Why hadn't I thought of it earlier? Why had I lied? It tormented me all through Maths. I couldn't concentrate on my geometry worksheet and just sat in a daze, shamefully poking holes through my new pencil case with my compass.

Another thought struck me: I was used to telling people that my dad was an actor. I'd done it for the whole of the last term. *What was so different now?*

I gave Ruby a poke with my compass.

"Ow!" she exclaimed. "What?"

"Why do I feel so guilty?"

"Because you just stabbed me with your compass?"

"No. I've been feeling like this since Ms Sorenson's class."

Ruby gave me a funny look. "What do you mean?"

I shifted uncomfortably and whispered, "I feel bad for saying my dad is an actor. But I've never felt bad about it before."

Ruby gave a long nod and grinned. "That's the Holy Spirit."

"The what?" I turned around sharply. "Where?"

"Inside you."

"What?"

"When you asked Jesus into your life, he gave you the Holy Spirit. It's God, inside you." She shrugged as though she were explaining something as simple as me eating a funny pie.

My jaw dropped open. "God is *inside* me?"

"Yup."

"Like actually inside my body?"

"In your spirit." Ruby grabbed some paper and did a quick sketch of a box. "Imagine a massive temple," she said, scribbling furiously. "God's presence used to be in the most sacred part of the temple, inside a place called the *Holy of Holies.*" She indicated the box. "It was kept behind a curtain where only the priests were allowed to go. Nobody else could get near..." She drew a stick man falling dead at the sight of the box.

I raised an eyebrow.

"When Jesus died, the curtain got ripped in two." Ruby slashed her drawing violently and beamed at me. "Now, there's no need for the temple because the *Holy of Holies* is God's people. God lives in *us* and *we* are the priests."

"I'm a priest?"

"Yup."

"An actual priest? Like, will I get some robes and stuff?"

Ruby giggled. "Well, no. It just means you can go directly to God. You can talk to him and hear from him and *know* him yourself. You don't need somebody else to go on your behalf. Do you get it?"

I had no idea. I thought for a moment and then muttered, "So... I can't lie anymore?"

Ruby smiled oddly. "Well, you *can*. But you might not want to."

I let out a long sigh. "God is *inside* me?" I repeated.

"Yeah."

"Just because I said a prayer?"

"Yeah."

"This God stuff is weird."

Ruby kept grinning. "You'll see."

~ **3** ~

I don't feel any different

The following Sunday, I announced that I would be going to church that morning.

"Again?" my sister said in surprise.[10] "Watch out or they'll convert you!"

I forced a laugh and reached for some toast. "Yeah, whatever."

Jill eyed me suspiciously. "Isn't it boring?"

"It's alright. Sometimes the preaching drags on. But I like the songs."

She wrinkled up her nose. "We had to sing hymns at primary school. I never saw the point."

"They're not really hymns. At least, I don't *think* they are. They're kind of like pop songs but about Jesus."

"Oh." Jill gave an indifferent shrug and sipped her tea.

I munched on my toast and tried to think of something interesting to say. "Sometimes Stanley dances in the aisle."

"What?"

"Ruby's dad. He dances."

"What do you mean, *Ruby's dad dances?*"

"You know..." I waved my arms about in a floaty manner. "Like this."

Jill burst out laughing. "What an idiot. You'll have to take a video on your phone for me."

I felt my cheeks burn. I hadn't meant to make fun of Stanley. I was just trying to trick Jill into thinking she was missing out. I thought for a moment before saying casually, "You've never been to church, have you?"

"I've been to plenty of weddings," she replied shortly. "And three funerals."

---

[10] I'd gone twice that month already.

"Normal church is a bit different."

Jill gave me a funny look but didn't reply. She finished her tea and went to pour herself another.

I lingered at the table, fiddling with my chair leg. "Do you have any other questions?"

"No." Jill opened a heavy folder and started to do some work.

"Okay."

I watched her in silence, wishing I knew what to say next. Before I could think of anything, there was a loud knock at the front door.

I stood up. "That will be Ruby."

Jill nodded and gave a careless wave. "Have fun with the crazy God Squad."

I attempted a smile before heading for the door.

Ruby's church is called *King of Kings* or *King's Church* for short. They don't have to dress up smart and they don't even meet in a church building. They meet in a school hall and their services are a lot livelier than I'd expected them to be.

Today, as we made our way across the school car park, I tentatively asked whether they were a *'happy-clappy'* church. I'd heard the term on a television show and just wanted to check I wasn't getting into anything too strange.

Stanley laughed. "We *are* happy. And we *do* clap a lot..."

This didn't particularly put my mind at rest. "So... *Are* you a happy-clappy church?"

Violet rolled her eyes and snapped, "We're not a cult, if that's what you're thinking."

I blinked at her. I hadn't been thinking that... I was now.

"We're a little bit happy-clappy, I suppose," Ruby admitted.

"We prefer the term *'charismatic,'*" Belinda added.

That sounded even weirder. I took a deep breath and followed them into the hall. A smiling member of the welcome team handed me a newsletter and said it was nice to see me.

"You too," I muttered.

We wandered over to a row of seats near the front and I plonked myself down, trying to ignore the bustle of happy-clappy charismatic people around me.

Ruby began a conversation with a couple behind us and Violet, who is always in the middle of some bizarre art project, was keen to show off her latest creation: a shabby-looking bag for her Bible. It was made from woven pieces of straw and emblazoned with the words, *'Do not be wise in your own eyes.'* The clasp was shaped like an eye made of buttons. I watched scornfully as the couple told her it was nice.

"Thank you!" Violet grinned before thrusting it in my face. "Some people say it's offensive. But I say God's word is only offensive if you're in sin."

I raised an eyebrow. "Who says it's offensive?"

"A girl in my class. I showed it to her because she's a practising witch. I tried to warn her that she's doing the work of the devil but she took it personally."

I shrugged and turned to the newsletter. There were notices about some upcoming events as well as a handful of prayer requests. Someone by the name of 'Harry Turner' needed prayer for a chronic illness. I looked round in my seat, trying to guess who he might be.

Suddenly, Ruby's mother leant over and gave me an uninvited hug. "Oh Livi!" she trilled. "It's so wonderful to have you here!"

I wriggled out of her grasp. "Thanks."

Belinda is quite dramatic at the best of times but, ever since I told her I was a Christian, she's been almost unbearable. "How's your sister?" she continued earnestly. "Is she keeping well?"

"Yeah, she's fine." I pretended to be engrossed in the newsletter.

"She didn't want to come then?" Belinda persisted.

"No. She doesn't really like church." I didn't add that Jill had called them the *'Crazy God Squad'* before I left.

Belinda gave a soft smile and said nothing.

A few minutes later the worship band came to the front and started playing a song. Most of the congregation got to their feet and began to sing but I stayed in my seat and watched.

The first song contained the line, *'With all of my heart and all of my soul, I love you, Lord. I give you my all.'*

It sounded a little intense. I wasn't sure I could sing those words with any sincerity. I didn't exactly *love* God just yet. I barely knew him. I could perhaps have sung, *'I think you seem rather nice and I'd like to get to know you better...'* but that was as far as my passion would go.

I looked across at Ruby. Her eyes were shut and she had a big dreamy look on her face.

God probably really likes her, I thought with a pang of envy.

I got to my feet, determined to join in with the next song.

'You give the pauper robes
To take the place of kings
You give the weary strength
To soar on eagles' wings...'

I had no idea what it was about but I did my best to sing along with the words on the screen. By the third verse I was feeling more confident. I'd got hold of the tune and even had the fleeting desire to perform my *Eager Eagle* impression during the chorus. As the song came to an end I sat down with a satisfied sigh. *That will do for today,* I thought proudly.

Halfway through the next song, Stanley started to dance. He sort of shimmied into the aisle and hopped about on one leg. I watched him out of the corner of my eye feeling rather unsettled. Was he an idiot, like Jill had said? Or could God possibly find it nice? *Is God happy-clappy?* I wondered in horror. I tried to ignore Stanley as I read the newsletter for the third time.

The singing finally came to an end and a man got up to preach. I sat up straight and forced myself to pay attention as he read a passage from the Bible.

"How great is the love the Father has lavished on us, that we should be called children of God! And that is what we are!" He looked up from his Bible and said, "If you're a follower of Jesus here today then you are a child of God. Do you know that?" He pointed to people in the congregation. "You're a child of God... You're a child of God..." He seemed to look right at me. *"You're a child of God."*

I blushed and ducked my head.

"And, as his child," the man continued, "you have direct access to his throne room."

I cast a glance at Ruby. I wondered if this was the same as the God-in-a-box stuff from the other day.

"When you accepted Jesus as your Saviour, your entire identity changed," the man went on. "You were born again as a child of God and something inside you came alive..."

I exhaled slowly and put a hand to my chest. Had something *really* come alive inside me? Was that the Holy Spirit, as Ruby had said? How could it be possible for everything to be suddenly so different just because of one little prayer to Jesus? And, if I was really God's child now, shouldn't I feel special somehow? I frowned. *Did I definitely, definitely do it right?* I looked at my hands and arms and then peered down my top, looking for some kind of sign that something had changed. Then I glanced up and caught Violet staring at me. She raised her eyebrows and tapped the message on her Bible bag.

I sniffed and tried to concentrate on the preach.

"Since we are God's children, we have been adopted into God's family..."

"That means we're sisters!" Ruby whispered.

I grinned at her and then realised that would make Violet my sister too.

"...and we have a perfect Father who will never let us down."

I bit my lip and looked away. It's all very well having some perfect heavenly Father *somewhere out there*, but it's not the same as having an actual physical dad living in my house.

The man talked for a while longer before concluding his preach by asking whether there was anyone there who hadn't met Jesus yet. "We would love to pray for you if you'd let us," he said.

I debated approaching him privately and saying, "When you talk about meeting Jesus, you really should clarify what you mean. Because I said the prayer but I still haven't actually *met* him yet."

I looked around, curious as to whether anybody would respond. The last couple of times, nobody did. But this week, a man at the side put his hand up.

The preacher nodded and went across to him as the band came up for one last song.

I stood up with the rest of the congregation and attempted to sing along but the song featured the word *'Father'* about twenty times which made me feel increasingly uncomfortable. I was grateful when it was over and sat back down with a heavy sigh.

Ruby sat beside me and grinned.

I forced a smile in return.

"Do you want anything?" she asked.

"What?" I squirmed. I wanted *many* things.

"A drink?" She indicated the rest of her family who had wandered off to join the queue at the refreshments table.

"Oh!" I gulped. "No thanks."

Ruby looked at me curiously. "Are you alright?"

"Yeah," I said quickly. "I was just thinking about the preach."

"It was good, wasn't it?"

"What he said about being God's child..." I shrugged before admitting, "I don't feel any different."

"That's okay. Just keep going."

"To church?"

She giggled. "I mean going on with life. With God."

I opened my mouth to ask what she meant but, before I could say anything, two boys came over.

I felt myself blushing as we stood up to say hello. I had met them a couple of times and knew their names were Joey and Mark but I was yet to have any substantial conversation with either of them as I kept forgetting who was who. It didn't help that they both had blond hair and were about the same height. As they greeted Ruby, I stood awkwardly beside her and looked for ways to tell them apart. One of them had a mole on his chin and a bag covered in badges. The other one had piercing green eyes and bright green trainers. I watched as he swept some hair from his face and scratched his ear. Now that I was staring so intently, I realised that he was actually quite nice-looking. I don't mean that in the soppy teenage girl kind of way. It was just an observation. He suddenly turned to me and I forced a smile and tried to pretend I hadn't been staring.

"How are you, Livi?" he asked.

Hearing a boy say my name made me feel somewhat embarrassed. I'm not sure any of the boys at my school have ever addressed me by my name. They sometimes call me *'New Girl,'* or, *'Country Bumpkin,'* or, with mild distaste, *'What's Your Name Again?'* And, outside of school, I don't really know any boys. Apart from Oscar but he's only three.

"I'm fine," I said shyly. "How are you?"

"I'm great. I made this yesterday!" He unzipped his jacket to reveal a bright red t-shirt emblazoned with the painted words *'J.C is cool.'*

Ruby looked over and laughed. "You're so weird, Joey!"

I made a mental note: *Joey is the one with amazing green eyes.*

"It's nice," I said.

"Do you get it?" He looked at me expectantly.

"Uh..." I could feel myself blushing. "Are they your initials?"

He chuckled. "Yeah, but also... you know, *J.C.* as in *The Great J.C!*"

I gave him a quizzical look.

"Jesus Christ," Ruby whispered.

"Oh!" I blushed again. "Yeah, I get it. Obviously."

Joey grinned. "Mark wants me to make him one with the words, *'History maker: Salt shaker!'*"

I forced a laugh and pretended to know what he meant.

"Because Jesus said we're the salt of the earth," Ruby explained.

"I *know,*" I said quickly.

Mark, who had been rooting around in his bag, emerged with a handful of flyers. "Check these out!" he said, handing them round.

I took one and looked at it. There was a clumsy cartoon of a man praying and another which looked like a man being set on fire. In big red letters was written, *'Repent and be saved! Jesus is coming!'*

"What are you going to do with them?" I asked.

"Hand them out, of course," Mark replied.

I gazed around the room. "Now?"

"No. In the city centre."

My jaw dropped open. "Seriously?"

"Yeah. Do you want to come?"

"No thanks," I said politely. I glanced over at Joey and wondered what he thought of it.

"Mark thinks the end of the world will come at any moment," he informed me.

I looked at Mark in shock but he just nodded proudly.

Then Violet came over and announced that it was time to leave.

Ruby smiled at the boys and said, "See you."

Mark said goodbye and Joey did some peculiar handshake and said, "Until next time, Livi!"

"Bye," I said awkwardly.

I attempted to give Mark his flyer back but he said, "It's alright. Give it to someone who needs Jesus."

I almost snorted as I imagined what Jill would say if I gave it to her. "Okay..." I muttered, shoving it into my pocket as I followed Ruby out of the building.

When I got home Jill asked if I'd had a nice time.[11]

I tried to be nonchalant as I said, "It was alright." I could hardly tell her that I'd learnt I was a child of God. She would think I'd gone crazy.

Jill doesn't mention Jesus much, other than as a swear word, and anything to do with faith tends to make her angry. A few weeks ago Belinda gave her a bookmark with a Bible verse on it and, although Jill received it graciously enough, as soon as Belinda was out of earshot she tore it up and branded her a *'Bible-bashing*

---

[11] What she actually said was, "Survived the God Squad unscathed, then?"

freak.' She says things like, *'People should keep their beliefs to themselves,'* and, *'Religion. It's the cause of all the world's problems.'*

A few months ago I would have agreed. I'd imagined that Christians were mainly self-righteous zealots (like Violet) or simpering do-gooders (like Belinda), and that anything connected with church was likely to be boring. I'd assumed faith in God was just something some people are born with, like a birthmark. I didn't realise that I had a choice in the matter. I never dreamt God could be relevant to *me*.

The church service was on my mind for the rest of the day. As I lay in bed that evening I thought about Ruby and her friends joking around and envied the way they talked about Jesus, as if he was their best buddy or something. I wondered what I should do to be as close to him as they were.

I sent Ruby a quick text. *'I'm not going to lie anymore.'*

A few minutes later, she replied, *'Cool.'*

I rolled my eyes and stared at the ceiling, wondering what else I would need to change. I hoped I wouldn't lose my imagination or my ability to perform animal noises and, more than anything, I hoped my transformation could take place without Jill having to know. I had a sudden moment of panic as I realised the flyer from Mark was still in the pocket of my jeans. Jill was always scolding me for leaving tissues and pens in my pockets before putting clothes in the laundry basket. What would she say if she found Mark's flyer? I didn't want her to call me a Bible-bashing freak. I leapt out of bed and ran all the way to the kitchen.

Jill was at the table eating a yoghurt. "Are you alright?"

I stole a glance at the untouched pile of laundry. "I left something in my jeans."

Jill watched as I trotted to the laundry basket and started poking around. I picked out my jeans and fumbled for the pocket.

"Got it," I said, stuffing the flyer quickly up my sleeve.

Jill raised her eyebrows. "That was close."

I gave a little splutter. "What?"

"I've told you hundreds of times not to leave things in your pockets. Can you imagine what would have happened if you'd left that in there?"

I forced a laugh. "Yeah, it could have been messy."

~ 4 ~

A day in the life of a liar

That night, I had a really odd dream. I dreamt I was walking through a field and came to a beautiful white pony. There was a man nearby and I asked him who the pony belonged to. He said it was my father's and that I could ride it if I wanted. Suddenly I was riding the pony and, even though I've never had lessons, I was cantering at full speed through a forest without falling off.

I told Ruby about it on the way to school. "It was so cool," I said. "I felt like I could do anything."

Ruby grinned. "It sounds like a dream from God!"

I looked at her in surprise. "God?"

"God sometimes gives messages through dreams."

I thought about it before saying flippantly, "Well, it's stupid. My dad doesn't own a pony."

"I don't think it's about your earthly dad," Ruby said quietly. "I think your father in the dream was God and he wants to assure you that you really are his child and... he loves you..." She trailed off.

"Oh." I bit my lip, feeling like I might cry. "So... my dad isn't going to come back on a pony?"

"Sorry, Livi."

I gulped and looked away.

We walked in silence for a bit.

"Do you want to talk about it?" Ruby whispered.

"No," I said quickly.

We kept walking.

With every step, my heart thudded painfully inside me. Eventually I sighed and muttered, "Part of me never wants to see him ever again..." I paused as we reached the school gates. "But another part of me misses him. I don't even know if he's still in Leeds." I let out a loud sob.

"Oh, Livi!" Ruby put an arm around me.

Another sob tumbled out. "If he really was an actor then at least I could get free films or something."

Ruby bit her lip. "I don't know what to say," she confessed.

I rubbed my nose with my sleeve. A few of our classmates were approaching. "Does it look like I've been crying?" I sniffed.

She gave an awkward shrug. "I've got a tissue."

Annie Button squeezed past us as Ruby rooted around in her bag. I turned away and pretended to be fascinated with the peeling paint on the school gates.

"What's wrong?" Annie asked nosily.

"Nothing!" I snapped.

She gave an uncomfortable smile and walked away.

Our first lesson was English. Our teacher, Mrs Tilly, had had quite a dramatic haircut[12] and the whole class said, *"Oooh!"* as she walked in.

"Good morning, everyone," said Mrs Tilly.

The class shifted noisily in response.

"I have some wonderful news for you."

"You've had a haircut, Miss?" guessed Annie.

Mrs Tilly gave a coy smile. "I have, Annie. But that wasn't my news."

Kitty gave Annie a shove and Molly said, "Loser!" which I assume must be high praise since they are her best friends.

"No... My news is a lot more exciting," Mrs Tilly continued.

The last time she teased us like that, she handed out worksheets on verbs. I took no notice and concentrated on some unfinished Maths homework.

Mrs Tilly gave a theatrical sigh. "You're going to create a newspaper!"

I looked up in shock. "An actual newspaper?"

"Yes, Livi. An actual newspaper."

I nudged Ruby. "That's so cool!" I whispered.

Ruby gave half a smile in response.

The rest of the class looked fairly disinterested.

"Will we have to write stuff?" Molly asked warily.

"Of course!" Mrs Tilly exclaimed. "You'll be writing the whole thing."

"What will we write?" demanded someone else.

---

[12] It used to be shoulder length and flat but was now in a thick, bouncy bob.

"I want features on everything. Current affairs, local news, sport, short stories... You'd better start thinking!"

Kitty and Molly exchanged sneers and a few people moaned. By this point, I already had three articles lined up[13] and could hardly believe that nobody else was as excited as me.

I raised my hand. "Can I be the editor?"

Mrs Tilly looked at me. "We'll be discussing that in tomorrow's lesson, Livi." She gave me a kind smile before adding, "Although it will need to be someone with strong reading skills."

"But I—" I stopped abruptly. Due to a careless lie the term before, Mrs Tilly believed that I was unable to read. I had tried every now and then to show 'vast improvement' but she seemed fairly impervious to it.

Behind me, Kitty gave a little hum as she raised her hand. "I'd like to be the editor, Miss," she said sweetly.

Mrs Tilly beamed. "Thank you, Kitty. I will bear that in mind."

I opened my mouth and then closed it again, feeling dizzy as our teacher went into further detail about the project. She had entered us into a local competition called 'Scribes of Yorkshire' in which our class would be competing with schools across the region to create the best newspaper.[14] The winning school, as judged by a panel of professional journalists, would be announced at a special ceremony in a place called Hull and the top prize was a day at a printers as well as two hundred pounds worth of books. We had until the end of term to create our entry and the editor would have the final say on *everything*.

As the lesson drew to an end, I approached our teacher's desk. "Miss, if I learn to read by next lesson, can I be the editor?"

Mrs Tilly shot me a sympathetic smile. "Livi, I'm so pleased with how you're progressing."

I gave her a desperate stare. "Is that a yes?"

She just took my hand and sighed.

That afternoon, we were in Art. Our teacher, Miss Appleby, had just showed off a lino print which she'd made at the weekend. I think the design was of a cat chasing a bird but, from where I was

---

[13] 1: 'How to survive in a new school,' 2: 'A day in the life of an animal impersonator,' and, 3: An as-yet-untitled interview with Ms Sorenson.

[14] According to Mrs Tilly, St. Augustine's School in York have won for the last four years in a row.

sitting, it looked rather shoddy. On our desks were scalpels and pieces of lino so that we could create prints of our own.

"Hey, we should make lino print portraits of each other!" Ruby suggested.

I stifled a yawn. "Yeah, alright." I would usually have enjoyed such a lesson but I was still reeling from our English class and desperate to work out a way to be editor.

At one point Ruby looked up from her work and said with a grin, "I hope you've not given me wonky eyes—" She looked at my untouched lino in confusion. "What are you doing?"

"I'm writing a poem," I said. "I'm going to tell Mrs Tilly that I banged my head in the night and am now miraculously cured. And I'll prove it by reading this out." I pointed to my poem and read, "'*A cacophony of speckled dachshunds arrived at the amphitheatre in Loughborough, ready to perform an exquisite symphony of Tchaikovsky, in honour of the pangolin's bar mitzvah...*' Those are some of the hardest words I could think of. I know it doesn't quite rhyme but does it make sense?"

Ruby was looking at me in bewilderment. "No," she said finally.

I growled at her. "Why not?"

She peered at me. "I thought you weren't going to lie anymore."

I gave a dramatic sigh. "I'm not. This is an old lie. I'm just fixing it."

"By telling another lie?"

I narrowed my eyes at her.

"Why don't you just tell Mrs Tilly the truth?"

I rolled my eyes. "What? That I've been able to read all along?"

"Well... Yeah."

"I want to be the editor," I said angrily. "There's no way she'll let me if she finds out I lied."

Ruby shrugged. "It's a bit far fetched— you learning to read in one night."

"Fine!" I grabbed my poem and tore it in half. "I won't lie."

She beamed. "Well done."

"But I really want to be the editor," I moaned. I had a sudden brilliant idea. "Ruby, *you* should be the editor!"

"Me? I don't want to be the editor."

"I know," I said pointedly. "But I would *help* you."

Ruby blinked at me. "No," she said firmly.

"Come on, Ruby! You wouldn't have to do anything. Just get yourself picked as editor and I'll do the rest."

"I don't want to."

"Please," I begged. "Don't let Kitty take this away from me!"

Ruby pursed her lips. "If I told Mrs Tilly that I wanted to be the editor then I would be lying. And I don't lie."

I glared at her. "What's the point in being a Christian if you can't do anything fun?"

Ruby frowned. "If you want to lie, then lie. You're free to do whatever you want." She turned back to her lino and started going over my hair, hacking at it a little too violently for my liking.

I gave a huff and ignored her.

We didn't speak for the rest of the lesson and I wondered whether this meant we had officially fallen out. But, on our way to Ms Sorenson's class, Ruby gave me a hopeful smile so I stuck out my tongue and gave half a smile in return.

As we entered Ms Sorenson's classroom, we saw that the chairs were set in a circle once again. However, this time when Ms Sorenson invited us to sit down, there was no wild chase for the chairs. We just ambled across the room and took our seats with quiet anticipation.

To my delight, Ms Sorenson took the seat beside me. She looked round at us all and held up her tin of beans.

Something uncomfortable churned in my stomach as I recalled our previous lesson. I eyed the tin with trepidation and wondered what we would have to talk about this time. I clenched my fists and made a vow. *God, I promise I won't lie this time...*

But, rather than give us a topic, Ms Sorenson simply smiled and passed me the tin.

I took it in shock and felt myself blushing. I bit my lip and gave the tin to Ruby. She looked equally alarmed and passed it on.

The tin got all the way round to Kitty without anybody saying anything. I started to relax.

But then Kitty cleared her throat, tapped the tin lightly and proclaimed, "Livi's dad isn't really an actor." She smirked at me.

My jaw fell open.

My classmates gasped and looked at me.

I tried to say, *'Yes he is,'* but the words wouldn't come out. At any rate, I didn't have the tin so I had no right to speak.

Kitty gave a triumphant grin and handed the tin to Molly. Molly let out a giggle and passed the tin on.

Nobody else spoke.

The tin got back to Ms Sorenson and I braced myself for what she might say in response to Kitty's revelation. But she didn't say anything. She just passed me the tin again.

I held it nervously in my lap. Across from me, Kitty and her friends were grinning inanely. The rest of the class were looking at me curiously, as if waiting to hear my defence.

I had no idea what to do. I didn't want to lie again. I *could* have done. But Ruby was right— it no longer felt good. Yet, at the same time, I didn't want to admit the truth and have everybody hate me.

Eventually, I bit my lip and said, "My dad *was* an actor. He's just taking a break." Immediately I felt like I wanted to cry.

I handed the tin to Ruby and she hurriedly passed it on.

The tin reached Kitty again and she said smugly, "Livi's lying. Annie heard her talking to Ruby about it on the way to school. Her dad was *never* an actor. She doesn't even know where he is."

Annie looked a little sheepish as she whispered, "I don't understand why you lied, Livi."

My cheeks prickled with shame. Now it would be even harder to admit the truth. I wondered whether I should say that *Annie* was the one who was lying... but that would make me an even *worse* person.

The tin positively flew back to Ms Sorenson as my classmates waited with bated breath to hear what I would say.

But Ms Sorenson didn't give me the tin again. Instead, she said, "Miss Warrington, could I have a word with you outside, please?"

Kitty gave a nonchalant shrug and got up, exchanging smirks with her friends as she sauntered out of the room.

Ms Sorenson followed her out and the class broke into excited chatter.

"Did you actually lie?" Connie Harper asked me incredulously.

"You're so weird," Molly sneered.

I shifted uncomfortably and attempted a smile. "It's not a big deal."

Nobody smiled back. Even Georgina Harris and Darcy Bell, who are usually reasonably friendly, were muttering in disgust.

Ruby gave me a sympathetic shrug and said nothing.

The only person to take my side was Rupert Crisp, the class geek. "Don't be so cruel," he chastised our classmates. "I, for one, admire Livi's tenacity in not yielding to the tyranny of the tin."

Our classmates shrieked with laughter and started throwing Rupert's briefcase around which, although unfortunate for Rupert, provided a welcome break for me. I sat as still as I could, not daring to look anyone in the eye in case I cracked.

A few minutes later, Kitty came back into the classroom and sidled up to me. "I'm sorry, Livi," she drawled. "I didn't mean to upset you."

I glared at her. "That's okay."

"I shouldn't have said what I said," Kitty continued loudly. She lowered her voice and added in a whisper, "After all, my mum always says we should be nice to orphans."

I clenched my fists in fury but, before I could respond, Ms Sorenson called me from the doorway. "Miss Starling. A word, please."

I felt my cheeks burn as I left the circle. A few of my classmates were giggling and I heard Molly hiss, "You're in trouble, Liar."

I followed Ms Sorenson out of the room, blinking quickly to keep from crying. She didn't say anything for ages and I stared at the floor, sniffing and feeling dreadful.

Eventually, she asked, "Are you alright?"

I nodded dumbly.

"Is there anything you want to say?"

I shrugged before muttering in a whisper, "My dad isn't an actor." A tear slid down my nose. I braced myself and focussed on my feet but Ms Sorenson didn't reply.

"Take a break," she said finally. "And come back in when you're ready."

I looked up in surprise. "Aren't you going to tell me off for lying?"

She smiled grimly. "I don't need to, do I?"

This made me want to cry even more. I sniffed noisily and wiped my eyes with my sleeve. "Sorry," I sobbed.

Ms Sorenson put a hand on my shoulder. "Don't be so hard on yourself." She gave me a soft squeeze before returning to the classroom.

I ran straight to the toilets and locked myself in a cubicle. I sat and cried for ages, not knowing which I felt sorrier for: breaking my promise to God or Ms Sorenson knowing I was a liar.

Everything in me wanted to curl up inside that cubicle and hide until the end of the day. Yet I was also aware of the pressing need to return to class as swiftly and sensibly as possible. If I was absent for too long, my classmates would be sure to take note. It's one thing to be caught out as a liar but being seen to be a coward would be even worse.

After crying into almost a full roll of toilet paper, I blew my nose and unlocked the door. I looked at myself in the mirror. My face looked red and blotchy. I slapped myself a few times and practised smiling.

"I don't care," I said to myself, my voice cracking slightly. I cleared my throat and tried again. "I'm fine, actually."

After slapping myself a bit more, I went back to the classroom. Ms Sorenson acknowledged me with a nod and some of my classmates stared at me as I crossed the room. I forced a smile and rejoined the circle.

Ruby glanced at me in concern. "We're naming fruits," she whispered.

It was Wayne's turn. He said, "Watermelon," then tossed the tin to Ruby.

"Banana," she said shyly before handing it to me.[15]

I felt like I would burst into tears all over again if I tried to say anything so I just stared straight ahead and passed it on.

---

[15] Ruby loves bananas. Well, actually, she loves banana *stickers*. She has over 800 of them. The other day we befriended the owner of the Polish supermarket down the road and he gave us a bag of mouldy bananas (complete with nine Polish stickers) for free.

~ 5 ~

A cunning way to convince Mrs Tilly

M_y classmates were rather divided following my public exposure. Most of them asserted that I was a complete weirdo. But several others seemed to be torn between hating me for lying and pitying me for being 'an orphan,' and the rest accepted the lie that my dad *used* to be an actor and that if I wanted to embellish the truth slightly then that was up to me.

For the whole of Maths I overheard sly comments and the odd snigger in my direction.

At one point Rupert Crisp slipped me a note which read, *'Alterius non sit qui suus esse potest.'* I had no idea what it meant but I knew being seen asking him would invite further ridicule.

"My dad is a spaceman," Kitty said loudly behind me. "No, wait. He's not."

"Mine is a lion tamer," Molly added with a snort. "Hold on, I'm lying. I don't even know where he is!"

A few people laughed. Others gave me pitying stares although they didn't dare challenge Kitty and her gang.

I tried to pretend that I didn't care and concentrated as hard as I could on my work. I didn't even want to look at Ruby. I was scared she might say, *'I told you so.'*

As the lesson came to an end, our teacher, Fester,[16] called me back and asked, "Is something wrong, Livi?"

"No," I said. "Why would something be wrong?"

"Because you did more work in this one lesson than you did for the whole of last term." He gave a wry smile.

"So?"

Fester raised his eyebrows. "Is everything alright at home?"

---

[16] His real name is Mr Lester. If he was an animal, he would be a scarab beetle. He's slightly nicer than a regular beetle but you still wouldn't want him in your house. I'm speaking from experience since Jill dated him briefly last term.

"Of course!" I forced a laugh. The last thing I wanted was him making any contact with Jill.

"Then why the sudden burst of hard work?"

"Sir," I said loudly. "I love Maths. I always have. It's my favourite subject and I'll probably want to study it at university. It just took me a while to feel confident doing it with other people in the same room." I waved my calculator at him and flounced out. *Well, if I'm going to be a liar,* I thought, *I might as well go the whole hog.*

Ruby and I walked in silence all the way home. I was feeling irritated and, although I knew it wasn't Ruby's fault, I did all I could to make it clear that I wasn't in the mood for talking.

Ruby glanced at me occasionally, as if considering saying something, but each time she seemed to think better of it and just sighed loudly instead.

We reached our street where we lingered uncomfortably in front of Ruby's house.

"Want to come and hang out?" Ruby asked tentatively.

I sniffed and fidgeted with my bag. "Yeah," I said finally, smiling awkwardly as I followed her in.

We went into the kitchen where Violet was cooking something smelly.

"Ew," I muttered. "What's that stink?"

Violet looked up from a saucepan. "I'm making soap."

I wrinkled up my nose and went towards her. "Isn't soap meant to smell *nice?*"

Violet pushed me away. "I'm not finished yet."

"Oh..." I peered into her pan. "Why is it yellow?"

"It's cheese flavour."

I let out a splutter. "Cheese flavoured soap? That's so weird!"

Violet ignored me and kept stirring.

I looked at Ruby and she shrugged. I turned back to Violet and tried to think of something funny to say. But, before I could come up with anything, I was hit by something worse than the smell of cheese soap: a pang of guilt. It occurred to me that, although Violet *is* rather weird, it perhaps isn't always nice to point it out.

"Hey, Violet, I didn't mean to offend you or anything. I've just not seen cheese soap before."

"It's fine."

I attempted a smile. "Cool."

"Anyway, I don't expect you to understand me," she continued smugly. "I'm ahead of my time— like the caveman who wanted to fly to the moon."

I raised an eyebrow. "What?"

"Let's go upstairs," Ruby said, pulling me into the hallway.

"They told him it was too small," Violet yelled after us.

"Pardon?" I called back.

"The moon!"

I shook my head and followed Ruby up the stairs. We entered her and Violet's bedroom where I let out a long sigh and threw myself onto Ruby's bed, narrowly missing Ruby's matted old teddy.[17]

"Today was awful," I moaned.

Ruby nodded sympathetically. "It was mean of Kitty to say—"

"Do you think Ms Sorenson hates me?" I interrupted.

"Of course not."

"*Everyone* hates me."

"Not everyone. Rupert seemed rather impressed."

I let out a growl and covered my face with my hands.

"It will be okay. They'll all forget in a day or two."

"It's not just that. I really want to be the editor for the newspaper but Mrs Tilly is going to let stupid Kitty do it because I 'can't read.' I can't believe my luck!"

Ruby gave a snort. "It's not really luck..."

"I know, I know! It's my own fault. Don't rub it in."

"I'm not," Ruby said quickly. "I'm sorry." She paused and added, "You'd be a really good editor."

"I know I would!" I gave her a hopeful smile. "Are you sure you won't say *you* want to do it?"

Ruby shook her head. "Sorry."

~*~

I racked my brain all night for a way to convince Mrs Tilly to let me be the editor. By the morning I concluded unhappily that it was

---

[17] Noah, an orange moose, is actually a hot water bottle cover. Ruby keeps her Bible in it so that she can '*hug God's promises*' while she sleeps. I tried sleeping with my Bible for a while in the hopes that this would prove to be a clever alternative to actually reading it. But, without a handy cover to protect it, I ended up rolling over and creasing half of the pages.

impossible to do this in a way which didn't involve lying or telling the truth. I ate my breakfast in silence, shooting the odd heavy sigh in Jill's direction.

Eventually, Jill looked up from some work and said, "What's wrong?"

"We're making a class newspaper," I said glumly.

"And that makes you sad? I thought you liked writing?"

"I *do.*"

"Then, what's the problem?"

I gave another sigh. "It doesn't matter."

She looked at me in confusion before turning back to her work. "Okay then."

I gave a moan and flicked some toast across the table.

Jill looked up irritably. "Do you want to talk about it or not?"

I shrugged. "You wouldn't understand."

She rolled her eyes. "Fine."

I watched her for a few minutes and felt a surge of self-pity. Big sisters are supposed to be cool. They're supposed to know exactly how you're feeling and give you cunning tips for how to get ahead. They're meant to say things like, *'Here's what you need to do to convince Mrs Tilly...'* But there was no way I could tell Jill about my dilemma. She would just tell me off.

I finished my breakfast and muttered, "I'm going to school now."

"Alright," Jill said without looking up. "Have fun."

I sighed again and left.

Ruby met me on the pavement. "The editor is being chosen today!" she said brightly, as if I could have forgotten.

I grunted. We didn't have English until the very end of the day so I had a further six hours of turmoil ahead of me.

"Have you thought about what you'll do?" Ruby continued.

I rolled my eyes. "Obviously. But there's nothing."

"Well, I've been thinking about it..."

My heart leapt. "You're going to pretend you want to be the editor?"

"No. I've thought of something *you* can do."

"Really? What?"

"It involves telling the truth..."

I gave a groan and threw my hands up in the air. "Ruby!"

"Just listen to me!"

I turned huffily. "What, then?"

She took a deep breath. "You just have to be brave and explain as honestly as you can that you made a mistake and that you feel really bad about it. Make it clear that it wasn't something you did to be naughty or to get out of doing work. You were just nervous because you were in a new school and you didn't mean for it to get out of hand. I'm sure Mrs Tilly will forgive you if she knows that you're truly sorry. *And,*" she added, before I could protest, "coming clean in a serious manner will show that you have the maturity needed to take on the role of editor."

I pursed my lips as I considered this. "Do you think it will work?"

"It might... Plus, you'll feel better once you've done it. Once, when I was little, I stole a sticker from a shop and stuck it on the bathroom mirror. Mum saw it and took me all the way back to the shop to own up. I was petrified but the manager just thanked me for saying sorry. I felt loads better afterwards."

I giggled. "What kind of sticker was it?"

Ruby blushed. "It was from the Christian bookshop. It said, *'Jesus is my friend.'*"

I gave a hoot of laughter and she grinned.

"Just think about it," she continued. "After all, she'll find out at *some* point, so it might as well be now if it means you could get to be the editor."

I could see that she had a point. "Okay. How should I do it?"

"Ask to have a private word with her. And say it all very carefully."

I nodded. "I'll do it."

I spent most of the day rehearsing my confession with Ruby. She did a rather good Mrs Tilly impression, right down to the way her lips quiver when she's concentrating. By the time the lesson arrived, I had a confident script committed to memory and had perfected the phrase, *'I'm a person who takes my schooling very seriously.'*

I lingered in the doorway, keen to approach our teacher before the lesson began. But, at the last moment, I lost my nerve. Mrs Tilly didn't appear to be in a very good mood and the first thing she did was give Wayne Purdy a detention for being on his phone. I hurried away from the door and took my seat, shooting Ruby a sheepish glance.

"It's alright," she whispered. "Wait till she's done the register and then put your hand up."

I nodded and chewed my lip.

Mrs Tilly fumbled for her spectacles and began calling out our names. All the while my heart clanged heavily inside me. I took several deep breaths as I tried to keep myself from shaking. Finally, Mrs Tilly finished the register and gave us all a big smile.

"Now!" Ruby hissed, elbowing me in the ribs.

But, before I could summon up the courage, Mrs Tilly stood up and said grandly, "Right then, it's time to pick our editor for the class newspaper!"

A few people shifted lazily and, behind us, Molly let out a loud yawn.

I looked helplessly at Ruby. She elbowed me again.

"So, who would like to be considered for editor?" Mrs Tilly stood at the white board, poised with a pen.

Kitty threw her hand up with fervour, clipping the back of my head as she did so.

I turned in anger and she smirked.

"Wonderful, Kitty." Mrs Tilly wrote her name on the board and beamed. "Who else?"

Nobody said anything. I glanced at Ruby. "What do I do?"

"Ask to have a private word with her," she muttered.

I half raised my hand and then lowered it again. I felt sick. "I can't do it," I whispered.

Ruby shifted awkwardly. "Yes you can."

"Help me."

"How?"

"Anybody else?" Mrs Tilly repeated, gazing keenly through her spectacles.

Kitty shot the class a dark look, as if daring anyone to challenge her. The class avoided our teacher's gaze. I shot Ruby a beseeching stare but she just shrugged.

"Well then!" Mrs Tilly said briskly. "If we're all in favour—"

I threw my hand up in the air. "Ruby should be the editor," I squeaked.

Ruby frowned at me and put her own hand up. "Livi should do it," she said shakily.

Kitty gave a hoot of annoyance and Mrs Tilly looked at us in confusion. "Ruby? Do you want to be the editor?"

Ruby shook her head. "I think Livi should do it."

Mrs Tilly smiled and tried to be kind by saying softly, "Well, Livi and I discussed this last lesson—" but she was interrupted by Molly who scoffed, "Livi can't be the editor because she can't read."

I turned in my seat and glared at her.

"Well, you can't," Molly sneered, sticking her chubby nose up at me.

"Yes I can," I snapped back.

"No you can't."

"I can!"

"Girls!" Mrs Tilly said loudly. "That's quite enough. If we have no more nominations then Kitty will—"

I got to my feet, pointed to a poster on the wall, and read at the top of my voice, *"In the event of a fire, form an orderly queue and make your way to the fire assembly point outside the Performing Arts block. Do not attempt to tackle the fire and under no circumstances should you return to the building unless authorised to do so. Please note that anyone found tampering with this sign will face immediate suspension. If you are concerned about fire safety, please speak to your form tutor and to read this information in braille please contact Mr Papadopoulos!"* I finished with a roar, gripping the side of the desk to keep myself from falling over.

Mrs Tilly gaped at me. "How on earth did you do that, Livi?"

I opened my mouth to say that I had been practising but burst into tears instead.

"Livi, what's the matter?"

"I'm fine," I said with a whimper. "I just..." I took a deep breath and tried to pull myself together. "I want to be the editor so much," I sobbed.

Behind me, Kitty let out a splutter.

"What a freak," Molly whispered.

Ruby leant over and took my hand.

"I *can* read, Miss," I continued through tears. "I'm sorry."

Mrs Tilly stared at me, her lips quivering violently.

Before she could say anything, Rupert Crisp stood up. "Kitty, I really think you should withdraw your interest in the post of editor. Livi seems to want it more than you."

At this, Kitty and her gang erupted into hysterics.

"Rupert loves Livi!" Melody sang.

Rupert shrugged and said, "There's nothing laughable about common courtesy."

I felt my last ounce of dignity evaporate as our classmates tittered.

"Thank you, Rupert," Mrs Tilly said awkwardly. "That was very considerate of you. But I thought Kitty was rather keen on being editor herself, weren't you, Kitty?"

Kitty was laughing too much to respond.

"She doesn't care, Miss," Annie said on her behalf.

Mrs Tilly seemed stunned. She looked from Kitty to me and gave me a somewhat patronising smile. "Well, if it means that much to you, Livi..."

"Yes please."

"And you *can* read?"

"Yes, Miss."

Mrs Tilly shook her head in disbelief. "Why on earth did you say you couldn't?"

"I... I don't know, Miss," I blubbered. "It just came out and I didn't mean to trick you... I'm not naughty, I'm a serious person at schooling, I just—" I gulped and burst into tears again.

"That's alright, Livi," Mrs Tilly said quickly. "Just sit down."

I nodded and took my seat, my whole body trembling like jelly.

Mrs Tilly wrote my name in big letters on the board. "There we go," she trilled. "We have our editor."

A wave of relief flooded through me as I gazed at my name.

"Well done," Ruby whispered.

I wiped my eyes and gave a shaky smile. "Is that what you meant?"

Ruby blushed. "Yeah, sort of."

~ 6 ~

A Christian thing

About once a fortnight Jill drags me into town to help her with the shopping. Our general routine involves buying cheap fruit from the market, browsing the odd charity shop and visiting the pound shop to stock up on toiletries. It's a hugely painful experience since Jill's combination of stinginess and hypochondria make her a somewhat miserable shopper.[18]

Today in the pound shop, as Jill stopped to compare the hypoallergenic qualities of two different body lotions, somebody mistook her for a shop assistant and asked if she sold verruca cream.

Jill looked rather affronted. "I don't work here."

"Oh!" The stranger eyed Jill's blue shirt which looked uncannily like the store's uniform.

"I don't work in a shop," my sister insisted. "And this top was from *Impress*."[19]

The stranger shrugged and walked off.

"That was really funny!" I said.

Jill scowled and headed for the checkout. "Some people are so stupid," she muttered as she slammed our basket down. "How could she think I worked here?"

"Because your top was the same colour." I rolled my eyes. "Get over it."

Jill glared at me. "No, Livi. I won't *'get over it.'* Do I look like the kind of person who would work in a pound shop?"

I shot the girl at the till an apologetic smile.

---

[18] She quibbles over every penny and scrutinises each banana for deformities.
[19] That was true, although she *had* bought it second hand from a charity shop.

"That's alright," the girl said snootily as she handed Jill her change. "I'm just working here part time to get through medical school. I wouldn't even *shop* here, myself."

Jill blushed, snatched our shopping, and stormed out.

I followed at a trot. "At least we saved 20p on toothpaste."

Jill grunted.

As we crossed the street, a voice behind us yelled, "Hey Livi!"

My stomach lurched as I turned and saw Ruby's friend, Mark, balancing precariously on a skateboard. I forced a smile, desperately hoping that we hadn't stumbled upon him handing out his crazy Jesus flyers.

He did an awkward spin on his skateboard and nearly fell off. "I'm Mark," he announced to Jill.

She gave him a friendly, if somewhat condescending, smile. "Are you in Livi's class?"

"He goes to Ruby's church," I said quickly.

Jill nodded. "That's nice."

Mark grinned at me. "Are you coming tomorrow?"

I tried to sound evasive as I began, "I haven't really thought about it..."

Before I got any further Mark pointed and yelled, "There's Joey!"

I spun round just in time to see Joey go flying off his skateboard.

My stomach lurched again. But this time it was a different kind of lurching. The kind of lurching that makes you wish you were wearing make-up.

Joey picked himself up off the ground, apologised to a little old lady whose toes he had run over, and came hobbling over to us.

"Hi," I said breathily.

"Hey Livi!" He gave a sheepish smile and held up his bleeding wrist.

Jill recoiled and dug around in her bag. "Here, I've got some antiseptic."

Joey blinked at her. "Thanks." He dragged himself over to a nearby bench and rolled up his trousers. Blood was dripping from his knee.

"This is my sister," I muttered.

Joey nodded. "Nice to meet you."

"You too," Jill replied. She squeezed some antiseptic onto a tissue and offered it to him. "Can you do it yourself?" Jill can't stand other people's blood.

Joey stretched his hand out and winced.

"I'll do it," I offered.

I took the tissue and began to dab at Joey's wounds. As he scrunched up his face and whimpered, I patted him as gently as possible, feeling an odd combination of compassion and delight as I marvelled at myself as his nurse.

"There you go," I whispered when I'd finished.

Joey gave me a brave smile and said, "Thanks." Then he added mournfully, "We were going to learn how to do a kickflip with some guys in the park. Now I can't even stand."

I tried to look sympathetic. "At least nothing's broken."

"We should pray!" Mark suggested.

I coughed. "Well, it was nice to see you both. We'd better go."

Mark looked disappointed. "Don't you want to pray for Joey's leg?"

I grabbed Jill's arm. "Maybe another time," I said rapidly. "We've got to go to the market."

Jill looked a little confused as I dragged her away.

"Bye then!" Mark yelled after us.

"Thanks for the antiseptic!" said Joey.

"You're welcome!" I called back.

As we headed down the high street, I glanced carefully at Jill. She was looking at me rather strangely. I braced myself as I waited for her to ask what Mark had meant by the idea of praying for Joey's leg.

Instead, she said with a smile, "They seemed nice."

I shrugged. "I don't really know them."

When we got home[20] I wandered over to Ruby's so that she could help me make plans for the class newspaper. Mrs Tilly had suggested I draw up a list of tasks so that people would know what their roles were. I also needed to come up with a name.

"How about *The Daily Fire*?" I suggested, grabbing some paper and a pen from Ruby's drawer.

"It's not daily though," Ruby said. "We're only making one."

"Oh yeah..." I thought for a bit. *The Fire?*

Ruby wrinkled up her nose. "I think that's a nightclub in town."

"Oh." I tapped my teeth with the pen. "This editor thing is hard."

---

[20] And after unpacking the shopping and listening to Jill hark on about being mistaken for a shop assistant for the seventeenth time.

"That's why I didn't want to do it." Ruby gave a wry smile. "But I'm sure you'll be very good at it."

I rolled my eyes and shifted onto my back, gazing round her room for inspiration. *"The Happy Moose?"*

"Sounds like a fast food chain."

"The Writing Desk?"

"Too old-fashioned."

"The Odd Sock?"

"That's just weird."

I thought for a while longer before giving up. Then I glanced across to see what Ruby was doing. She was in the middle of drawing a picture of a camel. She gave it great saggy cheeks and hairy ankles.

I gave an absentminded *Clumsy Camel* impression before saying gingerly, "I saw some of your church friends in town."

"Really? Who?" But, before I could reply, she leant over and grabbed something from her shelf. "That reminds me... Church is starting up a youth group on Friday nights. Do you want to come?"

I looked at her. "Who's going?"

"Lots of people. Me... Violet... Probably Mark..."

I gave a careful nod. "What about the other one? Joey, was it?"

"Oh yeah. Joey will probably be going."

I exhaled slowly and tried to sound vague as I said, "Yeah, could be fun."

Ruby grinned. "Cool! You just need Jill to sign this." She handed me a form.

My heart sunk. "Does Jill *have* to know?"

Ruby looked at me strangely. "You need permission from a parent or guardian. But what's wrong with that? Jill will let you, won't she?"

"She might wonder why I suddenly want to go to a church youth group. She already thinks it's weird that I'm going to church."

"Just say it's a Christian thing."

I rolled my eyes. "That's the whole point. Jill doesn't know that I'm a Christian."

"Ohh." Ruby gave me a long look. "Hmmm."

"I'm not telling her!"

Ruby just stared at me.

I tutted. "Stop staring."

"I'm not." Ruby folded up the permission form and slipped it into my coat pocket. "I'm doing my Geography homework." She pointed to her camel picture.

I gave a growl. "You think I should tell Jill, don't you?"

"If you want to."

"I *don't* want to!"

"Then don't." She opened her Geography textbook on a passage about the Sahara Desert and smoothed down the pages. There was a short pause and then she asked, "Why don't you want to?"

I gave an irritated sigh. "Firstly, because she might get angry. And secondly, because it's weird."

Ruby laughed. "Do you think you're weird?"

"No, *I'm* not! But the rest of you are."

Ruby looked a little wounded.

"Sorry," I said quickly. "I just mean that she won't understand."

Ruby sniffed. "Well, it starts this Friday so think about it."

~*~

I didn't go to many clubs when I was younger[21] and the idea of a youth group sounded really cool. I spent the whole of the next week summoning up the courage to ask Jill's permission. I knew the best thing to do was to admit that I had become a Christian but I was terrified of her response. Would she shout until I changed my mind? Or force me to speak to Aunt Claudia? Or perhaps even ban me from seeing Ruby? Just that week Belinda had posted another Bible bookmark through the door and Jill had muttered under her breath, "I wish they still fed Christians to lions."

What made matters worse was that Jill had been extremely stressed all week because she was behind on her targets at work. I debated writing her a letter or perhaps leaving my Bible on the kitchen table with a note proclaiming, *'Look who joined the God Squad!'* I even considered asking Belinda to come round and

---

[21] Except for an after school Keep Fit Club but that one wasn't out of choice; Jill made me go because she had recently read an article which linked poor concentration in Maths with a lack of exercise.

explain things to her but I dismissed this idea on Tuesday evening after Belinda referred to Jill as a *'dear lost lamb.'*[22]

By Thursday night I still hadn't told her. I stood in the kitchen, texting Ruby frantically.

'I'm gonna tell Jill now. Totally freaking out!'

'Do it quickly, like ripping off a plaster!'

'She's gonna be so mad!'

'I'll pray for you!'

I sighed. What I really needed was for her to pray for *Jill*. If she would just discover God for herself then everything would be alright.

"Can't you *make* her believe in you?" I begged God. "Just zap her or something..."

I supposed I could just not go to the youth group but it sounded really fun, especially since Ruby had said there might be free sweets. I gave a growl and tried to pull myself together. *How bad could it be?* I reasoned. *Jill won't stay angry forever. It's not like I've killed somebody.*

"No more lying, no more pretending, just *do* it!" I lectured myself as I paced backwards and forwards.

I could hear my sister in the next room, laughing at some stand-up comedy. At least she was in a better mood. I took a deep breath and went in.

"Hi," Jill said cheerily, patting the seat beside her.

I bit my lip as I shuffled towards her and perched on the sofa. "I need to talk to you."

She looked up in surprise. "What's wrong?"

"Nothing... I just need to tell you something."

Jill raised her eyebrows and switched the television off.

I took a deep breath and counted to ten. "Please don't be angry..." I stole a glance at her. She was looking concerned. I looked away and said very quickly, "I'm a Christian."

To my horror, Jill burst out laughing. "I thought it was going to be something serious!" she exclaimed.

"This *is* serious," I said weakly. "I decided after Christmas. I want to be a Christian." A huge part of me couldn't believe what I was saying. It sounded so daft now that I had said it out loud. I tried to look like I knew what I was talking about.

---

[22] Ruby and I had been discussing the situation whilst doing some homework together. Belinda had overheard us and assured me, "I know Jill's a dear lost lamb right now, Livi, but she's on her own special journey to the Lord."

Jill gave me a quizzical look. "Well, whatever makes you happy."

"Can I go to youth group?" I begged. "It's on Friday nights. I can get a lift with Ruby." I crossed my fingers and then remembered Christians weren't meant to do that.

"Does it cost anything?"

I shook my head.

"Then, yeah, you can go."

I let out a sigh. "Thanks."

Jill chuckled to herself and turned the television back on.

I sunk into the sofa and pretended to watch it with her but my brain was buzzing. I was glad that I was allowed to go to youth group but I couldn't help feeling somewhat irritated by her response. I would much rather have her yell at me than *laugh*.

~ 7 ~

What is faith?

The youth group leaders are called Eddie and Summer Lake. According to Ruby, they are two of the coolest people at King's Church. Eddie used to be the England Rubik's Cube champion and was on route to be a professional coach but he gave it up to be a preacher. And Summer has long blonde hair reaching down to her thigh. They live in a house on the 'nice' side of Leeds and they have twin two-year olds called Alfie and Felix.[23]

We were amongst the first to arrive and followed Summer expectantly into the living room.

"Make yourselves at home," she said, rushing back into the hall to answer the door again.

Seconds later, Joey wandered in and said, "Good, you came!"

I couldn't work out whether that was directed at any of us in particular and tried to act cool by glancing nonchalantly round the room.

Unfortunately, there weren't any sweets. Instead there was a tray of freshly baked flapjacks. I have never liked flapjacks. They have a particular aroma of other people's mothers and are high on the list of things that make me miss my mum, shortly followed by roast dinners, Christmas stockings, the words 'Apple of my eye' and people asking what my name means.

"Want a flapjack?" asked Joey.

"Er, yeah, I don't mind," I said, following him across the room.

He handed one to me and grinned. "I love flapjacks," he said, ramming a whole one into his mouth.

I bit into mine. It was a bit dry but I nibbled it as gracefully as I could, cupping a hand to my mouth to catch any stray crumbs.

---

[23] "I'm one of the few people who can tell them apart," Violet informed me as we chatted in the car on the way.

I was about to ask Joey how his day had been but, before I could get the words out, Mark came into the room and yelled, "Flapjacks!"

Joey gave him a friendly punch and said, "Hey dude!"

Mark grabbed a flapjack. "So I finally nailed that kickflip!"

"Seriously?" Joey looked impressed and a little envious.

I lingered awkwardly as they discussed skateboard tricks. Just as I was about to pluck up the courage to ask Joey if his leg was any better he wandered off to greet two boys who had arrived. I shot Mark a quick smile and pretended to examine the flapjacks.

"Livi," he said suddenly. "Are you on FriendWeb?"

"What's that?"

"It's an online social network. Like FaceBuddy."

"Oh." I shook my head. "A few people used FaceBuddy at my old school but it never really took off."

"Get on FriendWeb," Mark insisted. "It's loads better. You get to create your own Spiderface."

"What's a Spiderface?"

"It's you as a spider. Mine wears a top hat."

I chuckled. It sounded really weird.

"Seriously. Everyone's on it. You can share photos and videos and everything. Also, you can list your top eight friends— one for each spider leg. And, if lots of people have you on their legs, your profile is in gold to show you're really popular." He gave me a hopeful smile.

I wrinkled up my nose. "What else?"

"You can leave people flies on their wall."

"Flies?"

"Yeah. It's like a short message. Just dropping you a *fly*, you know?"

I raised an eyebrow. "I'll think about it," I said, rushing away before he could continue.

I crossed the room and joined Ruby on the sofa. She was talking to a girl who I'd not met before.

"This is Nicole," Ruby said to me. "And this is Livi."

Nicole and I exchanged friendly nods. Then Ruby excused herself to go to the bathroom and left us staring at one another.

We sat in silence for a while until I said dumbly, "Er, there are flapjacks over there."

"I know," Nicole replied. "I had one when I got here."

"Oh."

Fortunately, Eddie came in at that point. He got our attention and gathered us into a circle. Ruby returned from the toilet and squeezed in beside me as Eddie and Summer welcomed us all to their house.

"It's great to have so many of you here," said Eddie. "Now, we know some of you already.[24] But, for those who don't know us, I'm Eddie and this is my wife, Summer."

Summer beamed. "Hello everyone."

We murmured shy hellos in response.

"Perhaps you could go round the circle and introduce yourselves," Summer suggested. She turned to Violet.

Rather than give her name, Violet smiled at her and asked with a simper, "How are the boys?"

"They're great, thanks."

"Is Alfie's cold better?"

"Actually it was Felix who had the cold. But he's fine now, thank you."

Violet blushed and cleared her throat. "I'm Violet," she said quickly to the group. She looked at me.

"I'm Livi," I said.

We went round and said our names.[25] Then we played a few rounds of a game called *Bad Teeth*[26] before being told to get into pairs.

Ruby and I grabbed one another and grinned. There was a bit of commotion as the rest of the group sorted themselves out and a few people started to chatter. Joey took the opportunity to grab a handful of flapjacks.

Eddie waited for us to settle down before saying merrily, "Right then, we have a question for you. *What is faith?*"

"You've got five minutes to talk about it," added Summer.

We broke off in our pairs and I looked at Ruby expectantly. "Well, what is it?"

She thought for a moment. "I think it's believing in something even if you can't see it."

I nodded.

---

[24] Violet gave a smug smile at this.

[25] There were six girls (Ruby, Violet, Nicole, two girls named Grace, and me) and four boys (Joey, Mark, a really lanky boy called Rory and a short one called Bill). Violet was the oldest and Bill was the youngest.

[26] In which you answer questions about yourself by puffing out your cheeks and you're out if you show your teeth. I deliberately went out to avoid a question about family.

"How about you?"

"Yeah, what you said."

"You have to have your own opinion," Ruby scolded. "What do *you* think it is?"

"I don't know! Can't we just say your answer?"

We thought for a while longer before Summer got our attention and said, "So, what is faith?" She looked round at everyone.

Joey put his hand up. "I think one day I'll be better than Mark at skateboarding. That's faith."

Summer laughed. "Fair enough. Anyone else?" She turned to me and Ruby.

"Believing in something even if you can't see it," I said shyly.

She smiled. "Thank you, Libby—"

"Livi," I muttered.

"Oh!" She raised a hand to her mouth. "I'm sorry. I thought you said Libby earlier."

"No... It's Livi."

"Livi?" Rory, the lanky boy, piped up. "It did sound like Libby."

"I thought she said Lizzy," said one of the Graces.

"No, it's Livi," I insisted, feeling myself blush.

The group looked at me curiously.

Finally, Nicole asked, "What does it mean?"

I gave an uncomfortable shrug. "It doesn't mean anything."

Summer steered us back to the question. "Any other thoughts on what faith is?"

"It's sort of hoping God's out there," Bill ventured.

Violet coughed and read from her Bible, *"Faith is being sure of what we hope for and certain of what we do not see."* She looked round at everyone. "You can't just *hope* God is there. You should know."

"You can't *know*," I countered. "That's the point. It's faith, so you believe it but you don't know for sure." I looked at Eddie and Summer.

Eddie grinned and dragged a chair into the middle of the circle. "Come and sit on this chair, Livi."

I went over and sat down, feeling a bit coy as everybody stared.

"Do you trust the chair to carry you?"

I carefully rocked backwards and forwards. "Yeah."

"Lift up your arms and legs and let it take your whole weight. Do you know that you're safe?"

"Yeah..." I repeated, feeling like an overturned beetle with my limbs in the air.

"Is that faith?"

"I guess so…"

"How do you know it's not just a hope? Blind faith, perhaps?"

"I, er…" I thought for a moment. "Because I have my eyes open?"

He nodded. "Anything else?"

I chewed my lip. "I don't know."

Eddie looked round at the rest of the group. "Anyone?"

"She's sat on chairs before," Mark suggested.

"It's likely to be safe because that's how chairs are made," Ruby added.

Nicole put her hand up. "And she tested it first before she put all her weight on it."

"Great," said Eddie. "So perhaps we could say that faith is putting complete trust in something based on what we believe to be true?"

We nodded.

"Not just *perching* on a chair," Violet chipped in. "But with all your arms and legs in the air like Livi." She pointed at me.

Summer chuckled. "You can put your legs down now, Livi."

I gave an embarrassed smile and put them down.

Eddie talked about faith for a while longer. Once or twice I found myself stifling a yawn but I tried to look attentive since I was still in the middle. I sort of understood what he was saying but I wasn't sure how to apply it. Was God supposed to be a chair? Could I sit on him with my arms and legs in the air and know that he was definitely there? Believing in him still felt very much like a *hoping* rather than a *knowing*.

Eventually, Eddie called the meeting to an end and led us in a time of prayer. I kept my eyes shut the whole time for fear that he would pick on me and ask me to pray for everyone. I didn't want to have to explain that I was only a beginner at the whole *faith* thing.

"That's it for tonight!" Eddie concluded. "Thanks for coming."

"We'll see you next week," added Summer. "Take some flapjacks with you— there are loads left."

The boys ran to the table and filled their pockets.

As Ruby and I went to put on our coats Violet wandered over, holding her phone. "Dad's texted me," she said. "We're getting a lift back with Janine because the car wouldn't start."

"Oh, alright," said Ruby.

"Who's Janine?" I asked curiously.

"My mum!" Joey yelled in my ear. I jumped and he grinned. "Come on then!" he said, pushing open the front door.

I grabbed Ruby's arm and followed him out.

Joey's mother was tall and pretty. She wore a lavender scarf and smelt of vanilla. As usual when I meet people's mothers, I assessed her quickly to see whether she was *Mother Material*.

Five things that make somebody Mother Material
1. *Being kind and understanding.*
2. *Always having time to talk.*
3. *Taking control in a crisis.*
4. *Having a good sense of humour but not in a 'I'm-trying-to-be-your-friend' kind of way.*
5. *Having a certain level of glamour. A celebrity mother would be particularly cool.*

As we climbed into the car, Janine rubbed Joey's cheeks and said, "You look like you've had a *faith* lift!"

I suppressed a smirk as Joey squirmed. His mother ranked fairly high in the glamour department and she was kind to be giving us a lift home but she didn't quite have the sense of humour. That's the trouble with mothers. They rarely have it *all* just right. Belinda, for example, is kind and understanding and always has time to talk but she is not at all glamorous, her jokes are dire, and she usually starts crying in a crisis. Even though I know deep down that my own mother would have had failings too, I still can't help comparing everyone else's mother to my perfect image of her.

"So, what did you do?" Janine asked as she started the car.

"We had some amazing flapjacks," Joey said.

Janine chuckled. "Glad you learnt something."

"Oh, I did! I learnt that I can fit three flapjacks in my mouth at once!"

Ruby giggled. "Have you seen the *Flapjack Boogie?*"

Joey blinked at her. "The what?"

"It's online. I'll show you some time."

"Cool."

I tried to think of something funny to add to the conversation but the best I could come up with was, "I learnt that I could sit on a chair!" I sniggered at my own joke but nobody else laughed.

Joey looked at me in bemusement and his mum nodded slowly. Violet shook her head and started flicking through her Bible.

"Check out my drawings," Joey said suddenly, handing me a wad of paper from the glove compartment.

I peered at the top picture. It was of a man with rabbit ears and a lion's tail. It was good, if a little strange.

"This guy is called *The Ferret Ranger.*" Joey pointed to the next one. It was of a man climbing a ladder made from ferrets.

I wanted to show an interest but was starting to feel travel sick. I made eager noises as I pretended to study each drawing but the bulk of my energy was going into not throwing up on them. I was hugely relieved when we pulled up on our street.

"Thanks, Janine," Ruby and Violet sang as they slid out of the car.

"Yeah, thanks," I said queasily.

"You're welcome, girls." Joey's mum gave us a warm smile and started to turn her car around.

Violet marched straight into her house, keen to get to her journal.

"Oh, Ruby," Joey yelled through the window. "Don't forget the *Flapjack Boogie.*"

"I won't!"

"Send me a link on FriendWeb."

"Yeah, okay," she yelled back, waving as they drove away.

I looked up in surprise. "You're on FriendWeb?"

Ruby shrugged. "Yeah. Mark made me join a few weeks ago. Something about spider legs."

"And Joey's on it too?"

"I think most people are."

I followed her into her house, feeling slightly out of the loop. "Why didn't you tell me about it?"

"Everyone knows about FriendWeb. I assumed you weren't interested."

"I'm not. It sounds silly. But you still should have said."

"Do you want to see my profile?" Ruby pulled a laptop out from under the sofa.

"Okay," I said coolly.

When the computer had loaded up, Ruby tapped in the FriendWeb address and logged on.

A purple page covered with an overload of photos and status updates filled the screen. A message was flashing in the corner. *'New friend request.'*

"Oh, hold on..." Ruby clicked on the link. A photo of Wayne Purdy popped up and, without a moment's pause, Ruby accepted the friend request.

I raised an eyebrow. "Wayne?"

"Yeah," she said indifferently.

Another message popped up. *'Congratulations! You now have 245 friends in your web.'*

I stared at her. "Two hundred and forty five friends?"

Ruby nodded and clicked on a shiny web at the top of the screen. The web unfurled, showing a list of Ruby's friends. A dazzling photo of Kitty Warrington jumped out at me.

"You're friends with Kitty Warrington?" I asked in shock.

Ruby shrugged. "She's in my web. But we don't talk or anything."

I looked down her list. Half our school were listed as her friends. "You don't talk to *any* of these people!" I exclaimed.

"I know," Ruby said sheepishly. "It's kind of different online. You can be friends with someone but not actually *friends*, if you know what I mean."

I opened my mouth and closed it again.

"This is my profile," she continued, clicking on another link. Her profile page featured a massive photo of herself smiling awkwardly at the camera. Under her name was written, *'A good day for banana stickers!'* "That was my status update on Wednesday," she explained.

Suddenly, a pink spider with googly eyes and an orange quiff walked across the screen.

"What's that?" I asked in repulsion.

"That's my Spiderface."

"I don't like it."

Ruby ignored me and scrolled down the page to her 'wall' where a number of messages had been left by various 'friends.'

"Oh." She pointed to one in particular. "Joey left me a fly."

"Go on then," I said quickly. "Sign me up."

By the end of the night I had my own FriendWeb page. Ruby hadn't been able to help me because it was already late and Violet had come in and offered to walk me home. I took that as a hint to leave so I said a hasty farewell and sprinted back to mine, making a dash for the computer in the living room. I loaded up the website as fast as I could, afraid that Jill would come in and tell me to go to bed before I'd managed to figure it all out. It suddenly felt incredibly vital that I join FriendWeb before doing *anything* else.

For my profile photo, I uploaded a close-up shot of my eyes. I felt this made me seem mysterious. And I tried to make my Spiderface as friendly as possible by giving it wings and a unicorn hat.

I added Ruby as a friend and then sent her a text telling her to accept me. A few minutes later, a message popped up on my screen. *'Ruby Rico has accepted your friend request. Congratulations! You now have 1 friend in your web.'*

I sucked in my cheeks. *What next?*

My heart pounded as I explored Ruby's profile. I didn't know Joey's surname but found him in Ruby's web listed as *'Joseph the Dreamer.'* His Spiderface wore a multicoloured robe. I kind of wanted to add him to one of my eight spider legs but I wasn't sure if that would be making some kind of social statement so I didn't. I continued to go down Ruby's list and added Violet, Mark and a handful of my classmates. Then I hovered over the profiles of the more elite girls in our year. Molly Masterson had forgotten to make her page private and I spent a good thirty minutes poring over her photo albums. I contemplated adding her and Kitty as friends but didn't quite have the nerve to do so. In the end, I just added the people who I was fairly sure would add me in return but this didn't turn out to be very many.

I wasn't sure what to do next and hastily typed *'Audrey Sorenson'* into the search field. She didn't seem to have a profile. Not that I would have added her if she did.

I wrote a quick status update[27] before scrolling absentmindedly down Ruby's wall to read her flies.

At quarter past eleven, Jill came in. "It's getting late, Livi."

"Okay!" I tried to log out before she saw what I was doing. I was fairly sure she would disapprove.

To my disappointment, she saw and asked, "Is that FriendWeb?"

"Yeah," I muttered. "I'm just seeing what it's all about."

"Well, you might as well add me then."

I gaped at her. *"You're* on FriendWeb?"

"Of course. Everyone's on FriendWeb."

---

[27] *'What is faith? That is the question.'*

~ 8 ~

Awaiting acceptance

I checked FriendWeb systematically throughout the weekend. By Sunday morning, I'd been added by Violet, Mark and Jill,[28] but Joey's profile remained closed with the words, *'Awaiting acceptance.'*

As I got ready for church, I gave a growl and wondered why he was snubbing me. Surely he'd have been online by now to receive the link for Ruby's silly *Flapjack Boogie?* I had half a mind to blank him when I saw him. But, as soon as Ruby and I arrived at church, he came running over in excitement.

"I'm having a party on Saturday," he said, handing us a couple of bright green invitations. "You'd better be free."

"What's the party for?" I asked in surprise, all thoughts of blanking him gone.

"My birthday, of course!"

"Oh yeah, obviously." I blushed and glanced at the invitation.

Joey had drawn a picture of a cat being eaten by a shark being eaten by a horse. Inside the cat were the words, *'Come bowling!'*

"Nice drawing," I said.

He beamed. "Can you come?"

I looked at Ruby and she nodded. "I'm free."

"Me too," I agreed.

"Great!" He grinned and waved the rest of his invitations at us. "I'd better give these out."

"Oh, Joey," I said coolly, before he could rush off. "I'm kind of on FriendWeb now. I think I added you."

"Nice one! I'll accept your friend request when I get home."

"Yeah, if you want."

---

[28] Jill had also left me an annoying fly which read, *'Get off FriendWeb and do your homework.'*

He grinned again and ran off.

I smiled at Ruby and we went to find seats at the side of the hall. I recognised the two Graces from Friday night and gave a tentative wave. Then I sat back in my chair and waited for the meeting to begin. Ruby had given me a couple of CDs of worship music and I was hopeful that some of the songs would be featuring today. I had been practising.

Eventually, the band started to play and I got to my feet with the rest of the congregation. To my excitement, I knew the first song and joined in with great gusto.

'I have a wonderful Father
Who holds me in his hands
And wrote me into creation
For a wonderful plan...'

Halfway through the song I glanced across at Stanley and saw him sidle into the aisle. As he started to dance Oscar ran up to him and jumped into his arms. Stanley caught him and spun him round, the two of them singing with joy. It wasn't as funny as it usually was to see Stanley dancing. Instead, for some reason, I felt kind of sad. I shook my head and tried to focus on the song, but the words were starting to grate on me.

'I have a wonderful Father
I'm always on his mind
He will never, ever leave me
Till the very end of time...'

After another chorus I sat down and stared straight ahead. Even though Ruby had told me many times that I was now a part of God's family, I still felt like I didn't quite belong. I could imagine God as a grand and majestic King who made the universe and everyone in it. But a *Father*? As far I was concerned, fathers were pretty useless. To be surrounded by a throng of people singing about a Father who would never leave made me want to cry.

During the next song a lady came to the front and began speaking into a microphone. "I sense God wants to say that some people are struggling with the idea that God is your Father; perhaps because your earthly father hasn't been very reliable so you're finding it hard to trust that God wants to be a loving Father to you. But he does."

I sniffed and glanced around the room, as if to say, *'Who's that about then?'*

I stood up again and tried to join in with the next song but I couldn't concentrate. The words *'God is your Father'* kept going round and round my head and it made me feel annoyed. I wondered whether God had truly told the woman to bring that message or whether it was just a lucky guess. And if it *was* from God, well I didn't want to be *told* that he was a loving Father; I wanted to *know* it for myself.

If you're my Father, I muttered silently to God. *Then why do these songs make me feel sad?*

I waited for a moment and then sat back down. I decided I would give Ruby her CDs back.

The worship came to an end and Jim, one of the church leaders, got up to preach. He opened with a little anecdote about a man who had been trapped in a cave for many years, spending all his days crying for help, until a rescue party dug through to save him. *"...The man looked at the rescue party in horror. 'Who are you?' 'We've heard you calling,' they replied. 'We're here to save you.' 'Save me?' the man exclaimed. 'But now there's a big hole in my cave. You've destroyed everything!'"*

I laughed along with the rest of the congregation and wondered how the man could be so daft.

"Sometimes we can be like the man in the cave," Jim continued. "There's a whole new world out there but the familiar darkness is too comforting."

I imagined a man trapped in a cave for many, many years and wondered whether I could develop the story into an article for the class newspaper. This sent me off into a daydream and I spent the rest of the preach making editorial notes in the back of my Bible.

Once or twice Violet looked over and gave me an approving nod. I tilted my Bible slightly so that she wouldn't see my doodle of me accepting the prize for *Best Young Yorkshire Scribe*.

By the end of the service I had given roles to everyone in our class[29] and had created a list of articles that needed to be written. I was still struggling with a name but had whittled it down to my top two: *'The Hoot'* and *'The Grim Reader.'*

---

[29] I'd tried to be fair and give everybody something exciting to work on apart from Kitty Warrington and Molly Masterson who I had put in charge of traffic and weather.

"'*The Hoot*' because I'm thinking of making it into a funny paper, you know, with lots of jokes and cheesy bits," I explained to Ruby in the car on the way home. "Or '*The Grim Reader*' if I decide to be more serious. It depends on what happens in the news over the next few months."

Ruby nodded thoughtfully. "How about '*The Traffic Light*'?"

I wrinkled up my nose. "What kind of name is that?"

"Think about it!" Ruby waved her arms around. "You could have the headlines in red with a sign saying '*Stop Press!*' And lighter news could be in orange. Sports could be green..."

I exhaled slowly. I had to admit it was quite a good idea, although I rather wished I'd thought of it myself. "I suppose..."

She beamed. "Maybe I could've been the editor after all!"

I rolled my eyes and wrote her suggestion in my Bible.

As we pulled up outside the Ricos' house Belinda turned in her seat and asked, "How did you find church today, Livi?"

"Yeah, fine," I said. I forced a smile and slipped out of their car. "Bye then!"

The rest of Ruby's family said goodbye and headed into their house but Belinda got out of the car with a heavy sigh and stood staring at me. "How's your sister?"

"She's fine."

Belinda didn't look convinced. "I'll just pop in and see her."

"She's alright," I insisted.

Even so, Belinda put an arm on my shoulder and followed me into my house.

Jill was doing some work in the living room. She looked a little stressed but forced a smile when she saw us.

"Hi," I said. Then, in case she'd missed her, I added, "Belinda's here."

Jill gave a quick nod. "Hi Belinda."

"Hello Jill," Belinda said softly. "I brought round a bookmark for you the other day. Did you get it?"

"Yes," Jill replied through gritted teeth. "You stuck it over the keyhole. I couldn't have missed it."

Belinda smiled and nodded, as if unsure of what to say next. She glanced around the hallway and gasped as she caught sight of the garden gnomes on the stairs. "Goodness, Jill, what are they?"

My sister bit her lip. "They're gnomes, Belinda."

Belinda went over and examined them. "Aren't they terrific?"

Jill grunted.

"You can have them if you want," I offered.

"Oh, I couldn't do that! They're yours."

"We don't like them," I said. "Do we, Jill?"

Jill shrugged. "Have them, Belinda."

Belinda clutched her heart as though we had just offered her a share of the moon. "Are you sure?"

"Absolutely." Before Belinda could protest, Jill strode over to the stairs and gathered the whole pile into her arms. "I'll help you take them home."

Belinda was close to tears as she said, "You're so kind, Jill. I don't know what to say." She poked around in her bag. "Here..." She pulled out a small white Bible. "I want you to have this."

Jill forced a smile. "Honestly, Belinda. You don't need to give us anything."

"Oh but I must! I'd feel awful if I didn't."

"Okay then." Jill took the Bible and flung it onto the sofa before leading the way out of the house with the gnomes.

Belinda followed her across the street at a trot and, as I watched from the window, I sniggered at the sight of Stanley almost falling over in shock as he answered the door. Funnier still was Ruby's text a few seconds later: *'There are gnomes in my bathroom. What were you thinking???!'*

Jill returned to the house and shut the door with a chuckle. "That woman is crazy!"

I nodded and watched her as she picked up Belinda's Bible.

"Do you want this?" she asked. "Or should I chuck it?"

"Don't throw it away! It's a Bible."

Jill rolled her eyes. "I know what it is, Livi. But I don't want it."

"Well, I'll have it if you don't want it."

She threw it to me. "Knock yourself out."

I caught it awkwardly and said, "Thanks." I flicked through it and made a mental note not to doodle in this one. Then I cleared my throat and said gingerly, "If you ever want it—"

But she shook her head and went back to her work.

I took this as a hint to stop talking so I went over to the computer, keen to see whether Joey had accepted my friend request yet. I logged onto FriendWeb and clicked on my web. A few more people had added me that morning but there was still no sign of Joey. I sighed and tapped my chin, afraid that perhaps he didn't actually like me and was evading my request on purpose. Maybe he'd only invited me to his party because he *had* to. Perhaps I shouldn't go.

I stared at the screen for ages until, finally, a glorious message popped up in the corner. *'Joseph the Dreamer has accepted your friend request. Congratulations! You now have 9 friends in your web.'*

I breathed a sigh of relief and perused his profile. There were eighteen photos of him standing on his head as well as several albums devoted to his cartoons. I read his most recent status update[30] and wondered whether I should create a cool online name too, perhaps *'Lionheart Livi'* or *'Livi the Great.'*

Finally, after scrolling through his photos three times and reading every fly on his wall, I turned the computer off and did some homework.

---

[30] *'Joseph the Dreamer says: I want chips.'*

~ 9 ~

Nobody needs a hero

Our class was reasonably impressed with the name 'The Traffic Light.'[31] Mrs Tilly remarked that it had 'a certain flair to it' and a few people even caught my eye and smiled.

I was about to confess that it had actually been Ruby's idea but, before I could do so, Rupert Crisp put up his hand and suggested a comic strip entitled 'The Little Green Man.'

"It could depict the tales of an unlikely hero and his attempts to warn the people of Planet Earth of impending doom from an intergalactic warlord," he said dramatically.

"Or a man trying to cross the street," Wayne Purdy interjected. "And repeatedly being run over."

A few people sniggered.

Rupert gave an irritated tut. "How juvenile."

"I like that idea," Kitty said to Wayne. "He could live in an old bus."

"And wear a traffic cone on his head," Molly added.

"And have a pet zebra," Annie piped up.

Half of the class murmured in agreement.

"That's a ridiculous idea!" said Rupert, his cheeks growing crimson.

"Well yours is boring!" Kitty retorted. "There are millions of superheroes out there. Nobody needs another one."

I watched them arguing back and forth and then realised that Mrs Tilly was looking at me.

"Well, Livi!" she trilled. "We seem to have a little conflict. Since you're the editor, I believe the last word falls on you."

The class turned to me expectantly. Even those who couldn't care less about the comic strip nudged one another and grinned,

---

[31] Apart from Kitty who made a comment about it sounding like an ice cream.

keen to see who I would side with. I felt my stomach lurch as I considered my response. I liked Wayne's idea but, since Kitty and Molly were backing it so fervently, I couldn't possibly permit it. However, picking Rupert's idea was bound to give everyone cause to believe that I liked him.

I looked across at Ruby and she shrugged.

"Well, *Editor?*" Kitty drawled. "Are you going to pick our idea? Or do you *fancy* Rupert's?"

The class giggled.

I sucked in my cheeks and prayed for a way out. "Perhaps we could combine both ideas," I suggested. "It could be about a man who saves others from being run over."

Kitty scowled and Wayne wrinkled up his nose.

"That's stupid," Molly sneered.

The rest of the class looked confused.

"Thinking out of the box," Rupert said with a nod. "I like it. Could I be the illustrator, Livi?"

"Yup," I said briskly, shooting Mrs Tilly a beam which I hoped said, *'Aren't you glad you let me be the editor?'*

She gave me a bemused smile and said, "Good."

Kitty put her hand up to protest but Mrs Tilly said firmly, "Our editor has spoken, Kitty. Now, let's have some work in silence. You've all got assignments to be getting on with."

I turned in my seat and smirked.

Kitty glared at me and Molly muttered, "This will be the worst newspaper ever."

"If you're struggling with your weather report, I can always give it to somebody else," I retorted.

"We'll give you weather," Kitty hissed.

For the rest of the lesson Ruby and I were pelted with soggy balls of paper whenever Mrs Tilly's back was turned.

At one point, Ruby begged, "Can you stop that?"

But they just laughed and said, "How do you like the rain?"

"Ignore them," I whispered to Ruby. "Don't let them know that it's bothering you."

So we pretended not to notice in the hopes that they would soon grow bored but, unfortunately, the 'weather' continued all day with the 'rain' turning into 'hail' (crusts of bread during lunchtime) and, finally, 'thunder and lightning' (a box of crayons in Art).

By the time we reached Ms Sorenson's class we were covered in small bruises. We grabbed some seats as far across the circle as possible from Kitty and her gang.

I watched Ms Sorenson as she picked up her tin of beans and took a seat nearby. In our previous lesson she'd asked us to talk about things we liked and disliked about school. I rather hoped we would do it again. I had a few words to say about people throwing things. But Ms Sorenson had quite a serious look on her face. It seemed today's topic would delve a little deeper than school politics.

Once everybody had settled down Ms Sorenson held up her tin and said, "When the tin gets to you, and only if you want to, I'd like you to tell us about a time when you were disappointed."

I felt my stomach lurch. What came immediately to mind was my father's disappointing departure at Christmas and all the grisly details that had preceded it. But, of course, there was no way I could share that. There's telling the truth and then there's plain stupidity. I bit my lip and wondered what I should say.

Ms Sorenson handed the tin to Ritchie Jones. He shrugged and said, "When Leeds United got relegated." He passed the tin to Wayne Purdy.

"Yeah, me too," Wayne said nonchalantly.

"Me three," said Fran as the tin glided past him.

I wondered whether Ms Sorenson would tell them to be more original. But, as usual in her tin exercise, she just smiled and let us get on with it.

The tin made its way round the circle and my mind went into overdrive as I tried to think of something appropriate to say. It had to be interesting, with an air of tragedy, but nothing too deep or personal. I could say I was disappointed when Jill first announced that we were moving to Leeds. But people might take that the wrong way and tell me to go home. I could say I was disappointed when I ran out of green paint for my bedroom. But that might make me sound poor. I could make a joke and say that I was disappointed that not many people had added me on FriendWeb yet, but that too could disastrously backfire.

Molly had the tin. She sniffed and said pompously, "I was disappointed this morning when Livi failed to notice a perfectly good idea for the class newspaper." She wagged the tin at me and added, "Editors ought to be fair, you know."

I glanced at Ms Sorenson, hoping she wouldn't think I was abusing my position of power.

Kitty grabbed the tin from Molly and said with a big sigh, "We got burgled a few years ago. The thieves went into every single room in our house, even my walk-in-wardrobe. They took all of my jewellery, half of my clothes and my whole collection of *Tizzi Berry* eye-shadows."

I screwed up my nose and wondered what a thief would do with a load of half-used pots of eye-shadow.

"They even took my horse riding boots," Kitty continued. "And the shock of it was so great that my hamster died." She squeezed a little tear out for dramatic effect and Molly leant over and put a chubby arm round her shoulder.

Ruby and I nudged one another and rolled our eyes.

"Of course," Kitty went on, "it ended up okay because the police caught the thieves trying to sell my clothes at the market. We got everything back and my dad bought me two rabbits to replace my hamster. And now we've got a guard dog called Bruno."

Annie reached for the tin but, before she could take it, Kitty yanked it back again. "I forgot to say," she added with a simper. "During the time of the burglary, I was actually looking for a new horse with my mum because my first horse had just died. So the whole burglary was extra traumatic."

I tried to pretend I wasn't listening but I couldn't help feeling a deep pang of envy. It wasn't fair that someone as mean as Kitty had such a doting family, a massive house and all the animals she could ever want.

I felt Ruby poking me. "I don't know what to say," she whispered.

"Neither do I," I admitted.

Saying *anything* of any value meant being incredibly vulnerable. I'm pretty sure that was our teacher's intention but, although I would never usually disagree with the wisdom of Ms Sorenson, she didn't appear to understand that vulnerability was not a safe option for a teenager.

"You could talk about the time you dropped a banana down the toilet before you'd managed to take the sticker off," I whispered to Ruby.

Her eyes widened. "Thanks!"

I gave her an optimistic smile, hoping she would return the favour. But she just grinned and waited for the tin.

Finally, the tin got to me. I took it awkwardly and bounced it on my lap.

"I've never really been disappointed," I blurted out. "I mean, I have," I corrected myself hurriedly. "But I think, if you try hard enough, then you can always make disappointments into an opportunity." I passed the tin on, feeling my cheeks burn as I did so.

Ms Sorenson caught my eye and smiled and I gave a shy smile in return.

When the tin got back to her, Ms Sorenson said, "I thought what Livi said was very interesting."

The class turned to stare at me and I shifted in my seat and tried to look humble.

Across the circle, Kitty and Molly stuck up their noses and sneered.

"Every disappointment brings with it a potential opportunity," Ms Sorenson continued. "That can be your homework this week... The next time you're faced with a disappointment, think about how you can turn it into an opportunity."

I sat up straight and nodded, determined to do just that. Perhaps the next time Kitty and Molly pelted us with the weather I could gather up the paper and make a collage.

For the remainder of the lesson I lost myself in a daydream. In part, I was replaying the wonderful moment when Ms Sorenson noted my contribution as *very interesting.'* For the rest of the time I imagined myself as a happy-go-lucky superhero: *Golden Opportunities Girl,* making the most of every situation.

As it happened, I didn't have to wait long before a wonderful disappointment presented itself. I arrived home from school just in time to catch Jill crying in the living room.

As soon as she saw me she fixed a smile on her face and said, "Hi Livi."

I raised an eyebrow. "What's wrong?"

"Oh, nothing. I've just had a hard day."

"Do you want to talk? I might be able to help."

Jill rolled her eyes. "I don't need your help."

"But I have lots of good advice," I insisted. "Today I settled a dispute about a comic strip for the class newspaper and, in Ms Sorenson's class, I helped Ruby think of a good answer when it was her turn with the tin..."

"Good for you."

"So... What's wrong?" I wanted to add that I was now *Golden Opportunities Girl* and could surely help her turn any disappointment into something worthwhile.

She gave me a withering look. "Go and do some homework."

"Fine," I said, feeling stung.

I stomped up the stairs, peering through the banister as Jill pulled out some work and slammed it onto the sofa. I was sure that, whatever her problem was, I could help if she would just let me. I shut myself in my room and spread out on my bed, feeling resentful that my talent for good advice was being stifled due to Jill never trusting me to use it.

As I wallowed in self-pity, Ms Sorenson's words danced through my mind. *'The next time you're faced with a disappointment, think about how you can turn it into an opportunity.'*

I sat up quickly. If Jill wouldn't let me help her, perhaps I could create an advice column for the class newspaper and help *everyone else* instead! I would put a post-box in our form room and sift through the letters daily to choose those with the greatest needs. Not all the letters would feature in the final newspaper but I would endeavour to reply to as many as I could. If it got popular Jill might hear about it in the local press and think, *'Oh, I should have trusted Livi.'* And, of course, Ms Sorenson would be very proud.

I leapt off my bed and grabbed some paper. *'Livi's Great Advice Column,'* I wrote in big letters. *'I can help you with your problems. I've had lots of experience...'*

As I read it over, I feared it might sound as though I'd lived a troubled life. Perhaps it would work better if I kept my identity a secret...

After much thought, I settled upon a mystery agony aunt called *'Auntie Amber.'* In keeping with the traffic light theme, she would wear red and green wire-rimmed glasses and a zebra-striped bouffant wig. I spent the next hour creating a massive poster for our form room, decorating it with pictures of people crying cut out from various magazines. I signed the bottom of the poster with a curvy autograph.

'Auntie Amber's Advice Anonymous,'[32] I wrote. *'Tell it to someone who cares.'*

As I added a final silver streak to Auntie Amber's wig I heard Jill coming up to her room.

"It's alright that you don't need me," I yelled through my door. "I'll have plenty of people to help soon."

I hoped she would be curious and come and tell me her problems after all, but she didn't reply.

---

[32] Or *'A.A.A.A'* for short.

~ 10 ~

To be normal

The rest of the week passed rather uneventfully. Our form tutor, Miss Fairway, let me make an announcement about the advice column during morning registration on Tuesday but, by Friday, I still hadn't received any letters.

"I don't get it," I moaned to Ruby on the way home. "Teenagers are meant to be full of angst. Surely somebody has a problem they need help with."

"Maybe they just don't want help from *you*," Ruby suggested.

"It's not *me*. It's Auntie Amber." I had been careful to tell the class that the letters would be received by an *'anonymous counsellor.'*

Ruby chuckled. "Don't forget that it's Joey's party tomorrow."

I pretended to look surprised although I had, of course, been counting down the days all week. I even had my outfit sorted[33] and, after a thorough search of the local shops, had found him the most amazing present: a four-foot bar of Polish chocolate called *'SuperPoke.'* It was shaped like a finger, complete with a shiny sugar fingernail.

"Oh yeah," I said nonchalantly. "Bowling, wasn't it?"

Ruby nodded. "My dad can take us."

"I could ask Jill," I suggested. "Your parents always give us lifts."

"They don't mind. But you can ask Jill if you want."

"Yeah," I insisted. "She's not busy tomorrow."

---

[33] This had taken quite a lot of thought. We were going bowling, which is not exactly a posh affair, so it would be embarrassing to over-do it. But, then again, it was a *party* and I didn't want to look scruffy. I also had to take into account the funny-looking shoes that we would be forced to wear as it would be awful if my clothes clashed. In the end, I had decided upon a casual blue dress over leggings.

As it happened, Jill *was* busy. Very busy with a pile of stupid work.

I had asked for a lift in the most polite and considerate manner but she just waved a handful of papers at me and said, "I can't. I'm doing this."

"It would only take ten minutes!" I exclaimed.

"I'm sorry, Livi," she said, in the least sorry voice I have ever heard. "I haven't got time."

"Ten minutes!" I repeated. "You haven't even got ten minutes to do one tiny little favour?"

Jill threw her work down and put her head in her hands. I thought she might tell me off for being rude but, instead, she said very quietly, "I'm sorry, Livi. Not right now."

I opened my mouth and closed it again. I wanted a better explanation than that but experience told me that I was unlikely to get one. Jill is what Aunt Claudia calls *'a brooder.'* Supposedly, this means she is a deep thinker, grappling with life in a way that the average person wouldn't appreciate. But, in reality, it means she is in an almost constant state of depression for reasons known only to her.

I gave a sigh and flicked the doorway. "Never mind. I'll ask Ruby."

Jill shot me half a smile and turned back to her work.

Of course, Ruby didn't mind in the slightest about asking her dad to take us. And Stanley, who was slicing some homemade bread when we approached him, leapt up with a beam and said, "It would be my pleasure!"

I followed them glumly to their car, shooting a glance towards our house in the hopes that Jill would be standing at the window feeling guilty. As we set off, the two of them began a discussion over who had won the last time their family went bowling. Stanley insisted that it had been Violet but Ruby was adamant that Oscar had got a sneaky strike right at the end to clinch the victory.

I forced a smile and pretended to be interested but, in truth, I was timing the journey on my phone[34] and composing a secret poem entitled, *'To Be Normal.'*[35]

We arrived at the bowling alley and Stanley pulled up right outside the door. "Have a great time, girls!" he said.

Ruby gave him a hug and I said an awkward, "Thanks," before following her out of the car.

---

[34] It actually only took seven and a half minutes.

[35] I didn't get very far: *'I want to be normal. I want to be like you...'*

As Stanley waved and drove away, I fixed a smile onto my face and turned to Ruby. "I wonder if Joey's here yet."

"What did you get him?" she asked, peering curiously at my humungous bag.

I whipped out the four-foot chocolate finger with a grin.

"You can't give him that!" Ruby exclaimed. "Chocolate makes him sneeze."

"Sneeze?"

"Yeah. Once he ate a chocolate coin and sneezed non-stop for fifteen minutes." Ruby giggled.

I gaped at her. "Why didn't you tell me?"

She shrugged. "I thought you knew."

"How would I know?"

She shrugged again.

"So, is he allergic? Will it kill him? Or will he be okay if he eats it very slowly?"

"I don't know. That's quite a lot of chocolate."

"What am I going to do?" I started to panic.

"Don't worry about it. He won't mind."

I looked at her in desperation. Maybe we could share her gift. "What have you got him?"

Ruby chuckled. "A colour changing toothbrush... It's kind of a private joke."

My heart sunk.

"He won't mind," Ruby repeated, pushing open the door of the bowling alley. "He's a boy."

I frowned as I followed her in. "I know he's a boy," I said awkwardly.

"Boys don't care about presents."

I wondered how she could possibly know that since she was hardly an expert on boys and her own brother had once refused to let us enter the kitchen until we'd paid him with stickers and marbles.

"Some boys might," I muttered.

Ruby gave me a funny look.

I coughed and pretended to be interested in a rack of leaflets by the door. I hastily picked up a handful. "Oh look! The *Yorkshire Sausage Festival* is taking place in Leeds this year."

Ruby giggled and grabbed my arm.

As we made our way through the building Joey saw us approaching and ran over to greet us.

"Happy birthday!" Ruby sang, handing him her gift.

He pulled off the wrapping paper and fell over in hysterics at the sight of the toothbrush. Then he threw it to Mark who started laughing too.

"That's hilarious," Joey said to Ruby. "I can't believe you still remember that."

She sniggered and I attempted a cool chuckle beside her, feeling ridiculously left out.

Joey turned to me. "Hey Livi! I'm glad you could come."

"I, uh, didn't know that chocolate makes you sneeze," I mumbled, handing him the massive eyesore. "I also got you these..." I gave him the leaflets I had picked up at the door. "There's a voucher for the Leeds City bus tour in that one."

He gave me a bemused nod. "Thanks."

"You're welcome." I blushed and hurried to sit down.

Joey's mother, Janine, was lingering by the ticket desk. She waved at me and Ruby and asked for our shoe size. "And what do you want to drink?" she added. "Oh, and don't worry, I'll be staying out of the way. I'm just here to watch." She held up her camera and grinned. Then she blew a kiss to Joey who grimaced and said, "She insisted on coming!"

A few of his friends laughed and gave him a friendly shove but I thought it was kind of sweet. For the briefest of moments I imagined my own mother sitting with Janine, cheering us on and taking photos.

Once everybody had arrived, Joey did a head count and divided us into two teams. To my delight, Ruby and I were both on Joey's team.

"We're the Vikings," he said, handing us homemade Viking badges. He pointed to the other team. "And you're the Farmers."

"Farmers?" Mark screwed up his nose but passed the badges round regardless.

"Right then," Joey said, gathering us Vikings round for a pep talk. "We have to beat those Farmers. Everybody try really hard and... get lots of points."

The rest of our team chuckled but I couldn't help but feel slightly anxious. I'd only been bowling once before. I didn't want to let everybody down.

Our team went first, with Joey striding confidently towards the line. He gave us a determined nod and then turned and released his ball with ease. It glided down the centre of the lane and knocked down all ten pins. We got to our feet and cheered as he ran back to give us all a high five.

"The Vikings have landed!" he cried, blowing the Farmers a friendly raspberry.

In the next lane, one of Joey's friends took a turn and scored 8.

Ruby went next for us and got 9.

"That was close," Joey said as Ruby's second ball missed the last pin by a whisker.

Somebody else had a turn and got about half of the pins.

"Livi, you're up!" Joey nudged me.

I got uneasily to my feet. My stomach churned as I grabbed a ball and approached the line. *Please God, help me get a strike...*

Feeling the back of my neck turn red as every eye watched me, I raised my ball before carefully releasing it down the lane. Unfortunately, it had barely left my hands before it careered straight into the gutter.

My team mates let out a cry of disappointment as the Farmers cheered.

I blinked quickly before running back to my seat where I bent down and pretended to re-tie my shoelaces.

"Don't worry," Ruby whispered. "It's a hard game."

I shrugged as if I had no idea what she was talking about. I was about to sit back and pretend to be interested in the next person's turn when Joey yelled, "Second ball, Livi!"

"Oh..." I gulped and got to my feet, avoiding everybody's gaze as I picked up a new ball and walked all the way back to the line.

I squeezed my eyes shut before uttering one last desperate prayer. *Please God, help me get a spare...*

I took a deep breath and raised my arms. This time, I swung with such exuberance that I completely lost control of the ball. I watched in horror as it bounced out of my hands and catapulted into another lane, colliding with the ball of a serious-looking bowler who threw his hands up and ran to get an attendant. Behind me, I heard a roar of shock and laughter.

I turned shakily and forced a smile, desperate for the ground to swallow me up.

"That was amazing!" Joey exclaimed. "Did you do that on purpose?"

I looked at him in surprise. "No..."

"Well, it was cool!"

I shrugged shyly and went to join Ruby on the bench.

"That was so funny," she whispered. "That man nearly jumped out of his skin."

I gave an uneasy giggle. "Cool."

As my turn drew near again, I found myself growing worried. Should I try to repeat my previous entertaining shot? Or was there any hope that I could do it properly this time? I picked up a ball and walked slowly to the line.

"Hey Livi," Joey called behind me. "Want me to help?"

"Uh..." I bit my lip. "Okay."

He grinned and strode over to me. "Well, first of all, you see those three holes?"

I glanced down at the ball. "Yeah."

"Put your fingers in them. Like this..." He took the ball off me and showed me how to hold it properly.

"Oh." I blushed. "Thanks."

"And keep your arm straight," Joey continued, demonstrating beside me.

I nodded solemnly and stared straight ahead. Then I swung my arm and tentatively let the ball go. It drifted down the lane at about two miles an hour, almost coming to a standstill before it reached the pins. Eventually, it made it to the end and two pins fell down.

"You did it!" said Joey. "Well done."

I blushed again and muttered, "Thanks." I went to fetch another ball for my second shot, taking the whole thing slowly again. This time, the ball went straight into the gutter.

"That's okay," Joey assured me. "You did really well with the first shot."

I gave an uncomfortable smile and sat down.

As the game went on, my shots barely improved. I don't think I ever got more than three pins at a time. But the glorious compensation for my inaptitude was Joey's constant encouragement that I was 'getting better.' I watched in awe as he got several strikes in a row. Then I joined in with a group photo of the rest of us as pins being knocked down by Joey's mighty Viking arm.

In the end, and despite my poor efforts, our team won. But it didn't seem to matter. As we lined up at the counter for ice cream, my disastrous second throw remained the highlight of the match.

"It literally bounced about five times," one of Joey's friends said, re-enacting the moment with a scrunched up napkin.

"It was so loud," Ruby added.

"My mum got a good photo of that bowler shaking his fist at you!" Joey said, holding up Janine's camera.

I pretended to be embarrassed although I was secretly enjoying the attention.

"Well, that was fun." Mark pulled off his Farmer badge and tossed it into the bin.

"Good game," said someone else.

Around me, everyone started to dispose of their badges. But I took mine off carefully and tucked it into my pocket.

Jill was still working when I got home. I joined her in the living room and tried to tell her about my epic throw but she just nodded and said, "That's a shame."

"No!" I insisted. "It was funny. It went like this..." I grabbed a cushion and bounced it across the room. "And it went down another lane..."

She nodded again. "Okay."

I gave a growl and snapped, "Never mind."

Jill looked up. "What? Oh no. I'm sorry, Livi. I was listening really. I just have—"

"—to work," I finished bitterly. "I know."

Her face dropped. "I'm sorry."

"It's fine."

She shook her head and shut her folder. "Let's do something together. What do you want to do?"

I gave a careless shrug.

"Do you want to watch a film?" she suggested. "Or go and get an ice cream?"

"I had an ice cream at Joey's party."

"Well, you could have another one."

"With three scoops and a flake?"

"Yeah, if you want."

I gave a splutter. "Okay!"

So we drove into town and went to a fancy ice cream parlour in the centre. Jill ordered me the biggest ice cream on the menu and even asked for extra cream and sprinkles. It was massive and, as soon as I started it, I realised it would be a struggle to eat the whole thing. I was still full from the snacks at Joey's party.

"Is it nice?" Jill asked when I was about halfway through.

I offered her my spoon.

She shook her head. "You have it."

I smiled and forced down another gulp.

"So, you had fun at your friend's party?"

"Yeah."

"That's good."

I had a few more spoonfuls and stopped. My stomach was starting to ache. I was also shivering slightly. It was February, after all.

"Have you had enough?" Jill asked.

I looked up sheepishly. "Sorry to waste it."

"That's okay."

"Thanks," I added quietly.

"You're welcome... We should do this more often."

I nodded.

"It's good to get out of the house, isn't it?" she continued. "You know, do something normal?"

I nodded again, glancing round the empty ice cream parlour as the rest of my poem formed in my mind.

> *'I want to be normal. I want to be like you,*
> *Doing all the normal things that normal people do.*
> *Like chatting and caring*
> *And sisterly sharing,*
> *Eating ice cream in winter and wasting it too.'*

~*~

Later that evening I logged onto FriendWeb, wondering if Joey had uploaded any photos of his party yet. A flashing message at the top of the screen announced, *'New friend request.'* I grinned and clicked the link, half-hoping it would be Kitty Warrington just so I could snub her.

But it wasn't Kitty.

My stomach lurched as a picture of my dad popped up, accompanied by the words, *'Charlie Teeson wants to be your friend.'*

I gripped the sides of my chair and stared at the words in disbelief. His photo was a casual shot of him holding up a beer. He looked happy. Like a normal person. Like a normal father.

Along with the friend request was a private message. The subject said simply, *'Hello.'*

I bit my lip as I clicked on it.

'Hi Livi,
I keep meaning to call but can't quite find the words. I'm really sorry about everything. Drop me a line if you want.
Dad.'

I gaped at it for about ten minutes. He had left so suddenly and so *awfully*. I hadn't expected to hear from him ever again.

Eventually, a message came up. *'Do you know Charlie Teeson?'* I contemplated the two options: *'Add to your web,'* or, *'Cut loose.'*

I wished there was a third option: *'Keep on hold, just in case.'*

Without thinking, I accepted his request. Another message proclaimed, *'Congratulations! You now have 22 friends in your web.'*

I chewed the inside of my cheek.

Suddenly a chat window popped up at the bottom of the screen.

'Hi Livi.'

I almost fell backwards off my chair. It was him.

"What do I do?" I muttered, searching desperately for some kind of *'Hide'* button.

'Are you there?'

"No!" I moaned. "No, no, no."

'How's tricks?'

I stared at the screen with my mouth wide open. Perhaps, if I sat perfectly still, it would all go away.

'Livi?'

I gave a moan and leant towards the screen, my hands hovering over the keyboard as I pondered what to say. *'Good evening.'* Too formal. *'What do you want?'* Too abrupt. *'Sorry, I didn't realise I was logged on.'* A blatant lie since I had just accepted his friend request.

In the end, I decided I would simply say, *'Oh hi!'* but, before I could begin to type, another message popped up. *'Charlie Teeson is now offline.'*

I exhaled slowly. "Stupid FriendWeb."

Farther God

I remember the first time I realised that I didn't have a normal family. It was the Christmas after my dad first left and we were staying at Aunt Claudia's.

Christmas day was drawing to an end and I was sitting by the fire with my sister and aunt, my new presents strewn before me on the rug. Jill had bought me a couple of dolls and a brand new teddy[36] and I was lining them up and pretending to be their mother.

"Time for a bedtime story," I told them as I stroked their heads. I looked over at Jill and Aunt Claudia and added, "I wish I had a story." I tried to say this loudly for Aunt Claudia's benefit because, despite the fact that I had circled many books in the *Story Farm* catalogue and posted them to her several weeks before Christmas, she had bought me a dictionary and encyclopaedia and inscribed them with the words, *'Don't be a fool. Work hard at school.'*

My aunt didn't notice so I sighed and picked up the dictionary. "I'm going to read this whole book," I told my toys. "But we mustn't tell Miss Hoover."[37]

Before I'd even got past the first page, I found myself growing sleepy. So I curled up on the rug with one of Aunt Claudia's cats and closed my eyes.

---

[36] Sausage-Legs, who at that point was named Turkey-Eater.

[37] Miss Hoover was my year two teacher. She used to tell us that she had eyes in the back of her head which I didn't doubt because she looked a little like an alien and several of the older children claimed that her hair was really a wig. I assumed she'd been sent to Earth on a special mission to find out more about human life and, consequently, I endeavoured not to tell her very much, especially during *'Show and Tell.'*

Just before I drifted off I overheard Jill say to Aunt Claudia, "I really hate Christmas."

Aunt Claudia replied, "You're thinking about your mother, aren't you?"

"Not so loud!" my sister hissed.

I sensed them looking at me so I squeezed my eyes shut and willed myself not to move.

"She's asleep," our aunt said flippantly. "She's overwhelmed by all her presents, bless her."

"Do you think she's alright?" asked Jill. "Am I messing her up?"

"Don't be daft. You're doing a fantastic job."

"I don't know. This family is so... dysfunctional."

Our aunt sighed and muttered something about needing to put the leftover turkey in the fridge. She asked Jill if she wanted a cold chipolata and Jill said no. Then they turned the television on and switched through the channels to find a good film.

I gave them a few more minutes and then, when it became clear that the serious talk was over, I arose from my slumber with a dramatic yawn.

"Did you have a nice sleep, love?" Aunt Claudia cooed, giving me a squeeze as I got off the rug.

"Yeah," I said sweetly, shooting them a grin before running upstairs to look up *'dysfunctional'* in my new dictionary.

~*~

It was Wednesday night before I plucked up the courage to log onto FriendWeb again. My dad had sent me another message. I wasn't sure whether I was pleased or peeved about this. As I clicked on the link I pursed my lips and reminded myself to remain cool in the face of his grovelling apology.

'Hey Livi,
How has your week been? Mine has been pretty good. I've been working in the local crayon factory for less than two months and have already been promoted to Shift Manager. I get an extra break and am being trained to operate the wax machine. I suppose I should tell you that I'm living in Hull now. I live near a nice park. I think you'd like it.

Get in touch when you can.
Dad.'

I felt a rush of anger as I stared at his message. The casual manner of it left me feeling extremely affronted. How dare he write so carelessly, as if nothing had happened between us? *'I suppose I should tell you that I'm living in Hull...'* Who did he think I was? His penpal?

I deleted the message and quickly located the *'Remove Friend'* button on his profile.

'Are you sure you want to delete Charlie Teeson from your web? This cannot be undone.'

I hovered over the *'Yes'* button, feeling the blood rush to my cheeks, but, for some stupid reason, I just couldn't bring myself to click it. Instead, I stared dumbly at his profile page, wondering how far away Hull was and whether it had a cinema.

Suddenly, a smiling spider popped up at the bottom of the screen, accompanied by the words, *'Game request! Charlie Teeson challenges you to a round of Football Frenzy.'*

I burst into tears and switched the computer off, vowing never to go online again.

I felt pretty miserable for the rest of the week.

Ruby could tell there was something wrong but, when she asked, I shrugged and said, "Don't know." When she pushed further, I yawned and pretended to examine my fingernails.

By Friday afternoon she seemed to have got the hint and only spoke to me if absolutely necessary.

"Are you coming to youth group tonight?" she asked tentatively during Maths.

I scribbled across my worksheet and gave a half-hearted nod.

"Livi Starling!" Fester barked from over my shoulder. "How are you getting on with those equations?"

I screwed up my work. "I need to start again."

He raised his eyebrows and handed me a clean sheet.

"My dad can give us a lift," Ruby continued awkwardly after Fester had gone back to his desk.

I grunted and dragged my pen across my new worksheet. I didn't particularly want to go to youth group. Every time somebody said the words *'God'* and *'Father'* I felt like screaming, especially when they were used in the same sentence. But I didn't want to be a bad Christian and not go. I was meant to be God's child. I wanted to make him proud.

I made a determined effort to look normal when we arrived at Eddie and Summer's that evening. I joined a few of the girls in a corner and forced a happy smile onto my face.

"I wonder what we're doing tonight," Ruby said, indicating Eddie who had removed all the cushions from the chairs and was arranging them in a higgledy fashion across the room.

One of the Graces laughed and said, "It looks like an obstacle course."

"Yeah," I muttered. "Or like the sofa threw up."

Out of the corner of my eye, I saw Joey coming in with Mark and made an extra effort to look relaxed and happy.

"Let's start with a game," Eddie said once everyone had arrived. "I want you to get into pairs."

Ruby grabbed my arm and grinned. I forced a smile in return although I couldn't help but glance across the room to see who Joey was partnering with.

"You're going to race towards these..." Eddie shook a bag of sweets and put them on the floor in the corner of the room.

Everyone burst into eager chatter and Joey and Mark leapt up and rubbed their hands together.

"But," Eddie continued loudly. "Only one of you will be able to see." He held up a handful of scarves.

Summer took the scarves from him and handed them round. "Decide who's going to be blindfolded," she said. "The other person has to lead them round the obstacles to reach the prize."

Ruby looked at me and giggled.

I pretended to be excited as I asked, "Do you want to be blindfolded?"

"I'm scared! You do it!"

I shrugged and put the scarf round my face.

Ruby secured it tightly. "Can you see?"

"No." I got to my feet and waited for the game to begin. With my eyes closed and my face covered I listened to the buzz around me and felt strangely detached from the world.

As Eddie yelled, "Go!" I began to amble mindlessly in the dark, caring very little about anything at all.

Once or twice I almost lost myself, drifting into a daydream about nothing in particular. I could have been anywhere, doing anything. But then I came to my senses and remembered I was *here*, in a random house in Leeds, with a scarf over my face, racing a Christian youth group for a bag of sweets. It seemed so bizarre.

"Left!" Ruby squealed. "No, I meant right! Right! There's a cushion. Stop!"

I followed her instructions as best I could but, from the roars and cheers at the other end of the room, I gathered we were miles away from winning the prize. At one point I walked into a lamp because Ruby got her left and right muddled up.

A shriek erupted across the room and Ruby moaned, "Oh, Bill and Rory have won."

I pulled off my blindfold and saw that I was facing a pot plant, further from the sweets than when we'd begun. "Oh well," I said indifferently.

The others jabbered away as Eddie and Summer gathered us into a circle. The prize was meaningless since they had several more bags of sweets which they passed round as we sat down.

"I hope you all enjoyed that!" Eddie said.

I joined in with the animated nods.

Summer grinned. "Did you feel safe in your partner's hands?"

I eyed Ruby carefully and caressed the bruise on my leg. *Not really.*

"Life can sometimes feel like walking with a blindfold on," Summer said. "We need clear direction from God because he's the only one who can see what's coming. But that requires trust…"

I stifled a yawn and looked around the room. They must have really liked owls because there were seventeen dotted around the room, including a tiny crystal ornament on the mantelpiece and a clock which hooted the time on the hour. Most of the books on their shelf seemed to have a Christian title and one in particular caught my eye: *'Godly Parenting. Stewarding the Heart of your Child.'* There was a row of photos of Alfie and Felix along the windowsill. I envied them for having *godly parents* like Eddie and Summer.

I turned back to Summer who was sharing a story about a time when she and Eddie weren't sure whether to stay in Leeds or go to Germany.

"We really had to listen to God," Eddie chipped in. "Because on our own we would have been lost."

I knew I ought to be listening, and that God was probably disappointed in me for not even trying, but I just couldn't concentrate. I found it so frustrating. I had asked God *many* questions. I'd asked him what was wrong with Jill and I'd asked him whether my dad would be coming back. I'd even asked him about insignificant things like what to put in my scones for Food Technology. But he never seemed to say *anything* in reply. On several occasions I had resorted to Violet's technique of opening the Bible at a random passage, but he didn't speak to me in that way either. How could he possibly be as close as Summer and Eddie claimed? Unless everybody else was hearing him and I just wasn't doing things right.

After she'd finished speaking, Summer told us to get into small groups to pray together. "Perhaps you're struggling with something right now," she suggested. "God wants to help you know where to walk."

I felt a surge of irritation but tried to look interested as Nicole and one of the Graces joined Ruby and me.

I hoped I could just blend in if I looked nonchalant enough but, without warning, Nicole turned to me. "Let's pray for you, Livi."

"No, it's alright," I said. "I don't need any prayer."

She looked at me in surprise. "Oh."

I blushed as a lump formed in my throat. "I mean, I just need the toilet." I got up from the circle and ran out of the room.

Ruby followed me and grabbed my arm in the hallway. "Livi, wait!"

I pulled away and ran up the stairs but Ruby chased me up and lunged in front of the bathroom door. "Can I come in too?"

I sighed huffily and rubbed my head.

"Or do you actually need the toilet?" she added nervously. "Because I'm not trying to watch, if you do."

I laughed despite myself and said, "You can come in."

She smiled and followed me in, locking the door behind us. "Are you okay?" she asked, sitting beside me on the bathmat.

I took a deep breath. "My dad sent me a message on FriendWeb."

"Oh!"

"Two messages actually. He's working in a crayon factory." I screwed up my nose.

Ruby gave me a tentative pat on the shoulder.

I squirmed. I didn't want to be stroked like a dog. "I'm fine."

She bit her lip. "What did you say to him?"

"Nothing. I'm not going to reply. He's an idiot."

She gave a slow nod. She looked as though she was about to say something but at the last moment she shook her head instead.

"What?" I snapped.

"Nothing."

"What?" I repeated. "Just say what you think."

She chewed her thumb and looked away. Finally, she whispered, "I think you need to forgive him."

I stared at her. "Forgive him? How can you say that?"

"Because you'll always be angry until you do."

"I *should* be angry! He lied. And he left— twice!" The lump in my throat doubled in size and I blinked furiously to keep myself from crying.

"I know," Ruby said quietly. "Forgiving him doesn't mean he was right—"

"He's not even sorry! He invited me to play *'Football Frenzy.'*" I paused before adding bitterly, "I *hate* football and I hate *him.*"

Ruby stared at me.

"I do," I insisted. "And I don't care if it's not very Christian. I'll never forgive him."

Ruby blushed. "We can talk about it another time."

I let out a growl. "No! You don't understand."

Ruby gulped and looked away. "Where is he?"

I gave a grunt. "Hull. Wherever that is."

"Isn't that where the awards ceremony for the class newspaper is being held?"

My stomach lurched. "What if he's one of the judges?"

"I doubt he will be..."

I put my head in my hands and moaned.

Ruby was about to say something else but, at that moment, Summer knocked on the door. "Are you girls alright in there?"

Ruby raised her eyebrows. I sighed and turned away.

"We're alright," Ruby called to Summer. She got up and unlocked the door.

Summer came in, her face full of concern. She looked from me to Ruby. "Do you want to talk?"

"No," I said, just as Ruby said, "Yes please."

I glared at Ruby but she said, "You should talk about it, Livi."

I shrugged and ran my finger along the bathmat.

"What's upsetting you, Livi?" Summer asked softly.

I frowned. "I didn't like that blindfold game. And I don't understand what you mean about being able to trust God to lead us. He feels so far away." I pursed my lips before adding defiantly, "Sometimes, I'm not even sure if he's there at all."

Summer didn't look remotely worried. In fact, she just smiled. "It's okay to feel that way," she assured me. She paused for a moment. "What's your relationship like with your parents?"

I scowled and turned away.

Ruby coughed and spoke up for me. "Her mum died when she was a baby and her dad left... twice." I tutted but Ruby carried on, "She lives with her sister."

Summer nodded slowly. "God is nothing like your earthly family," she said. "He won't leave you or let you down. Even when you feel like he's far away, his eyes are always on you."

A tear slid down my cheek. "I don't feel it."

Summer put an arm around my shoulder. "You will."

I gave a heavy sigh and put my head in my hands. I desperately wanted to believe her.

As Stanley drove us home, I spent the entire journey trying to compose myself so that Jill wouldn't see that I had been crying. But, as I got out of the car, Ruby called to me, "Remember that God loves you, Livi!" and I immediately burst into tears again.

I wiped my face and unlocked the front door as quietly as possible. Jill was emerging from the kitchen. I jumped in fright and forced a smile.

She looked at me in surprise. "What's wrong?"

"Nothing. I'm just a bit tired."

Jill gave me a long look. "How was tonight?"

"It was alright. A bit boring."

"You don't have to go, you know."

"I want to! I like it."

I can't have sounded that convincing because she gave me a pitying smile and said, "You don't have to do everything Ruby does. Don't try to be something you're not."

~ 12 ~

A fair fight

Aunt Claudia has a saying: *'The angry cat ruins the mouse.'* I had never quite understood her point. I'd assumed that surely an angry cat would *want* to ruin a mouse. And the average cat owner wouldn't deny their cat such a right. In fact, if you had a plague of mice, you would cajole your cat into being as angry as possible in order to exterminate the pests. Like much of what Aunt Claudia says, I had always responded to this bizarre expression with a scornful roll of the eyes. That was until this afternoon, when I became the mouse.

I had felt agitated all day. It began with an annoying assignment in French where we had to write a letter to an imaginary pen friend named Peppe, telling him all about our family.

"This is the most pointless subject ever," I complained to Ruby as Madame Maurel handed out French dictionaries. "When will I ever need to speak French?"

Ruby shrugged. "It could be useful if you ever go to France."

"I'll probably *never* go to France."

Ruby ignored me and turned to her work.

I flicked through the French dictionary, looking for inspiration. I wrote a few hasty sentences before leaning back on my chair with a sigh.

Madame Maurel eyed me from her desk. I tried to look busy but it was too late. Without a pause, she swooped over and picked up my work.

"*Cher Peppe,*" she read aloud. "*J'habite avec ma soeur*; I live with my sister. Good. *Mais assez parlé de moi; But enough about me...*" She scanned my work and then looked at me. "What ees zis, Livi?"

I took my book from her and read, *"Quelle est your opinion on human cloning?"*

Madam Maurel raised her eyebrows.

"I ran out of things to say," I mumbled.

"Nonsense!" Madame Maurel threw her hands up in the air. "You 'ave barely begun to tell Peppe about your family. What ees your sister's name? What about your parents?"

"And don't forget about pets!" Kitty piped up behind me.

"Exactement, Mademoiselle Warrington!" Madame Maurel trilled. "Peppe would like to know zese things!"

I scowled as she trotted back to her desk.

"Peppe can mind his own business," I muttered.

I was still brooding over the French class in Geography where I was caught off-guard by Mr Thomas asking me to summarise what he had just said about the deforestation of the rainforest.

Without thinking, I responded with a half-hearted toucan impression.

Mr Thomas gave me a perplexed stare and I heard Kitty and Molly snigger behind me.

"Er, the birds will die out," I explained weakly. "And the bonobos— they're a type of monkey." I finished with my *Bashful Bonobo* impression, forcing a shrug as everybody laughed.

After lunch, we had Maths, which did little to soothe my spirits, and my mood got even worse during Science when Ruby asked suddenly, "Are you coming on the weekend away?"

"What weekend away?"

"Bible Bash. Eddie mentioned it on Friday."

"Oh. I wasn't listening," I confessed.

"You should come! It will be fun."

"When is it?"

"In two weeks."

"Is it free?"

"Er..." Ruby stopped and thought about it. "It will be for you," she said finally.

"What do you mean for *me?"*

She blushed. "It's free if you're from a low-income family."

"I'm not from a low-income family!" I exclaimed. "Jill works in business. She gets bonuses every time she hits her targets."[38]

"Sorry. I didn't realise."

---

[38] That was true, although I couldn't remember the last time it had happened.

"Just because I don't talk about money, it doesn't mean I don't have any!"

"Sorry," Ruby repeated. "Well then, it's thirty five pounds."

I bit my lip. There was no way we could afford that. "That's fine," I snapped.

The bell rang to signal the end of the day and I slammed my book shut and gathered up my belongings.

Ruby scurried to catch up with me as I marched out of the room. "Where are you going?" she called weakly.

"Checking the post box." I fixed a firm expression on my face and strode towards our form room.

I had checked Auntie Amber's post box systematically since I put it there and was yet to receive any mail. But still, I didn't want to be unavailable should a need arise.

Some of our classmates followed us in and headed to their lockers. I tried to be discreet as I approached the post box and casually peered through the slot. My heart skipped a beat at the sight of a folded-up piece of paper. I had a letter! Unable to contain my excitement, I pulled the lid off the box and quickly yanked the letter out. Then, turning slightly to maintain a degree of secrecy, I unfolded it and began to read.

'Dear Auntie Amber,
There's a really weird girl in our class and we don't know what to do. We think she's part animal because she's always making strange noises and we're scared of catching something if we get too close...'

I stopped in disappointment. Behind me, I heard a squeal of laughter. I turned to see Kitty, Molly, Melody and Annie grinning inanely.

"*Ha ha,*" I said sarcastically.

"I'm surprised you could read it," Molly sneered.

"Maybe she couldn't," Kitty suggested. "Do you need some help?" She yanked the letter off me and read loudly, "*'There's a really weird girl in our class.'* That's you, Livi."

"How original," I retorted. I was aware that a few of our classmates were watching and was determined not to be seen to falter. I grabbed my bag and said nonchalantly, "It was almost funny. But you spelled '*weird*' wrong."

Kitty looked at the letter in confusion. "No I didn't."

"Yeah, you did. It's spelled *K.I.T.T.Y.*"

Kitty turned bright red as, across the room, Ritchie Jones said, "Smooth!"

I snatched the letter back and ripped it up. "Nice try though."

With her eyes narrowed and her ears almost standing on end, Kitty looked like a particularly unpleasant cat. I smirked and began to walk away, feeling like the mouse who stole the cheese. However, I did not factor for an even fiercer beast: Molly Masterson.

"Hey, Livi," she called after me. "Where did you get your bag? A charity shop?"

"Ignore her," Ruby whispered, pulling me through the doorway.

With hindsight, I should have listened to Ruby. But something in me snapped and I turned on my heels and marched back to Molly.

"What did you say?" I demanded.

"I *said*," Molly drawled, "Where did you get your bag? *A charity shop?*" She exchanged a glance with her friends and they burst out laughing.

I glared at her and said loudly, "Well, you would know, since that's where you got your ugly face."

Across the room, our classmates tittered.

Molly stopped laughing and swore. "At least I can read," she muttered.

"I *can* read!"

"No you can't."

"I can!"

"You can't."

"I CAN!"

Molly gave a sneer and said under her breath, "No you can't, because your mummy never taught you."

I gave a cry of annoyance. "Whatever." I looked her up and down. "At least I'm not fat."

Molly's mouth dropped open.

A stunned silence filled the room as the faces of our bemused classmates suddenly turned very serious.

"I can't believe you just said that," Kitty hissed.

I rolled my eyes. "She started it." I was aware of my classmates staring but gave a careless shrug as I said, "Ready to go, Ruby?"

Ruby looked as though she was about to cry. "Er, Livi…" She pointed behind me.

I looked round just in time to see Molly lunging at me, her hands coiled into fists as she pummelled me to the floor.

"How dare you call me fat!" she screamed.

"Get off me, you monster!" I shrieked, squirming under the weight of her heavy thighs.

Molly gave a cry of fury and pulled my hair.

I slapped her as hard as I could, thrashing wildly with one hand and shielding my face with the other.

I was vaguely aware of a rush of commotion as our classmates ran to watch. A few people got their phones out to film us, Wayne Purdy started commentating in the corner, and Kitty, Melody and Annie cackled as they urged Molly to poke my eyes out.

At one point, one of my shoes fell off and I considered whether anybody would notice my doodle of a horse on the insole. But I figured this wasn't the time to be self-conscious. I closed my eyes and wondered whether this was how I was going to die: suffocated under the weight of a hysterical Molly Masterson.

Just as I was about to aim a desperate kick towards Molly's backside, a pair of hands intervened and wrenched the two of us apart.

It was Miss Day, our Food Technology teacher. "Stop this senseless brutality immediately!" she exclaimed in a panic.

Miss Day scares easily. A few weeks ago Ruby accidentally set an oven glove on fire and Miss Day hasn't let her near an oven since. She pulled the two of us to our feet. "What on earth happened here?" She looked thoroughly appalled.

I grabbed my shoe and hung my head in shame. Miss Day is quite a nice teacher and I hated the idea of causing her such alarm. My only consolation was that it wasn't Ms Sorenson.

"She started it—" I began.

Molly opened her mouth to disagree but Miss Day said, "I don't care who started it. This kind of behaviour is absolutely unacceptable. I'm going to have to take you to Mr Riley."

My stomach sunk. Mr Riley is our head teacher. I'd only been in his office once before. It was on my first day when he had welcomed me with his booming Leeds accent and said he hoped I had a *smashing time at Hare Valley High.* I'm not sure this was what he had in mind.

Miss Day cleared her throat and gave us both a stern look. "Come with me."

Molly whined and I attempted a friendly smile, as if to say, *There there, Miss Day, we were only messing about!'*

But Miss Day's usually placid exterior had given way to a wild beast within and she positively snarled as she shook her head and roared, "NOW!"

The last thing I heard as Miss Day escorted us out of the room was Kitty exclaiming, "Oh my goodness, did you see the donkey drawn in her shoe?"

Molly and I had to wait outside Mr Riley's office for about half an hour. Miss Day had gone in to inform him of our arrival before telling us grimly that he would see us 'in a minute.' She had left us sitting on two ends of a thin wobbly bench, as far away from one another as possible. All around us, students were rushing through the corridor as they celebrated the end of another school day. At one point Ms Sorenson hurried past and I tried to smile, as if to pretend I was waiting for Mr Riley for a good reason. She smiled back and walked on.

Eventually, it grew very quiet in the corridor. I wondered if I should try to say something to Molly. Perhaps we could sort things out between us and avoid the whole ordeal of seeing the head. I cast a cautious glance in her direction but her gaze was fixed straight ahead, a look of deep fury etched on her face. I sighed and picked my fingernails.

Finally, Mr Riley emerged from his office and addressed us gravely, "Girls." He waved a hand at his open door.

Molly sprang off the bench and waltzed into the office. I stood up rather more tentatively and followed her in.

Mr Riley closed the door behind us and ambled over to his desk. "Now then," he said. "What happened?"

I cleared my throat and attempted to look remorseful as I grappled for a mature response. "I think it was hormones," I began.

Before I could expand upon this, Molly burst into tears.

Mr Riley looked at her in surprise. "Are you alright, Molly?"

"She called me fat," Molly shrieked, her face scarlet with rage.

Mr Riley inhaled sharply. "Is this true, Livi?"

"She said I couldn't read!" I spluttered.

Mr Riley breathed heavily out of his nose. "Can you read?"

"Of course I can read!"

"Well then." He shook his head. "Livi Starling, do you realise how seriously we take bullying at this school?"

My jaw fell open. "I'm not a bully!" I exclaimed. "She started it. She said I couldn't read."

"But you can."

"Yes, but I—"

"Have you seen the school handbook, Livi? We have zero tolerance for negative comments regarding appearances."

I gaped at him. It seemed it was quite alright for Molly to taunt me for something that wasn't true but entirely forbidden for me to pick on something that was spot on.

"I didn't mean it in a bad way," I said weakly. "My aunt is fat."

I felt myself blushing as Mr Riley stared at me. Molly was still whimpering and wiping her snotty nose on the backs of her hairy arms.

Eventually, Mr Riley said, "Molly, you can go now."

Molly sniffed and picked up her bag. She cast me a quick glare before slouching out of the room.

I took a deep breath and faced Mr Riley.

"I'm very disappointed with you, Livi. I don't know what the standards were at your old school but this simply will not do."

I opened my mouth and closed it again.

"I'm going to need to talk to your parents..." He headed towards a filing cabinet containing student information.

I stared at him and waited for him to correct himself.

"I mean, sister," he said as he located my file. He ran his finger down the page and then reached for the phone. To my relief, he put it down again after several rings. "She doesn't appear to be in. Can I trust you to deliver a letter?"

"Yeah," I whispered.

I watched as Mr Riley pulled out a sheet of official letter-headed paper and started to write. I realised time was short so, in the most grown-up voice I could muster, I began, "Sir, I don't think this is fair—" But, before I could get any further, a lump caught in my throat and I started crying instead.

Mr Riley put the finishing touches to his letter and folded it twice. Then, without even reading it through, he crammed it into an envelope and sealed it with two licks. He held it out and said, "Straight to your sister and no funny business. I expect to hear from her in due course."

A lone tear rolled down my cheek as I took the letter and walked out. The whole school was deserted by this point and my shoes tapped noisily down the empty corridor as I ran to the door. I sped across the playground, completely desolate except for Ruby, sitting under a tree, looking forlorn.

"Hi Livi," she said when I reached her.

I gave a heavy sigh. "Hi."

"Are you alright?"

I waved Mr Riley's letter at her. "Stupid Miss Day. I'd have had it sorted if she hadn't come interfering."

Ruby gave me a funny look. "I got Miss Day," she admitted. "I thought you needed some help. Sorry."

I sighed again and rubbed a bruise on my shoulder. "Thanks."

Jill was late home from work that evening. This meant I had a long time to mull over the day's events and conspire against Molly and Kitty and their whole stupid gang. All the while Mr Riley's letter sat looking very grim on my bed. I glared at it for about fifteen minutes before grabbing it and holding it up to my lamp, trying in vain to read it through the envelope. I scrunched it slightly, catching sight of the odd word as the paper curled in my hand. I picked at the envelope. Perhaps I could rewrite Mr Riley's letter, pulling out the gist of it and explaining that Molly had admitted all fault.

"But I *can't* do that," I scolded myself. "That would be lying which is wrong, wrong, *wrong...*" I stopped and thought about it. "Or *is* it?"

I sat against my bed and scowled. The reason I was in trouble was because I had told the truth. Molly *is* rather fat. Admittedly, it was a somewhat insensitive comment to have made, but it was *true*. Yet my honesty had got me into trouble and Molly's lie was going unpunished. How was that fair? I gave a sniff as I considered that maybe lying wasn't so bad after all...

Five examples of Acceptable Lying
1. When somebody asks you if you like their new haircut and you don't.
2. When planning a surprise birthday party for a friend.
3. A magician claiming he got a coin out of your ear.
4. Hiding a Jew from the Nazis.
5. Taking special measures to ensure an already depressed sister doesn't grow more miserable...

Perhaps I could forge a letter from Jill informing Mr Riley that I had been appropriately punished and that the matter need not be discussed further. Nobody would need to know. I pulled out some paper from my bag.

Except, I reminded myself, *God would know. And God would not be pleased.* He'd probably mark me out as a lost cause, destined to be a liar forever. I could almost hear him mocking me: *I would never pretend that your bad haircut looked nice.*

I groaned and threw myself onto the bed. *Fine, I'll give Jill the letter,* I told God angrily. *But I don't think it's fair at all.*

I closed my eyes and distracted myself with a despicable daydream in which Molly ate all of Kitty's pets and got so fat that she exploded.

Eventually, I heard Jill's key turn in the lock, followed by her calling, "I've got a pizza, Livi!"

"Okay!" I yelled back, emerging from my daydream with a lurch.

I made one last plea to God. Perhaps when Jill opened the letter it could miraculously announce that I had won a prize instead.

'Dear Ms Starling, I am pleased to inform you that your sister has been named Sensible and Responsible Student of the Year...'

I dragged my heels all the way down the stairs and stood in the kitchen doorway.

Jill looked up from the pizza box and eyed my gloomy expression. "What's wrong?"

"I have to give you this," I said quietly. I slid the letter across the table and waited. "I started to open it but I didn't read it, I promise."

Jill looked at me in confusion.

I bit my lip and watched as she unfolded the letter, her eyes narrowing as she read it.

She put it down and stared at me. "I can't believe you tormented this poor girl."

"I didn't *torment* her," I spluttered. "She's horrible. She said—"

"You can't go round calling people names."

"She said I couldn't read..."

Jill ignored me and got up from the table. "I thought you were meant to be a Christian!" she said hotly.

I avoided her gaze. "Maybe I'm not."

~ **13** ~

For all my sins

As I came down for breakfast the next morning, I overheard Jill on the phone to Mr Riley. I stopped on the landing and listened.

"Absolutely appalling behaviour. I couldn't be more shocked... Yes, I know... Not at all..." She looked up and caught my eye but didn't return my smile. "What would you suggest, Mr Riley?" she continued into the phone.

I tried to get her attention. "Tell him it wasn't my fault!" I pleaded.

Jill turned her back on me and made approving noises into the phone. "I'm happy with that," she said before saying goodbye.

I gave a heavy sigh and plodded down the stairs.

Jill gave me a stern look and headed into the kitchen.

"What did he say?" I asked as I followed her.

"He said he was very disappointed in you."

"Anything else? I mean, am I going to get punished?" I had tormented myself all night with visions of being publicly stripped of the role of editor.

Jill pursed her lips and went to pour herself a cup of tea. "You're on report."

"*Report?*" My jaw dropped open. Being on report meant I would need a signed statement from a teacher at the end of every lesson. Such a penalty was usually reserved for the most disruptive of students, like Wayne Purdy when he filled his French book with swear words and Sheena Ali for setting fire to a table. It wasn't something I had ever imagined could be fitting for *me*. What would Ruby say? How could I face my classmates? An even worse thought struck me: *What would Ms Sorenson think?*

"How long for?" I asked desperately.

"Till the end of the week."

I let out a small sigh of relief. We didn't have Ms Sorenson until Monday.

"If you're good," Jill added. "Longer, if not."

I frowned. "I don't deserve this. It was Molly's fault."

Jill stirred her tea and ignored me.

I scowled at her. "You should have stood up for me."

She gave a bitter laugh. "You're old enough to know better."

"But she started it! She said—"

"I don't care, Livi! I've got enough on my plate without you causing trouble at school." She stood up so fast that she spilt her tea and swore as she hunted for a tea towel.

I gave a growl, wishing I could find the words to defend myself. When nothing mature came to mind, I settled for screaming, "Whatever!" before grabbing my bag and marching out.

Our first lesson was Maths. I sidled miserably up to Fester's desk and put my planner in front of him. He looked at me in confusion.

"I'm on report."

"Report?" He almost fell off his chair. "*You're* on report?"

"Yes."

He stared at me for ages before asking, "What did you do?"

I gave an irritated tut. "I don't want to talk about it."

He kept staring at me in disbelief. "Who'd have thought it? Livi Starling on report!"

I would have made some snide comment except that I needed him to write a nice statement.

"I'll go and do my work then," I said, forcing a smile.

As I wandered back to my desk I caught Kitty's eye and she nudged Molly and grinned. *"Who'd have thought it?"* she sang under her breath. *"Livi Starling on report!"*

I turned to appeal to Fester but he was busy hunting in his drawer for a pen.

Kitty sniggered and hissed, "Bet you feel awful!"

"It's only being on report," I said coolly, forcing a shrug as if to say I was tough enough to have endured much worse.

Kitty passed a note to Molly and they both laughed.

I ignored them and hurriedly took my seat.

"Don't worry," Ruby whispered. "Things can't get much worse."

"Yes they can," I muttered. "We've got Drama next."

Despite making every effort to shine in our Drama classes, our teacher, Miss Waddle, is yet to spot any potential in me. She took my planner with mild surprise and enquired, "What did you do?"

"Just said something I shouldn't have," I mumbled.

Miss Waddle gave me a disapproving stare. "Well, make sure you behave this lesson."

I nodded and turned to see Molly and Kitty giggling. I narrowed my eyes at them as I joined Ruby on the other side of the room.

Miss Waddle got everybody's attention and told us to sit in a circle. She held out a ball and said, "This is anything you want it to be." She demonstrated this by standing in the middle of the circle and stroking her own head with it. "This is my hairbrush," she said dreamily. She raised the ball. "Who's next?"

Wayne Purdy took it and rubbed it under his armpits. "This is my deodorant," he said with a grin.

Everybody squealed and refused to touch the ball after that.

As Miss Waddle gave in to the crowd and went to fetch a clean ball, I wondered what the ball could be for me. I thought perhaps it could be a bird landing in the outstretched hand of a stone statue. I closed my eyes and practised staying perfectly still.

Miss Waddle interrupted my efforts with a shout. "Livi? Are you paying attention? Don't forget you're on report." She waved my planner at me and the class tittered.

I gaped at her. "I *was* paying attention, Miss!"

She raised her eyebrows and asked who wanted to go next.

I watched irritably as my classmates took turns with the ball.

Even Ruby plucked up the courage to have a go. She pretended the ball was the first ray of light at the start of creation and dropped the ball dramatically to demonstrate this.

Molly went next and threw the ball at the wall, narrowly missing my head. "It's a bomb!" she yelled.

Kitty took the ball and rocked it in her arms. "It's a tiny little baby who hasn't learnt to read yet," she simpered. She smirked at me as she sat back down.

"Fantastic," Miss Waddle trilled. "Who's next?"

I pursed my lips and avoided her gaze. I felt like I would cry if I did anything other than sit quietly at the side of the room.

As I went to fetch my planner at the end of the lesson, I overheard Connie Harper ask, "Why is Livi on report?"

"She called Molly fat," Kitty replied, casting a dark look in my direction.

I glanced at Miss Waddle. She looked horrified.

I tried to explain that Molly had started it but the words wouldn't come. So I waited for Miss Waddle to sign my planner then ran out as fast as I could.

I approached the rest of my lessons with a growing sense of dread. Every time a teacher asked what I'd done to warrant being on report, I felt more and more ashamed. But then I'd catch sight of Molly and Kitty sniggering in the corner and I'd start to wonder if expulsion wasn't a small price to pay to go over and strangle them both.

By the end of the week, my planner was adorned with ten signed statements. They ranged from, *'Livi was as good as gold,'*[39] to, *'Livi spent most of the lesson sulking in the corner.'*[40] I had resisted the urge to scrawl over that one because I still needed to show them to Mr Riley. I knocked on his office door last thing on Friday afternoon.

"Hello Livi," he said in his booming Leeds accent.

"Hello Sir," I replied politely, holding out my planner.

I watched as he read through each report. His moustache trembled every time he took a breath and if I screwed up my eyes it looked a bit like a dying rodent.

Eventually, he nodded and gave me my planner back. "Right then. I trust you've had time to think about the way your behaviour affects others?" He accidentally spat in my eye when he said this.

I blinked. "Yes, Sir."

"Good. Keep things up and we'll review the situation after school on Monday."

"Monday? But I thought it was just till the end of the week."

Mr Riley gave me a solemn stare. "I'm not interested in whether you can tow the line for a couple of days. I want to see clear signs that you're truly sorry."

Tears stung the backs of my eyes. "I *am* sorry," I muttered.

This was a lie. I had never been less sorry in my life. If Molly and Kitty had been standing there in that instant I'm not sure I could have held back from clanging their heads together.

Mr Riley nodded. "Come and see me Monday."

---

[39] From Mr Holborn, our History teacher.
[40] From stupid Miss Waddle.

~*~

As part of my punishment Jill declared that I wasn't allowed to go to youth group that week. This suited me fine as I had no desire to go anyway. The last thing I fancied was three hours of pretending to be a nice, normal Christian. Instead, I spent most of the evening wondering what would be worse: the disgrace of approaching Ms Sorenson on Monday with the news that I was on report or the regret of pretending to be ill and missing her lesson altogether. Then I wasted an hour trawling the internet for *'ways to get revenge without sinning'* before giving up and crawling into bed.

I awoke late on Saturday and lay in bed for ages, staring at my ceiling in self-pity. I could hear Jill moaning on the phone to Aunt Claudia.

"She's on report... Yes, it's very serious... Of course I was shocked... She called a girl fat."

I could imagine our aunt's indignant reply. Her double chin was probably wobbling in dismay.

I rolled onto my side and narrowed my eyes at the sight of my Bible. I'd barely opened it in the last few weeks. Every time I tried I felt hopelessly lost. I ran my finger across its edges and muttered, "Couldn't you have written something a bit shorter? I'll never read all this."

God didn't reply.

I sighed and closed my eyes. *It's bad enough having a hopeless earthly father; how am I meant to impress a perfect heavenly one?* I wondered whether God was sick of me yet. I was pretty sure he'd give me a poor report for all my sins.

I waited until Jill was definitely off the phone before getting dressed as I didn't want her to hear me and insist I talk to Aunt Claudia. Then I went downstairs and, like a dopey moth drawn to a flame, absentmindedly logged onto FriendWeb.

There was a new message from my father.

My heart skipped a beat as I opened it, hoping vainly for an outpouring of remorse and a grief-stricken appeal for forgiveness.

'Hi Livi,
Just thinking of you because there was a clearout at work and we have twenty four boxes of crayons left over. The packaging is slightly dented but they should work fine. Do you want them? I know you used to like drawing when you were

younger. Or have you grown out of that? Let me know and I'll post them. There are some interesting colours like Salmon, Sprout, Sunrise and Hashbrown.
Thinking of you,
Dad.'

I stared at the screen for about ten minutes, feeling a bubbling rage rising inside me. *Do I want some crayons? What kind of useless, useless, runaway father offers crayons?*

The frustrating thing was that I like crayons very much and have a shoebox full of them under my bed. When I was younger I had a lucky crayon called *Sweet Cheeks*[41] which I carried everywhere with me until I lost it at the swimming pool. I used to fill endless notebooks with my crayon drawings. These days I don't use them much for fear of breaking them but I like taking them out and lining them up in rainbow order.

I read my dad's message over and over, my heart throbbing at the idea of such exotic colours. But to accept them would mean authorizing his abandonment. It would forever give him reason to exclaim, *'It was good that I moved away. You got crayons.'*

I narrowed my eyes at the computer and shut it down. Then I got to my feet and said, "That's enough, God. I quit." I pulled on my shoes and marched across the street to Ruby's house.

When she answered the door, Ruby took one look at my face and said, "Oh dear."

I sniffed and said, "I don't want to be a Christian anymore."

She looked at me.

"I don't care what you say," I proclaimed. "I've made my mind up..." I started to tell her that I couldn't be happier with my decision but the moment was ruined by me bursting into tears.

"Oh Livi!" Ruby put her arms around me. "It's okay."

"No!" I said furiously. "It's not okay. I thought God was meant to make everything better but he hasn't. I'm on report, Jill's all moody with me, and my stupid dad wants to know whether I'd like twenty four boxes of crayons." I put my head on her shoulder and sobbed.

Ruby rubbed my back and said nothing.

"I quit," I insisted. "No more God stuff."

"Let's talk to my mum," she suggested.

"I don't want to..."

---

[41] Its official name was *Ladybird Red.*

But Ruby grabbed my arm and dragged me into the kitchen. We were met by the sight of Oscar perched on the table like a little monkey, wearing nothing but a pair of pants. Belinda stood over him, cutting his hair into ridiculous tufts.

"Hi Livi!" Oscar sang.

I eyed his haircut, which resembled something from the pet shop down the road. "Hello," I said.

Belinda looked up and beamed. "Hello Livi! How are you?"

"I'm—" I started to say that I was fine, but the words caught in my throat. "I'm... I don't know."

Belinda put her scissors down and looked from me to Ruby. "What's wrong?"

"Livi doesn't want to be a Christian any more," Ruby said quietly.

Belinda blinked at us. "What happened?"

I took a deep breath and looked at the floor. "I sort of got in trouble at school."

"She called a girl fat and had to see Mr Riley," Ruby filled in.

I gave a frustrated moan. "She said I couldn't read!"

Belinda just smiled. "Are you scared that you've let God down?"

"I— yeah," I admitted. "I've messed everything up."

Belinda shook her head and came round the table towards me. "You will never, *ever* mess things up. God loves you. Just keep choosing him." I opened my mouth to protest but she continued, "Do you really think God is shocked by the week you've had? Not at all! He saw it coming long before you did!"

I took a deep breath and let this sink in. "I *do* want to be a Christian," I said, fighting back the tears. "But I thought it would be easier than this."

Belinda patted my hand. "Becoming a Christian isn't the end of all your problems. It's the beginning of you facing up to them."

I was aghast. "You mean everything is going to get *worse?*"

"Not in the long run. Just let God do what needs to be done."

I let out a long sigh.

"He won't let you down," she added.

"But I'm rubbish," I said feebly.

"Great!" Belinda grinned. "Then you'll be a fantastic vessel for God."

"Vessel?"

"God uses the weak things!" Oscar piped up.

I stared at him. "What?"

Belinda tittered and put an arm round my shoulder. "The bottom line is: you can keep protesting but God loves you and there's nothing you can do about it."

I wriggled out of her grasp. "Okay…"

Ruby caught my eye. "It will be alright, Livi."

I felt a lump in my throat. "It's easy for you," I blurted out. "Your life isn't a mess."

"Neither is yours," Ruby countered.

I rolled my eyes. "You know it is!"

"Only from where you're standing," she insisted. "Not from God's point of view. He sees where you're going."

"Where am I going then?"

"How would *I* know?" Ruby gave me a playful shove. "I'm standing in the mess with you!"

I shoved her in return and gave half a smile.

"Facing your problems can be hard," Belinda said gently. "But now you have somebody to face them with."

I looked at Ruby. "You?"

"No!" Ruby giggled. "Jesus."

I blushed. "Oh yeah."

Belinda gave me a squeeze. "Is there anything I can do to help?"

I shook my head. "I'll be fine."

"Are you sure? Would you like a drink or some cake… or a haircut?"

"No. I'm alright."

She nodded and gave Oscar's hair one last snip. "There you go my little pumpkin!"

Oscar shook his head from side to side. "Does it look like a llama?" he asked me. "I want to look like a llama."

I laughed. "Something like that."

"Yippee!" Oscar gave his head another shake and ran out of the room.

Belinda waved her scissors at me. Then she wandered out of the kitchen and yelled up the stairs, "Stanley, your turn, darling!"

I caught Ruby's eye and giggled.

She grinned and pulled her own hair safely into a ponytail. "Let's go!"

"Oh Livi!" Belinda called after me. "Before you go, I've got something for Jill." She rooted around in a drawer before handing me one of her Bible bookmarks.

I suppressed a grimace and said, "I'll give it to her."

I gave the bookmark a hasty glance as I turned to leave. My heart leapt as I read the verse. *'I am sure that nothing can separate us from God's love—not life or death, not angels or spirits, not the present or the future, and not powers above or powers below. Nothing in all creation can separate us from God's love for us in Christ Jesus our Lord!'*[42]

Underneath, Belinda had written, *'Don't let anything stop you from coming to Jesus. He died for all your sins. Even the ones you haven't done yet.'*

I read it three times. He died for all my sins... Even the ones I haven't done yet... I could call Molly fat again and again and I'd still be saved...

"It's a bit cheesy, I know," Belinda admitted. "But I thought Jill might like it."

I gave a small smile. "Actually, Belinda... Jill doesn't like the bookmarks."

"Oh." She looked a little wounded.

"I do though," I said, reading the bookmark once more. "So... You can keep posting them... Just address them to me."

---

[42] It gave the reference (Romans 8:38-39) and featured a picture of a ladder reaching from a girl's heart all the way into Heaven.

~ 14 ~

Like a donut

Mrs Tilly was away on Monday morning. This was great as it meant I didn't have to worry about whether being on report would jeopardise my role as editor. The downside, however, was that the class (a *double* English lesson at that) was being covered by none other than Fester.

He looked at me in surprise as I plonked my planner in front of him. "Still on report?"

I gave an irritable sigh. "Yup."

He stroked his chin in amusement. "Now then, since this is a double English lesson, do you think I need to write *two* reports?"

"If you want." I went to take my seat before he could say anything else.

Fester turned to a note left by Mrs Tilly regarding the lesson. *"Continue with 'The Traffic Light,'"* he read in confusion. "Does that make sense to any of you?"

I quickly marched back to him and took Mrs Tilly's note. "It's our class newspaper, Sir." I turned to our classmates. "Basically, guys, I need you to carry on with your articles. Come and see me if you have any questions."

A few people groaned and Kitty rolled her eyes and said, "Ego trip or what?"

Fester looked at me as I sat back down. "Right then!" he said with a grin. "You heard Miss Starling. Get on with your articles!"

The class muttered and moaned as they pulled out their work.

I pretended not to notice their grumbling as I busied myself with rooting through my pencil case, as though in search of a particular pen. I settled on a tacky pink biro, a souvenir from Jill's recent work trip to Blackpool.[43] Then I pulled out some paper and began jotting down notes for an article on animal impersonation. Ruby and I had already designed an advert for the local donkey sanctuary and I figured my article would complement it nicely.

A short while later, Fester came over and asked, "How are you getting on?"

"Fine," I replied curtly.

"Can I see what you're doing?"

"You don't need to," I said, putting my hand over my work. "You're a Maths teacher. Besides, I'm the editor so I know what I'm doing."

I felt a pang of guilt as Fester raised his eyebrows and left my desk.

Ruby nudged me. "Are you okay?"

"I'm just nervous," I admitted.

"What about?"

"Ms Sorenson's class." I blushed. "I don't want her to know I'm on report. She'll think I'm awful."

Ruby gave me a sympathetic pat and returned to her work. She was writing an article about people dropping litter round the school. So far, she had written the title: *'The Rubbish Story! By Roving Reporter, Ruby Rico.'* I didn't want to break it to her but I wasn't sure it would make the final paper.

"Why don't you write about the new Sports hall?" I suggested.

She screwed up her nose. "It's not as relevant as the litter problem."

I forced a smile and turned back to my own article.

'Anybody can be good at animal noises. You just have to listen carefully and then get into the mindset of an animal. For example, to perfect my recent Helpless Hedgehog impression, I spent a long time curled up under my bed pretending I didn't know where I was...'

Ruby peered over my shoulder. "Can you teach me how to do a worm impression?"

"A worm?"

"Yeah. It's Oscar's birthday soon and he loves worms."

---

[43] It has a plastic hand on the lid emblazoned with the words, *'They didn't have my name.'*

"Well..." I thought about it. "Worms don't really make any noises."

"Oh!"

I giggled. "I could teach you how to do a *Serious Snake?*"

Ruby shook her head. "He's scared of snakes."

I laughed and went back to my work.

As the long lesson drew to an end, I packed up my bag and waited for Fester to write my report. He held my planner out with a grim nod. I snatched it from him and turned to see what he'd written. I had to squint to read his messy scribble.

'Livi worked steadily this lesson although her manners left much to be desired. I hope she will show a little less cheek in this afternoon's Maths class.'

I snorted and turned to leave. Then I sighed and said, "Sorry Sir. I didn't mean to be rude."

He nodded. "See you this afternoon, Livi."

Before Ms Sorenson's lesson, we had Art. Miss Appleby was joined by a teaching assistant called Mr Bradley. I assumed he was going to be weird because he wore clogs, a mismatched suit and glasses with bright yellow frames. Since he didn't appear to have any fashion sense, I wondered how he could possibly be any good at Art. But then he astonished us all by drawing a remarkably accurate portrait of Fran Gorman in thirty seconds flat.

As I approached Miss Appleby's desk with my planner I couldn't help but ask, "Can you draw one of me?"

"Perhaps another time, Livi."

I looked at him in surprise. "How do you know my name?"

"I heard that girl saying, *'Not everyone who wears clogs is a freak, Livi.'*" He pointed to Ruby.

"Oh..." I ran back to my seat. "You need to keep your voice down," I hissed to Ruby.

"What?"

"He heard us talking about his clogs."

Ruby looked over at Mr Bradley and he waved. "Whoops," she whispered.

I put my head in my hands. I was not at my nicest today. I'd already offended Fester and now I was passing judgement over a complete stranger. I scolded myself and glanced at the clock on the wall. Forty minutes until Ms Sorenson's class. I watched the minutes tick by, unable to concentrate on the untidy lino print that I was supposed to be crafting.

Finally, the lesson came to an end. I retrieved my planner from Miss Appleby and anxiously followed Ruby out of the room and down the corridor to Ms Sorenson's classroom.

"I'll save you a seat," Ruby said, heading towards the circle.

I gulped and looked towards Ms Sorenson. She was sitting at her desk, scribbling in her filofax. I took a deep breath and went over to her.

"Hello Livi," she said as I put my planner down.

"I'm on report," I whispered.

To my surprise, she replied, "I know. Miss Day told me about your fight with Molly."

I blushed. I hoped Miss Day hadn't also told her about the horse drawn in my shoe.

Ms Sorenson looked at me curiously. "Why isn't Molly on report too?"

I shifted uncomfortably and stared at the floor. "I sort of called her fat."

Ms Sorenson didn't reply and I felt a lump rising in my throat as I imagined the look on her face. I cautiously raised my eyes to look at her.

She smiled kindly. "What did Molly do?"

"She hit me," I said weakly. "That's why we were fighting."

Ms Sorenson shook her head. "I meant what did she do to warrant being called fat?"

"Oh." I looked down again. "It's just silly," I said, my voice cracking slightly. "She said I couldn't read. I know it shouldn't have bothered me but it did."

Ms Sorenson didn't reply. When I looked up again I found it hard to make out her expression. Was it pity? Or bemusement? She took my planner from me and said, "You can go and sit down now."

I nodded dumbly and went to join the circle.

Kitty was watching me like a hawk. She gave a smirk and whispered something to her friends.

Molly sneered and said, "I know!" She started to rock back on her chair, giving me a smug look as she did so.

I ignored them and took the seat next to Ruby.

Ms Sorenson took an empty seat across the circle and held up her tin. "Good afternoon, 9.1. Today we're going to talk about first impressions. What do you notice when you first meet people and what do you think—"

Before she could finish, Kitty put her hand up and said sweetly, "We should have rules, Miss."

Ms Sorenson stared at her. "Rules?"

Kitty nodded and cast a sly glance in my direction. "Not naming any names but, without rules, *somebody* might decide to start calling *somebody else* fat." She gave Molly a patronising pat on the shoulder.

Molly frowned at her. "I'm not fat," she snapped. "I've just got big bones. Plus, my grandmother was Russian."

The class looked at her in confusion.

"It's colder in Russia," Molly explained irritably. "So they have thicker skin. It's genetic."

Ritchie Jones let out a snort and said, "That's not true."

"Yes it is!" Molly insisted. "You can look it up on Google." She glared at us, as if challenging anybody to dare argue further.

For a moment, nobody said anything.

Annie Button gave a small cough. "Even if you *were* fat," she said cautiously. "It wouldn't matter, would it? It's what's on the inside that counts."

"I'm not fat!" Molly roared.

"I know," said Annie. "But, if you were. It would just be a fact. Like saying Aaron Tang is Chinese."

"Malaysian," Aaron corrected quietly.

"That's what I meant!" Annie gave Aaron a sheepish smile before adding to Molly, "You're not fat, by the way."

Molly breathed heavily out of her nose and swung back on her chair.

I glanced at Ms Sorenson. She was drumming lightly on the tin, seemingly happy to let the unauthorized conversation continue.

"What do *you* think, Livi?" Kitty asked suddenly. "Is Molly fat?"

"I don't know!" I spluttered. "It doesn't really matter."

Kitty was about to say something else but, before she could open her big mouth, Molly's chair gave way with a sudden crack and she fell to the floor.

A hoot of laughter erupted round the circle followed by shrieks of, "Molly fell off her chair!" and, "Look at the seat!"

Molly looked like she was about to cry as she pulled herself off the floor and rubbed her backside. "That chair's broken, Miss," she muttered.

"I can see that," our teacher replied. "Are you alright?"

112

Molly made a great show of wincing as she tested all her limbs. "I don't know. I can't feel my elbow."

"Can you *ever* feel your elbow, Miss Masterson?" Ms Sorenson gave a curious smile.

A few people sniggered at this.

Molly blushed. "I feel sick, Miss."

Kitty put her hand up. "Can I take her to the nurse?"

Ms Sorenson looked far from impressed as she said, "If you must."

"Can I go with them?" Melody piped up.

"And me?" ventured Annie.

Ms Sorenson gave them a withering look. "She only fell off her chair which, I should add, was her own fault as she was swinging on it." She turned to Molly. "Go to the nurse."

"Can Kitty come?" Molly whimpered.

"Yes. Hurry up." Ms Sorenson dismissed them with a wave of her hand and picked up her tin. "Where were we?"

I felt a little ripple of delight as Molly hobbled out, supported by a hapless Kitty.

Ms Sorenson looked at us expectantly but we avoided her gaze. I don't think anybody wanted to remind her that we had just been discussing whether or not Molly Masterson was fat.

Rupert Crisp put his hand up. "First impressions, Miss."

Ms Sorenson handed him the tin. "Thank you, Rupert. You can start."

Rupert beamed and said, "First impressions are wrought with deception. But so are second and third impressions... In fact, many a man has regarded his appearance in a mirror and known not whom he was seeing."

A few people giggled as Rupert gave a haughty sniff and passed the tin to Aaron Tang.

"First impressions are stupid," Aaron said. "You should get to know someone before you judge them."

He handed the tin to Darcy Bell who said, "Some of my favourite books have got the worst covers."

The tin got round to me and I held it in my lap as I carefully considered my words. "It's hard not to judge by appearances," I said, thinking about the teaching assistant in Miss Appleby's lesson. "But I think that's partly because we're always so worried about what people think of *us*. And often our first impressions say more about us than they do about the person we're judging, you know... like our own fears or whatever." I shrugged and passed the tin to Ruby.

"I think first impressions are silly," said Ruby. "We should keep our eyes closed when we meet people."

She started to pass the tin on but I quickly put my hand up. "I know I haven't got the tin but can I say something else, Miss?"

Ms Sorenson nodded and Ruby gave me the tin again.

I took a deep breath. "First impressions aren't *completely* silly. Sometimes they are a bit true. Like, if somebody was wearing a Leeds United shirt then you'd probably be right in thinking they're a football fan." I paused and bit my lip. "But it's not the *whole* truth. For example..." I took off my shoe and held it up. "I drew a horse in my shoe a few weeks ago because I had a dream that I was riding a pony and..." I shifted awkwardly as my classmates craned to stare. "Anyway, it was a really cool dream and I didn't want to forget it. But, if you just judged my shoe by what's on the outside, you'd never know it was there." I blushed and put my shoe back on.

Ms Sorenson smiled as I passed the tin back to Ruby.

Ruby looked at me. "I agree with Livi," she said. "First impressions are okay but the best bit is always what's on the inside." She grinned as she added, "Like a donut."

The class tittered politely.

As the lesson came to an end most of our classmates crowded round to inspect Molly's broken chair before heading off to Maths. I didn't want Ms Sorenson to think I was gloating over Molly's misfortune so I pretended not to be interested. Instead, I lingered by her desk and waited for her to write my report.

She scratched her cheek as she thumbed through my planner. Then she smoothed down this week's page and wrote a hasty sentence before handing it to me with a smile. "See you next week, Livi."

"Thanks, Miss." I took my planner and hurried out, my cheeks burning with shame. I hoped she hadn't been too influenced by Fester's report above.

As I followed my classmates down the corridor I paused behind the water fountain and nervously opened my planner. My heart raced as I located the page containing Ms Sorenson's report.

'Livi Starling was, as usual, a delight today. Her contributions to class discussions are always intelligent and insightful and today's lesson was no exception.
— Ms A. Sorenson.'

She had signed it with a great loopy signature which left Fester's untidy scrawl looking like a squashed bug in comparison. Everything in me leapt with joy. Ms Sorenson didn't hate me! She thought I was a delight! She didn't judge me for being on report or for calling Molly fat! I breathed a huge sigh of relief and ran to catch up with Ruby.

I glided through Maths, caring very little when Fester joked about having cramp from writing so many of my reports.

At the end of the day I went to see Mr Riley. I knocked proudly on his door and held out my planner with a grin.

He looked over it with his usual serious stare, hesitating slightly over Fester's morning report, before saying, "Well done, Livi. I think you've learnt your lesson. You're now off report."

I nodded and pretended to look humble. "Thanks, Sir."

I took my planner from him and carefully tucked it into my bag. Then I trotted down the hallway, enjoying the carefree tapping of my shoes as I ran.

Ruby was waiting for me in the playground. As I made my way towards her I saw Mr Bradley, the teaching assistant, heading to the staff car park.

"Hey, Mr Bradley!" I called to him. "I'm sorry I insulted your clogs. I expect you're really cool deep down. Like a donut."

He turned round and raised his eyebrows. "Pardon?"

"You're a donut!" I yelled.

He looked at me in confusion but I just grinned and ran on.

The first thing I did when I got home was cut Ms Sorenson's report out of my planner. I mounted it on a piece of card and slipped it into my starling box[44] next to the Viking badge from Joey's party. I lay on my bed and beamed as I considered that being on report was perhaps the most wonderful thing that had happened to me all term. It had given me rock solid proof that Ms Sorenson, the best teacher in the world, truly liked me. And, to top it all off, I now had her autograph!

---

[44] My keepsake box from Ruby.

~ 15 ~

A picture from Grace

The most pitiful thing Jill has ever done to attract the attention of a boy was grab the microphone and start singing during the toasts at the wedding of her best friend, Lorna. As the best man came over and politely informed Jill that he wasn't interested I buried my head in my hands and vowed never to follow in my sister's footsteps. I decided that if I ever found myself in the predicament of liking a boy I would simply tell him. No mind games, no soppy daydreaming, no turmoil over what he was thinking and whether he liked me back. That was, however, before I met Joey. It's not that I *fancy* him, as such; I would just rather like it if *he* fancied *me*. I've tried to remain sensible about the whole thing but unfortunately, this weekend, my careless attempt to impress him made Jill's rendition of '*Do you really want to hurt me?*' look almost respectable.

It was the first night of the *Bible Bash* weekend away and we were gathered in an old barn with youth groups from several churches in the region. In a moment of madness, I had volunteered to represent our church in a game to cram as many marshmallows into my mouth as possible.

As I glanced into the crowd before commencing the challenge I made eye contact with Joey and he yelled, "Go on, Livi! You're the best!"

I gave a steely nod. Then I grabbed a handful of marshmallows and shoved them into my mouth, determined to do Joey proud.

"Woah! Steady!" a youth leader named Martin said in surprise.

I just nodded and grabbed several more. I shot a sideways glance at my competitors and grinned.

"Livi! Livi! Livi!" I heard Joey's voice over the crowd.

I stuffed another handful into my already bulging mouth and turned to give Joey a wave. Then, out of nowhere, I felt the urge to

116

sneeze. In my attempts to suppress it, a clump of marshmallows shifted down my throat and I started to choke. For the briefest moment I saw my life flash before my eyes and the fear of imminent death was only exceeded by the greater fear that nothing I had done so far would be worth watching. I retched and strained, contorting wildly as my eyes came close to popping out of my head.[45]

Martin whacked me on the back and the mashed up contents of my mouth came pouring out, narrowly missing a girl on the front row.

I stumbled back, expecting an outburst of anger from the girl in front and a lot of pointing and laughing from the crowd.

But, to my surprise, the room filled with cries of alarm and the girl I had spat on leapt up and asked, "Is she alright?"

Summer came running over and put an arm round my shoulder. "Oh dear," she said. "I was afraid of that game getting out of hand." She gave Eddie a meaningful look as he came over to clean up my mess.

"Would you like a drink, Livi?" he asked.

Several people volunteered to get me some water and Martin had to shout over the commotion to tell everybody to calm down. The attention was a little bit much and I debated closing my eyes and pretending to pass out. I didn't dare look into the crowd at Joey so just covered my face with my hands and moaned. Summer led me out of the room, followed by Ruby and then Violet who was told to go and sit back down. We went to the kitchen where Summer poured me a glass of water.

I gulped it down rather ungracefully as I explained, "I needed to sneeze. That's why I choked. But I think I was winning before that point."

Summer laughed. "Yes, I should think you were. You had almost a whole packet in your mouth!"

Ruby looked close to tears. "I thought you were going to die."

"Me too," I admitted. I drank a second glass of water and closed my eyes dramatically.

Summer laughed again. "Have a rest and come back in when you feel better. Ruby can stay with you. Take as long as you need."

Ruby stared at me as Summer left. "Are you alright?"

---

[45] Ruby told me later that I'd looked like a turkey being slowly strangled. It's not an impression that I intend to add to my repertoire.

I nodded slowly. "Did anybody laugh? Like did Joey or Mark or anybody think I was stupid?"

Ruby's eyes widened. "No way! It's not your fault. It was just a dangerous game."

I nodded again and poured myself another drink.

In truth, I felt better within a few minutes. But I didn't want to face the embarrassment of going back into the meeting so Ruby and I explored the rooms at the back of the barn instead. It meant we had the first choice of where to sleep and we unrolled our sleeping bags in the furthest corner of the girls' dormitory as we discussed how cool it was to be spending two nights away from home.

"My mum cried!" Ruby said with a giggle. "You'd have thought we were going for a year, not a weekend. She even gave me this!" She held up a tearstained letter and grinned.

I roared with laughter, although I couldn't help but feel a pang of envy. Jill's last words had been, "Hopefully I'll get the house cleaned while you're gone."

I changed the subject. "What would you have done if I'd died?"

Ruby blinked at me. "Cried."

I gave a satisfied nod, feeling that the occasional near death experience was probably worthwhile if it gave people a chance to see how much I meant to them.

The meeting finished about an hour later and my stomach churned as the rest of the girls piled into the dorm. I was afraid of being mocked but, funnily enough, my little jaunt with death had made me rather popular and our side of the room filled up quickly as girls pitched their sleeping bags close to mine. One by one they came over to check whether I was okay and I perfected the art of rubbing my throat and meekly asserting that I would be fine.

"I like your pyjamas," one girl said.

"I like your sleeping bag," said another.

I shrugged shyly and thanked them, making sure to show off the hood on my sleeping bag. In actual fact I had borrowed it from Ruby's family. They had also lent me an old camping mat and I felt a little smug as I considered the number of people who had to make do with the hard cold floor.

When everybody had got ready for bed we gathered in small groups, huddled inside our sleeping bags as we exchanged jokes and stories. The girls had come back from the meeting with excitement over what Eddie had called 'God Moments,' so most of the conversations centred on tales of miraculous encounters and answers to prayer. Popular among our group was Nicole's story of being rescued from a river by an angel. I had no idea whether it was true or not but I couldn't help but gaze hopefully up at the rafters as I wondered what an angel might look like. I felt a combination of envy and awe as I made mental notes for a potential article for the class paper.

Eventually, one of the youth leaders came in and told us to settle down and the chatter continued at a whisper for a while until one by one we fell asleep.

At about two in the morning I was awoken by somebody shaking me roughly. For a moment, I had no idea where I was and wondered whether I had fallen out of bed. Then I heard a chorus of light snoring and remembered that I was sleeping in a barn, surrounded by thirty other girls.

The shaking continued, followed by Ruby asking, "Are you awake, Livi?" She bent over and shone her torch in my face.

I gave a groan and shoved her away. "I am *now.*"

"Great! Do you want to sneak out with us?"

"What?" I opened my eyes and came face to face with Noah, Ruby's moose.

Ruby giggled as I sat up with a jolt. Nicole and one of the Graces were grinning at me.

"You're sneaking out? That's not very Christian is it?"

"Well, no," Ruby said sheepishly. She put Noah down. "But we're only going to the back porch... You don't have to come."

"I want to!" I assured her. It sounded wild.

Five minutes later, we were huddled outside the barn. It was pretty much the same as huddling *inside* the barn except that it was cold.

"This is so exciting!" Grace whispered as she passed round a packet of sweets. She nudged Nicole who looked like she was about to fall asleep. "Wake up, Nicole!"

Nicole grunted and batted her away.

We sat silently for a while, shivering slightly as we passed the sweets backwards and forwards. I caught Grace's eye and smiled. Unlike the other Grace, who is the same age as me and Ruby, this particular Grace is a couple of years older.[46] She always comes up

---

[46] Her full name is Grace Verity Moore. I saw it written in her Bible once and couldn't stop reciting it in my head as it sounded so fancy. The other Grace is called Grace Fletcher. She has really small ears and giggles a lot.

with good answers in the discussions at youth group and I like listening to her when she prays. It's like she's really connected to God, like he's really close to her or something. This was the first time we'd spent any actual time together and I wondered how to summon up the courage to tell her that I liked the way she prays. In the end, I settled for telling her that I liked her slippers.

"Thanks!" Grace grinned before asking, "Hey, Livi, have you been baptised?"

"I don't know," I said. "I might have been christened when I was a baby. I'll have to ask my sister."

She shook her head. "That's not the same. Baptism is for those who know they want to follow Jesus."

"I *do* want to follow Jesus."

"Well, being baptised is a public declaration of that. Nobody can choose it for you." She gave me a very firm nod.

"Okay," I said with a shrug. If Grace said it was good then I believed her. "How do I do it?"

Before Grace could reply, Ruby pointed down the path. "There's a pond over there."

I looked at her in dismay. I wasn't sure I wanted to be choked and drowned all in one night.

"*Or,*" Grace said pointedly. "There's a baptism service coming up in a few weeks. You should ask if you can do it then."

I turned in alarm. "In front of lots of people?"

She nodded. "Yeah. That's kind of the point. Like a wedding."

I gave a long sigh. I wasn't sure I was ready for a public declaration. I didn't want to declare my faith in front of everybody only for somebody to say, *'What's she doing up there? She's not a proper Christian yet.'* Maybe I ought to read the whole Bible first, to be sure I understood exactly what I was getting into. "I'll think about it," I said.

Grace smiled.

By this point Nicole was fast asleep and had started to snore. Grace shook her and said, "Let's go back inside."

Nicole gave a tired whimper and began crawling up the steps.

Grace handed me and Ruby the rest of the sweets and turned to follow Nicole. She paused at the door before saying cautiously, "Oh, Livi... This might sound weird but I think God gave me a picture for you."

"A picture?" I hoped she hadn't taken a photo of me choking.

"Yeah." Grace chewed her lip. "I was praying for you earlier and I saw a picture of a bird in a cage. The cage door was open but the bird was too scared to go out even though it was free to." She paused before adding, "I hope that makes sense."

"Er, thanks," I muttered.

She shrugged and followed Nicole inside.

I turned to Ruby. "What was that about?"

Ruby bit her thumb. "Well... Maybe you're the bird and you need to step out of the cage."

"I'm not in a cage," I retorted.

"It's symbolic. You've been set free but you're not experiencing it yet."

I gulped. "How does she know?"

"God told her."

I looked at her in shock. "So people suddenly know all my secrets?"

"No. God only tells us things to help one another."

"Can't he tell me things himself?"

"Of course! But he also likes us to be connected. We're a family."

I gave an irritated sniff. "I hate the word 'family.'"

Ruby blushed.

"And I hate the word 'Father,'" I added fiercely. "Christians say that word a lot."

Ruby nodded slowly and stared at me.

"What?" I demanded.

"I'm just thinking."

"Well, don't." I shifted and wrapped my arms round myself.

"I know you won't like this," Ruby began. "But you should forgive your dad."

"Ruby!" I yelled. "We've been through this before! How can I forgive him after everything he's done?"

"God has forgiven *you*," she said simply.

"He doesn't deserve to be forgiven."

"Neither did you."

I glared at her. "I'm not going to forgive him. He's a horrible person and I don't want to speak to him ever again."

"It wouldn't mean he hasn't hurt you. And he'd still be responsible for everything he's done. But *you* would feel better."

I shook my head.

"You want to stay angry with him?"

"Yes."

Ruby thought for a moment. "How does it feel?"

"How does what feel?"

"Being angry with him. How does it feel?"

I sniffed as I thought about it. "Horrible," I admitted. "I feel sad and angry whenever I think about him. It's like, wherever I go, he's right there." I waved a hand across my shoulder.

"And yet you still want to keep feeling that way?"

I gave her a long look. I could see where she was going. "No," I said stiffly. "I don't want to keep feeling this way. But I don't want to forgive him either."

"Well..." Ruby cleared her throat. "You'll probably keep feeling that way until you forgive him..."

She was about to keep speaking but I interrupted with a growl. "Stop it! What if *your* dad left and I told you to just let him off?"

"I don't mean letting him off," Ruby insisted, her cheeks turning red. "I mean letting him *go*. My mum says unforgiveness is like drinking poison in the hopes that it will kill the other person."

I looked away, simmering at how insensitive she was being.

Ruby coughed and continued, "Once, I was halfway through a really good book when Violet told me how it ended. I was so angry with her that I decided to trash her room. Except her room is also *my* room so when I went to do it I couldn't think straight and broke my own mirror..."

"That's not the same," I said scornfully. "You have no idea."

"I know. I'm sorry. I just hate seeing you so... *trapped.*" She paused before adding, "You need to walk out of the cage."

I turned away as tears stung the backs of my eyes. "I can't. Even if I wanted to, I just can't."

"God can help you."

"How?"

"Just ask him to."

I stared at my hands. "I probably think about my dad more than I think about anything," I confessed.

"So... Do you want to keep being angry with him?"

I thought for a moment before shaking my head.

"Then will you forgive him?"

I sighed and put my head in my hands. I was starting to feel rather choked up. It was like having a clump of marshmallows wedged in my throat all over again. "I can't," I said. "It's too hard."

~ 16 ~

The most normal thing of all

I awoke with one prayer on my lips: *Dear God, please help me spend time with Joey today.* As I pulled myself out of my sleeping bag I yawned and added, *I don't mean to be selfish, God. I know I should probably pray for all the people in the world who are starving or dying. But still, if you don't mind, I'd like to get to know Joey better.* I looked up at the ceiling, hoping for an answer or at least a small sign that God had heard.

Beside me, Ruby was reading the letter from her mother and looking a little homesick.

"Good morning," I said.

She grinned and shoved the letter into Noah. "I wonder what we're doing today!" she said brightly.

"I wonder," I echoed.

The day was split into two parts, with group seminars in the morning to be followed by an afternoon meeting in the main barn. Through my careful eavesdropping over breakfast I discovered that Joey was planning on attending the seminar entitled, *'Sharing your Faith,'* so I made sure to express my interest in it to Ruby.

"Are you sure?" she asked. "I wondered if you wanted to go to *'Being filled with the Holy Spirit'?*"

I shook my head. "I want to know how to tell people about Jesus."

Ruby shrugged. "Okay. Then we're in Meeting Room 3."

I nodded and followed her down the corridor.

Joey arrived at the same time as us and I gave a little wave as I feigned surprise at seeing him there. Then I took a seat at the opposite end of the room so as not to appear too eager. The session was being led by a youth leader called Lucinda. Once everybody had arrived she got our attention and told us to get into pairs. I tried not to grimace as Ruby grabbed my arm.

"You have five minutes to get to know each other," Lucinda said. "Then you'll introduce your partner to the rest of the group." She smiled before adding, "Make sure you pick somebody you don't know!"

Ruby dropped my arm in disappointment. "Oh. I know you."

"Yes," I said, trying to look upset. "That's a shame."

Before Ruby could say anything else, I gave her a quick shrug and glanced around the room. Joey was several seats away, having a sneezing fit. I sucked in my cheeks and trotted over to him.

"Did you eat some chocolate?" I asked.

He shook his head and sneezed again. "I was staring at the lamp. Bright lights make me sneeze too."

"Oh."

"I also get nosebleeds when there's going to be a storm."

"That's cool!"

"Sometimes."

I watched him blow his nose before saying awkwardly, "Er... Can I be your partner? Because I was thinking we don't know each other *that* well..."

He patted the seat beside him. "You're right. We should hang out some time."

My heart skipped a beat. "Hang out?" I repeated.

"Yeah, you know. Get to know each other better."

I nodded and tried not to look too excited.

"So, Livi Starling..." Joey said eagerly. "Tell me about yourself."

"Erm..." I fiddled with my top. "I don't know what to say."

He shrugged. "What's your favourite animal?"

I chewed my lip. "I kind of like koalas. Their fingerprints look just like human ones and they make really cool noises, especially when they're angry."

"Really? Like what?"

I paused before giving him my best *Drunken Koala* impression.

His eyes widened. "That's amazing!"

I gave a coy shrug.

"Can you do a cat?"

"I can do three types of cat," I said proudly. *"Manipulative Cat, Sleepy Cat,* and *Newborn Kitten."*

"Wow!" I felt myself blushing as he stared at me. "What else do you like doing?"

124

"I like writing…"

Joey listened as I told him about my plans for the class newspaper. He asked me a few more questions about my likes and dislikes and then said, "Do another animal noise!"

"I've been practising my *Happy Fox*," I said, letting out a high pitched squeal.

The people beside us looked over and we giggled.

"You're funny," Joey said.

My stomach did a little flip. "Your turn," I said, feeling rather faint.

He grinned at me and I grinned back and wondered where to begin. There was so much I wanted to know about him.

"Tell me about yourself, Joey… Er…" I paused. "What's your surname?"

"My surname?" He went pink. "It's Cashbottom."

My jaw fell open. "Cashbottom?"

He nodded.

"As in… *bottom?*"

He blushed. "Yeah."

"Not *button?*"

"No," he said tersely. "Cash*bottom.*"

"Okay." I forced a smile. "So, er… what's your favourite animal?"

"Turtles."

I couldn't think of anything else to say. My mind kept screaming *'Cashbottom'* like a foghorn so we just sat in awkward silence for the next few minutes.

"Right then!" Lucinda clapped her hands together to get everybody's attention. "Let's get to know one another!"

We shuffled into a circle, squirming uncomfortably as Lucinda asked for volunteers to begin. Two boys from a church in Bradford offered to go first. I tried to concentrate on the facts that they were sharing but, in truth, I wasn't really interested. My brain was still reeling from the revelation of Joey's surname. One of the boys was named William Jackson and I found myself shaking my head as I thought, *'Jackson!' See, that's a proper surname!*

Ruby went next with her partner, the girl I had almost thrown up on the night before.

"This is Emma," Ruby said timidly. "She has three pet rats called Shadrach, Meshach and Abednego. Was that right?" Emma nodded so Ruby continued, "She likes painting and dancing and playing the flute. More than anything else, she just loves Jesus."

Emma cut in and added with a grin, "The funny thing is, when I said *'Jesus,'* Ruby thought I said *'cheeses!'*"

They looked at one another and burst out laughing. I felt a pang of envy. I hoped Ruby realised that rats were dirty.

Emma beamed and said, "This is Ruby. She collects banana stickers and once dressed up as a giant banana for non-uniform day. She likes reading and jigsaws. And her best friend is Livi." She pointed at me and smiled.

I attempted a small wave as everyone turned to stare at me.

Lucinda thanked Ruby and Emma and then looked at me. My heart sunk as she said, "Why don't you go next?"

I glanced at Joey and blushed.

He grinned and announced to the room, "This is Livi Starling. She's really good at animal noises. She likes writing and her favourite school subject is Personal and Social Development. She doesn't like eggs, clogs, or when flies fly into her mouth."

"Great!" said Lucinda. She turned to me.

"Er, this is Joey..." I paused. "Joey, erm. He likes turtles." I shrugged at Lucinda. "That's where we got up to."

"Okay. Thank you." She moved on to the couple beside us.

I stared straight ahead, avoiding Joey's gaze.

When everybody had been introduced, Lucinda talked about the difference between how we see ourselves and how God sees us and how identity is the key to telling others about Jesus. I'm sure it was interesting and very appropriate but I just couldn't concentrate. I had finally managed to pair up with Joey, a feat that had taken almost two months to orchestrate, only to discover his dreadful secret: his surname. *Cashbottom.* How did that even happen? Did his ancestors run a bank from their backsides or something? *Joseph Cashbottom. Joseph Cashbottom. Joseph Cashbottom.* It went round and round my head like a bad song. And then my imagination got the better of me: *Livi Cashbottom. Livi Cashbottom. Livi Cashbottom.* I rubbed my throbbing head and forced myself to listen to Lucinda.

As the seminar came to an end, Joey poked me and said, "So, when are you free to hang out?"

My stomach churned. How could I explain that he was perfect except for his awful surname? Hanging out with Joseph Cashbottom... It would be social suicide.

I cleared my throat. "I don't know. I've got a lot on at the moment."

He looked quite hurt.

"I've got to edit a whole newspaper."

"It's fine," he said, pulling on his jacket. "I'll see you later."

"Okay," I said weakly. Then, as he began to walk away, I called out the stupidest thing ever: "It's not because of your surname!"

At this, Joey shook his head angrily and left.

I felt awful for the rest of the day. I debated going over to Joey at lunchtime to try and make amends but the awful truth of the matter was that I wasn't even sure if I liked him anymore. As Ruby and I took our seats for the afternoon meeting I wondered how I could possibly be so shallow. I watched miserably as the hall filled up around me and sixty excited teenagers took their seats. All of them seemed so cheerful and *nice,* far more deserving of God's love than me. I slid down in my chair and grunted.

Ruby looked at me. "Are you alright?"

"Just bored."

She raised her eyebrows. "The meeting hasn't started yet."

"It *will* be boring though," I snapped. "We'll sing and then someone will talk and I'll feel rubbish as usual. I don't know if I can be bothered anymore."

Ruby shifted uncomfortably.

I closed my eyes. Frustration bubbled inside me as I muttered, "Am I doing things wrong? Like, do I need to be a better person?"

"No! You're doing great."

I sucked in my cheeks and tried not to cry as I grappled to find the words to express what I wanted. "Ruby, does it *really* feel like something?"

"Does what feel like something?"

I opened my eyes. "God. Can you really feel him?"

"Yes."

I looked her in the eye. "Promise?"

"Promise."

I took a deep breath. "Okay."

The worship band assembled at the front of the room and I stood up with everybody else and forced my way through the songs.

I uttered a hasty prayer: *Thanks for letting me talk to Joey. I'm sorry I messed it up...* but the confusion of not knowing whether or not God had heard me was almost too much to bear.

I drifted through the service, listening to bits and pieces but finding it difficult to focus. A youth leader from another church was leading the meeting and read a story from the Bible about Jesus offering water to a woman at a well. *"Jesus answered, 'Everyone* who drinks this water will be thirsty again, but whoever drinks the water I give him will never thirst. Indeed, the water I give him will become in him a spring of water welling up to eternal life.'"

I pursed my lips as I tried to concentrate. I wondered what kind of drinks they had in Heaven and imagined Jesus handing everyone a milkshake when they arrived.

"What Jesus is offering is a life source that will never run out," the youth leader explained. "This is free of charge and available to everyone..."

He talked for a while longer and then prayed that we would all experience more of this living water. I looked around while he prayed. Most people had their eyes shut. Ruby was beaming. Some people were crying. I felt nothing in particular.

The youth leader finished his talk by saying, "If you're not a follower of Jesus and you want to enter into new life today, then I'd like to invite you to come to the front and we'll pray for you."

As he called the meeting to an end, I saw a handful of people making their way to the front. They were met by smiling youth leaders who looked like they were saying something exciting. Without really thinking I got up and went to join them, my insides churning as I begged, *Please God, I just want to connect with you.*

I got to the front where Summer was looking at me curiously. "I want to be a Christian," I told her.

She took my hand. "You're already saved, Livi. You don't need to keep doing it."

"But I want more. I want to *feel* it. I want to be sure God has actually accepted me."

She smiled. "Your desire for more is wonderful."

I shifted uncomfortably. I didn't think she'd be quite so impressed if she'd heard me at the start of the meeting.

"You don't need to do anything else to be accepted by God," Summer continued as Ruby came over and stood beside us.

Joey was behind her. I tried to catch his eye but he kept his head down and carried on walking.

I sighed and turned back to Summer. "But I still mess up," I muttered. "And so does *she.*" I pointed at Ruby. "She snuck out last night."

Ruby looked at me in horror but Summer just laughed.

"We all mess up," she said. "But the point is, it's no longer who you *are.* It's not how you're known in Heaven."

I raised an eyebrow. "How am I known in Heaven then?"

She grinned. "Livi Starling, you're one of Heaven's finest flyers."

"Don't be stupid!" I exclaimed. I gulped before adding, "Sorry." My cheeks burned as I stared at the floor.

Summer cocked her head to one side and tried to catch my eye. "God is far more interested in who you're becoming than in what you're doing, Livi," she said softly. "He made you and he knows you— I mean *really knows* you— better than you know yourself. In fact, from the moment that you accepted Jesus, every situation in your life started to work together to mould you into who you truly are."

I opened my mouth and then closed it again.

"God is so proud of you."

I squirmed. She made it sound like God had no idea how awful I was.

As if reading my mind, Summer added, "The Bible says that you're the righteousness of God. That's not because of your own behaviour but because Jesus paid the price. You are who he says you are."

I curled my hands into fists. "But I still can't feel it," I said pathetically.

"You will."

"But I want it *now*. Some days I believe God loves me and other days I'm just not sure."

Summer put a hand on my shoulder. "God loves you perfectly *all the time*. Nothing can make him love you more or less, although blocks on your side of the relationship may affect how you receive his love."

"Blocks?"

"Yeah." Summer waved a hand about as she said blithely, "The way we see God, the way we see ourselves, past disappointments, bad habits, anger, unbelief, unforgiveness..."

My stomach churned.

"All kinds of things keep us from being fully free."

"Like being in a cage?" I whispered.

"You could say that!"

I gave a long nod and looked away, careful not to catch Ruby's eye.

"But don't worry," Summer said quickly. "God will remove every block in his time. Just keep trusting him. He knows what he's doing."

I exhaled slowly. "If you say so."

~*~

We had one last meeting on Sunday morning. I nestled myself into my chair, fixing a smile on my face as I prepared myself for one final push before going home. I was more than ready to get back to normal life. The novelty of sleeping on the floor had definitely worn off and I was beginning to get irritated with all the cheery faces. I approached the meeting in the same way that I always did; with a general sense of isolation and a doubt over whether it was even worth it. I certainly wasn't expecting anything exciting to happen. I stood up with Ruby and pretended to pay attention as Eddie opened the meeting with a prayer.

Then the worship band came up and the guitarist yelled into the microphone, "Hasn't God been amazing this weekend!"

The room erupted in applause and I gave a polite clap and forced another smile.

We had just finished the first song when I saw Lucinda approach the microphone.

"I feel like God wants to heal some deep wounds right now," she said. "Some of you have a lot of family stuff going on..."

I bristled at the word *'family'* and tried to look indifferent.

"In particular," Lucinda continued. "I feel like God wants to meet with those of you who are struggling to feel the embrace of a loving Father."

I bit my lip and stared at my hands.

"Don't be scared. Come to the front during the next song and we'd love to pray with you."

I swallowed hard and dug my nails into the palms of my hands. I didn't want to go to the front, in full view of everybody, and admit that my family was a mess. Besides, I'd already gone forward the day before and I didn't want people to think I was an attention seeker. As the band began the next song I tried to focus on the words, even raising my hands into the air as if to proclaim that I couldn't be happier with my life. But I couldn't concentrate and ended up watching to see if anybody was responding to what Lucinda had said. To my surprise, I saw that Mark had approached the front for prayer. So had Nicole and Emma, the girl I had spat on. I watched as Nicole started crying and wondered what on earth could be wrong with her life. She always seemed so happy.

"Why is Nicole up there?" I asked Ruby.

"Her dad died a couple of years ago," Ruby whispered. "Maybe it's about that."

I gave a slow nod. "What about Mark?"

Ruby shrugged. "I don't know." She carried on singing.

As the song reached its final chorus I chewed my fingers and tried to reason with myself. *I should go up for prayer... But I don't really need prayer, I'll be fine. And, anyway, I never feel anything so what's the point..? Mark and Nicole are having prayer and it looks like it's working for them... But maybe they're just hyping themselves up. I have to be careful about these things...* I gave a loud growl and shook myself.

Ruby looked at me in confusion.

"I need prayer," I said helplessly.

"Go on then."

I took a deep breath and stepped into the aisle. I kept my head down as I marched quickly through the crowd. *Come on, God,* I begged. *Remove a block. I can't do it.*

I approached the front of the room and one of the youth leaders came over to greet me. "Would you like prayer?"

I nodded stupidly.

"What would you like prayer for?"

"Uh, just family stuff," I mumbled.

She smiled kindly. "What's your name?"

"Livi."

"Libby?"

"Livi," I repeated awkwardly.

She nodded and put a hand on my shoulder. "Thank you for your presence, Lord," she began serenely.

I wasn't sure what to do and felt silly staring at her so I closed my eyes and tried to look serious.

"You are so good, Lord," the girl continued. "Thank you for choosing Livi before the creation of the world to be holy and blameless in your sight..."

It sounded rather grand. I hoped God didn't think I was thinking too much of myself. *This is so stupid,* I thought. *Just ignore her prayer, God. I don't mean to be so weird.* But then, without meaning to, I began to cry.

"Lord, come and reveal your Father heart to Livi..."

Ignore her, God. I don't really care about all that family stuff. I lifted my hands to cover my face.

The girl stopped praying for a moment to whisper to me, "I feel God would like to tell you that you're his very special child. He chose you and he *wants* you and you are his princess."

I nodded and tried to look nonchalant. *I know that already, God. You made us. You're our Father... But it's just words if I don't feel anything.*

The girl carried on praying and I closed my eyes and wondered whether the whole church thing was really for me. Sure, I believed in God and I believed Jesus died for me. But maybe all the rest of it— the singing and praying and actually *living* for Jesus— was only for the die-hard fans. I was about to wipe my eyes and thank the girl for her time. I would go and sit at the back and wait for Ruby and go home and get on with being normal.

But then he came.

Out of nowhere and quite uninvited, this heavy, wonderful, all-consuming presence flooded my heart and almost sent me off my feet. Like a wave of peace. And I knew. I mean, I *really knew,* in my *heart*, not just in my head. For one blissful moment, I *knew* that God was my Father.

I started crying again but this time I didn't care and the girl just looked at me and smiled.

As I stood there, engulfed by the presence of the Creator of the universe, everything that I thought was normal suddenly seemed so absurd and so mundane. Suddenly, the only thing that was *really* normal, really true, was the desire to stay in his arms forever.

That's when I realised that I have *no idea* how incredible God is and knowing him is what I was made for. It's the most normal thing of all.

~ 17 ~

Not at all hypothetical

I arrived home from *Bible Bash* with the same sense of awe as an explorer returning from an unspeakable journey into undiscovered territory. There were no words to express the weight of what I was feeling except to say that I had tasted the divine and there was no going back.

Jill met me at the door looking tired and painfully human. "Did you have a good time?"

"Yeah." I handed her a bag of dirty washing and asked, "How was your weekend?"

"Oh, rubbish." She started telling me about how the hot tap in the bathroom wasn't working properly. It sounded so bizarre and meaningless after the encounter I had just had. "I'm going to phone the landlord first thing tomorrow. It's completely ridiculous."

I gave a slow nod. "Well, I'd better unpack." I forced a smile and made my way up the stairs.

I went into my room and threw myself on the bed. On the surface, everything was just as it had been when I had left. My floor was just as messy, my walls were just as kiwi-like and Sausage-Legs looked just as dopey draped over my headboard. Yet, somehow, everything was irreversibly different. It's like I was seeing for the very first time. Where previously life had been various shades of grey, now suddenly there was colour. Even my pile of homework looked brighter. I wondered if life would ever be the same again. I truly hoped not.

I grinned and closed my eyes. *Thank you, God.*

I decided I should probably write down what had happened. As *Bible Bash* had drawn to an end, I had sidled up to Summer and whispered, "I just felt God."

She'd hugged me and exclaimed, "How wonderful, Livi!"

"I know that he loves me," I'd added.

"Guard that hope, Livi," she'd replied. "It's precious."

As I reached for some paper, I felt the urge to do something big. I needed to mark the fact that I finally knew for sure that I wanted to follow Jesus. I also wanted to thank God for showing me that he accepted me. I put the paper down and grabbed my phone, my heart racing as I dialled Summer's number.

It was Eddie who answered. "Hi Livi! Was it you who left the orange moose?"

"No. I... Is Summer there?"

"Hold on..."

I bit my lip as I waited for Summer to take the phone. I could hear Alfie and Felix squealing in the background and hoped I wasn't interrupting anything important.

Summer came on the line. "Sorry about that, Livi. Are you alright?"

"Yes..." I sucked in my cheeks. "I was just doing some thinking and I want to get baptised. Am I allowed?"

"Of course you can get baptised!"

I grinned.

"...As long as it's alright with your sister."

My heart sunk. "Does she have to know?"

"I'm afraid so. Being a Christian is your choice but we like to involve parents or guardians when it comes to being baptised publicly."

I gave a long sigh. "Could I just do it in the bath with Ruby?" I recalled the pond outside the barn.

Summer didn't answer for a while. "You could... But this is a good chance to share your faith with your sister."

"She won't understand!"

"She might— if you explain why it's important to you."

"She won't." I gave another sigh. "What is it, anyway?"

"What?"

"Baptism."

"Oh! It's a symbol of you dying to your old life and being born again. It's also a deeply spiritual experience—"

"I mean... what happens? Do I have to hold my breath?"

Summer chuckled. "You're not under the water for very long, Livi. You just go under and come straight up."

"And then I'll be a real Christian?"

"No! You've done that in your heart already. This is the outward expression of it."

"Grace Moore called it a public declaration. Like a wedding."

"That's right."

"I like the way she prays."

Summer laughed. "You're doing great, Livi."

I felt a lump in my throat. For a brief moment, I wished Summer was my sister. "Thanks," I said weakly.

I hung up and gave yet another sigh. Even the thought of having to talk to Jill about baptism was causing my previous joy to slowly seep away. *No,* I begged. *Don't leave me just yet. It felt so good.*

Before I could lose my nerve, I leapt off my bed and made my way downstairs. Jill was at the kitchen table pulling apart some ugly grey knitted thing. It looked a bit like a deformed elephant.

"What's that?" I asked.

"Belinda made it. I think it's meant to be a tea cosy." She gave a scornful laugh. "But she forgot to leave a hole for the spout. Stupid woman."

I forced a smile and went towards her. "Jill?"

"Yes?"

I cleared my throat. "I was thinking and I've decided I want to get baptised."

She gave me a funny look. "Baptised?"

"Yeah..." I coughed. "You kind of get dunked under water."

Jill looked alarmed.

"You come up again," I added rapidly. "It's sort of a symbol of dying to your old self and being born again."

Jill stared at me as though I had just suggested running naked through the centre of Leeds. "I don't think so, Livi."

"Why not?"

She rubbed her head. "It sounds a little strange."

"It's not strange!" I shot back, trying hard to keep my voice steady and reasonable. "Just because you don't understand it..."

This time, Jill gave me a warning look and said, "Look, I don't mind you going to church occasionally and calling yourself a Christian, or whatever, but I'm not having it take over your life."

I opened my mouth in dismay. All the way home, I had been specifically praying that God *would* take over my life.

"It's just a bit of water," I said. "Like swimming or taking a bath."

"Then go swimming."

"But it's the *symbol—*"

"I've said no."

Tears pricked the backs of my eyes. "But I *want* to."

"Livi, please!" Jill snapped. "You're being silly."

"Just *think* about it," I pleaded. "You can ask Belinda questions. She'll tell you it's not silly—"

Jill snorted. "I don't need advice from Belinda Rico on what is or isn't silly." She flung Belinda's knitted tea cosy across the table.

"Or you can ask my youth leaders, Summer and Eddie. They're not weird."

Jill shook her head. "I don't need any input from them either."

"But they're really nice. They care and they're not at all hypothetical."

"That's enough, Livi!" Jill barked. "You've been back less than an hour and you're already giving me a headache."

I let out a loud growl and turned to leave. "You don't understand!"

"And the word is *hypocritical!*" she yelled after me.

"Shut up!" I slammed the door behind me and stormed up to my room.

That didn't go right, I said to God as I flung myself face-first on my bed.

I felt tears bubbling up and hurriedly rubbed my face. I grabbed my Bible and flicked through it, praying as I did so. I opened it at a random page and read aloud from one of the Psalms. *"Cast your cares on the Lord and he will sustain you; he will never let the righteous fall..."*

This is really, really important, God, I prayed desperately. *You have to make her change her mind.* I recalled one of the posters from Ms Sorenson's classroom and stared at myself in the mirror as I chanted, *"Life is not a dress rehearsal!"*

With a renewed sense of boldness, I decided to try again. I strode back down to the kitchen and lingered in the doorway. "Please can I get baptised?"

Jill turned in frustration. "We've just discussed that, Livi."

"No we haven't! You said no without thinking. That's not a discussion."

She pursed her lips. "I don't want you to get baptised."

"Why?"

"Because it's ridiculous!" she exploded. "It's a daft religious ritual that doesn't mean anything."

I swallowed hard. "If it doesn't mean anything then why can't I do it?"

She gave me a fierce look. "Don't push me." I opened my mouth to protest further but she went on, "There's nothing out there, Livi. There's no God, no Heaven, nothing, and I don't want to hear any more about it!"

Tears stung my eyes as I clung to the door frame. I wanted to explain to her that God was really good, really important and really *real*. I wanted her to know that church didn't have to be boring or religious or full of hypocrites. I wanted to show her that I'd found something, or rather *someone,* who truly, truly mattered. But she looked so angry and I didn't want to make things even worse.

"Okay," I whispered.

I went into the living room and switched on the computer, feeling a combination of fury and helplessness. I swallowed hard as I loaded up FriendWeb and drafted an email to my father.

'Hey Dad,
Sorry I haven't replied. I've been busy with school. Oh yeah, before I forget, I've become a Christian and I want to get baptised...'

I paused and then started again.

'Hey Dad,
I'll keep this brief: I have been thinking about getting baptised. It's kind of a symbol of choosing to be a Christian and you sort of get wet while you're doing it. My youth leader said I should get permission from a parent so I just thought I'd ask you if—'

I stopped and put my head in my hands. I tried three more times but nothing sounded right. In the end, with tears of frustration rolling down my cheeks, I deleted the message and shut the computer down.

Jill was on edge for the rest of the day. I made every effort to stay out of her way, not wanting to do or say anything that might make her yell again. I'd known she didn't really believe but I didn't realise quite how *angry* she was about it. I flinched every time I recalled her words.

To make matters worse, Ruby rang me late in the afternoon and proclaimed, "We've got a dog!"

"A dog?" I exclaimed in envy. "How come?"

"He was wandering around the estate. The police said that if nobody claims him we can have him!"

137

"Wow..."

"Do you want to come and meet him?"

"Of course!" I forced myself to sound excited although, deep down, I was bubbling with jealousy. Why should this dog choose Ruby's family? They already had so much. I tried to remind myself that I had just met *God* and therefore didn't need a dog or a big family or any other earthly prize but I still felt pretty gutted regardless. I realised this must be precisely why Summer had told me to *'guard that hope.'* The cares of life robbed it so easily.

I drifted into the hallway and put my shoes on. "I'm going to Ruby's," I called to Jill. "They've found a dog."

"Oh yeah," she replied vacantly from the kitchen. "It was sitting outside the front door all morning."

My jaw hung open. "You mean it should've been *mine?*"

Jill didn't reply so I gave a cry of annoyance and left the house.

Ruby was waiting for me on her front step. I was mildly reassured by the fact that the dog was incredibly ugly. It had a tired-looking face, a scrawny grey body and skinny legs that wobbled when it wagged its scruffy tail.

"Isn't he gorgeous?" Ruby cried as I crossed the street.

I stood awkwardly as the dog came over and sniffed my feet. I wasn't sure I wanted to touch him. "He's a bit... dirty."

"That's because he's a stray," Ruby explained. "We're going to bath him and give him a haircut. Then he'll be fine."

I imagined the dog perched on the kitchen table for one of Belinda's haircuts and gave a slow nod. "What's he called?"

"We don't know. We've tried lots of names but he hasn't responded to any of them."

Oscar came running outside and flung himself on the animal. "Look at my dog!" he shouted.

I cocked my head to one side. "He looks like a *'Walter...'* or a *'Dennis.'*"

At this, the dog turned and barked at me.

"You got it!" Oscar said triumphantly. "You guessed his name!"

Violet emerged from the house and Oscar ran to her and exclaimed, "His name is Dennis!"

She raised her eyebrows. "I don't like that name."

Oscar squealed and covered the dog's ears. "Don't be mean!" He patted the dog and whispered, "It's alright, Dennis. I love you."

"Do you want to help us bath him?" Ruby asked me.

I shrugged. "Okay."

I followed them up the stairs, keeping a wide berth between myself and Dennis. He was nothing like the dog of my dreams. I had imagined a King Charles Spaniel with dainty paws and a perfectly round face, not this scraggly beast.

Violet had prepared a luxurious bath, complete with bubbles and scented candles. Dennis took one look at it and bolted for the door. It took several minutes and a lot of wrestling before the four of us managed to coax him into the bath. Once in, he wouldn't stop splashing and it didn't take long before we were all drenched.

"Peace, my furry friend!" Violet cooed as she lathered shampoo over his back. "We'll have you cleaned up in no time..."

"Would you like a sponge?" offered Oscar.

Dennis barked and shook wildly.

I wrinkled up my nose and whispered to Ruby, "Perhaps his name is 'Sponge.'"

She giggled and reached for the shower head. Dennis began to howl as she turned the shower on and rinsed the shampoo out of his coat.

"That will do," Violet said, wringing water out of her jumper. "Let's take him back outside to dry off."

We lifted Dennis out of the bath and he gave an almighty shake before sprinting out of the door and down the stairs. Violet and Oscar leapt up and ran after him but Ruby just looked at me. "Shall we wait up here till he's dry?"

"Yeah," I said in relief.

We grabbed a couple of towels and patted ourselves down.

"That was hard." Ruby grinned. "Imagine having more than one!"

I gave an absent nod and thought wistfully of Kitty's menagerie of pets. I wondered if she bathed them all or whether she had a maid to do it. "I wish I had a pet," I muttered. I leant against the bathroom wall and sighed.

Ruby was bending her towel into the shape of a chicken.

I watched her for a moment before saying, "I want to get baptised."

Ruby looked at me in amazement. "That's great!"

"Jill won't let me."

"Why not?"

I bit my lip and blinked hard. "I don't know. She got really angry. She said God doesn't exist and she doesn't want me to mention it again." I sniffed and looked at the floor.

"Oh Livi!" Ruby gave me a sympathetic pat. "That's awful."

"It's not fair," I said bitterly. "I wish I could just do it."

Ruby eyed the dirty bath water.

"Not now!"

She shrugged. "What are you going to do?"

"What *can* I do? She never listens to me. I want her to believe in God. I want her to come to church. I want her to meet Jesus for herself. But it's all too much."

Ruby thought for a moment before exclaiming, "One bite at a time!"

"What?"

"My mum says it a lot. It's how you eat an elephant."

"One bite at a time?"

"Yup! Just start at a corner and work from there."

I sighed. It wasn't as simple as that. There weren't any corners with Jill. It was one big impenetrable circle.

~ 18 ~

Kitty's secret

Apparently, sharing a bed with a stray dog is not as cute as one might imagine. When I met Ruby for school the next morning, she had a face full of cuts and a bruised neck.

"What happened?" I asked.

"Dennis slept on my head," she moaned, clutching the side of her face. "I think he broke my ear."

I suppressed a laugh. "Why did you let him sleep on your head?"

"Because Violet wouldn't let him sleep on hers. And one of us had to because he kept howling."

I chuckled and tried to be sympathetic as I picked dog fur out of her hair. "Why didn't you just put him out of your room?"

"We tried. He kicked the door down."

I raised an eyebrow.

"He's stronger than he looks!"

I giggled before saying nonchalantly, "Nobody claimed him then?"

Ruby shook her head.

"So... You officially own a dog?"

"I guess." She gave a soft smile.

I tried to look happy for her. It's not that I wanted Dennis for myself— he was far too ugly. It just felt fairer if neither of us had a dog. I changed the subject. "Only two weeks left to complete the class newspaper."

"Oh yeah!" Ruby grinned. "I wondered if I could do an article about Dennis. You know, 'A Diary of a Lost Dog,' or something like that?"

I sucked in my cheeks. "You'd have to call it something else. Freddie Singh has already done 'A Diary of a Toaster.'"

"Oh." Ruby shrugged. "Okay."

I forced a smile. "But obviously you can write it. It's everybody's paper."

~*~

Mrs Tilly began the morning's lesson by reminding us that the deadline for our newspaper was a fortnight away.

"Make sure you give yourselves plenty of time to check your work and make last minute changes..." she lectured us. "You still need to finalise the layout."

I nodded along so that she would know I was aware of this fact and completely on top of things. When she had finished, I stood up to make a brief announcement. "Just so you know, there's still time to leave a letter for the advice column." I coughed and added smoothly, "Auntie Amber said she still has lots of slots available."

The class stared at me blankly, apart from Kitty who sniggered and whispered something to Molly.

"Does anybody have any questions?" I continued. "About the advice column or the newspaper in general?"

Nobody said anything so I sighed and sat back down.

"Thank you, Livi," Mrs Tilly trilled. "Now then, let's have some silent working as I'm sure you all have plenty to be getting on with."

The class gave a moan and reluctantly pulled out their work.

Behind me, I heard Molly whisper, "I can't wait till this project is over."

"Yeah," Kitty hissed. "Then maybe *someone* can go back into their little hole."

I swivelled round in my seat. "Would you like me to check your work for you, Kitty?"

"You won't be able to read it," she sneered.

I rolled my eyes and turned away, determined not to take the bait.

To my delight, Mrs Tilly came over at that moment and said, "Kitty, you don't appear to be doing anything. Where's your work?"

"I forgot it," Kitty snapped.

Mrs Tilly looked a little affronted and held out a fresh piece of paper. "Then you'd better start again."

Kitty took the paper and slammed it down on her desk.

142

I turned to give her a quick smirk. Then I hummed and made a great show of enjoying myself as I carefully laid out my own work. In total, I had written seventeen articles. They were mainly informative pieces of writing,[47] with the odd humorous item[48] to liven things up. I decided a spot of poetry would complement the rest of my work nicely.

'I am a tin
I'm full of beans
But I am more
Than what I seem
And when you hold me in your hands
You'll know my weight
You'll understand...'

I sat back and chewed my pen, unsure of how to finish it.

Beside me, Ruby was working frantically.

"I'm writing a poem," I told her.

She gave me half a glance and continued scribbling.

I watched her with curiosity. "What are you doing?"

"An advert." She held up her work and grinned.

I took it from her and read aloud, *"For all you dogs out there who can't read this... You might need glasses..."*

"I'm going to take a photo of Dennis wearing my mum's spectacles!" Ruby said eagerly. "Or, as I plan on calling them, *sPETctacles!* What do you think?"

I wrinkled up my nose. "It's a serious newspaper, Ruby."

She looked disappointed. "Oh."

I sighed as I considered my poem. "You can do it if you want."

As the lesson drew to an end Mrs Tilly interrupted the class to announce, "If any of you need some help putting the finishing touches to your work, I'm sure Livi, as your editor, would be happy to look things over for you."

I stood up to agree but, before I could say anything, I was surrounded by a rush of people keen to dump their work on me. Within seconds, I had over twenty pieces of work in my possession, most of which was half-hearted, unfinished or unnamed. Several

---

[47] Such as a piece entitled, *'Reasons Why Smoking Isn't Cool,'* and a selection of spring recipes from Miss Day.

[48] Including, *'Strange Sights On The Way To School,'* and, *'Teachers Spotted Shopping.'*

articles contained only a title, eight different people had reported on a recent Leeds United football match and one piece of paper said simply, *'Livi is a loser,'* but there was the odd gem, such as Rupert Crisp's cartoon strip and Aaron Tang's *'Travels in Asia.'*

"I'll meet you in the canteen," I told Ruby as the lunch bell rang. "I just want to put this stuff in my locker."

She nodded and followed the rest of our class out of the room.

I picked up the work from my desk, feeling the weight of responsibility as I carefully packed it all into my bag. I grinned as I considered how amazing it would be if my newspaper[49] won the competition. I wandered down the corridor, almost walking into Mr Riley as I lost myself in a daydream.

"Hello Livi," he boomed, eyeing me somewhat suspiciously.

"Hello Mr Riley," I said politely. Then, in case he'd seen everyone's work poking out of my bag and was about to accuse me of theft, I added, "I'm the editor for our class newspaper." I began to assure him that I was still behaving myself and hadn't called anybody fat recently but he just nodded and walked on.

As I entered our form room, I saw Annie Button lingering by my post box. I watched as she sighed and dropped something in.

"Excuse me," I said loudly.

She looked up and blushed. "Hi Livi. I'm just leaving a letter for Auntie Amber."

I glared at her as she hurried out of the room. No doubt it was another of Kitty and Molly's joke letters. I marched over to the post box and yanked open the lid. I was about to scrunch the note up without even reading it but curiosity got the better of me and I unfolded it instead.

The letter was written on a scrap of yellow paper and was full of spelling errors. My jaw dropped open as I read the hasty scrawl.

'Deer Anty Amber,
I'm really worried about my frend. Her mum walked out 2 weeks ago and she hasn't seen her since. Nobody at scool knows exept me and she keeps getting into troble for not doing her work. What should I do to help her?
From Worried Frend.'

I read the letter three times. Was it meant to be a joke? It wasn't very funny if it was. Yet, if it wasn't a joke... who was it

---

[49] *Our newspaper,* I corrected myself.

about? Molly's mother had dropped her off in her brand new car that morning and I was pretty sure Melody's mother was one of the dinner ladies. And it surely couldn't be about Kitty since her life was so perfect...

The classroom door opened and I quickly shoved the letter into my pocket.

Kitty walked in, followed by Molly and Melody.

"Why won't you tell *me?*" Molly was exclaiming.

The three of them took one look at me and stopped in their tracks.

"Hi," I said nonchalantly, checking to make sure I had replaced the lid on the post box.

Kitty glared at me. "Let's go somewhere else," she muttered.

"Why should *we* have to leave?" Molly sneered. "We were here first."

"No you weren't!" I retorted.

"I mean here, in this school."

I rolled my eyes. "I was leaving anyway." I headed for the door, eyeing Kitty carefully as I did so. "How are your pets, Kitty?"

She gave me a funny look. "They're fine."

I nodded. "How about your parents?"

Kitty went bright red. "They're fine too."

"Have you and your mum gone horse riding recently?"

Kitty looked like she was going to explode. "Let's go to the library," she said to her friends. She adjusted her bag and came towards me. "Get out of my way!" she shrieked.

I sucked in my breath as she shoved past me and marched out of the room.

I met Ruby in the canteen and sat in stunned silence as I went over Annie's letter in my head. Kitty's mother had left home. Kitty didn't know where she was. I felt a sick kind of satisfaction as the realisation sunk in that Kitty's life wasn't so perfect after all. *And nobody knows except Annie—* my heart leapt— *and me.*

I thought about Kitty telling everyone that my dad wasn't really an actor and her comment about being nice to orphans. I thought about her jeering Molly on to punch me and taunting me while I was on report. I thought about how snide and sneaky and mean she was *every single day.* A ripple of anger and then smugness rushed through me. Now I had some ammunition for sweet revenge. Perhaps I could photocopy Annie's letter and put it up around school. Or I could 'accidentally on purpose' get caught passing it to

Kitty in a lesson and she would be made to read it out. I felt almost ashamed at how attractive that idea was.

"Livi, are you okay?" Ruby interrupted my dark plotting.

I looked up. "Yeah, I'm fine."

"What are you thinking about?"

My cheeks grew hot. I knew Ruby would disapprove of my thoughts and instantly felt guilty. "Er, I kind of found something out about someone."

Ruby raised her eyebrows. "What? Who?"

I looked around to make sure nobody was listening before whispering, "Kitty's mother left two weeks ago and Kitty doesn't know where she is!" I tried to keep the delight out of my voice but wasn't entirely successful.

Ruby looked at me in shock. "That's so sad!"

"Why is it sad?" I shot back. "Kitty's horrible. It serves her right if her family is a mess."

Ruby shook her head. "Maybe that's *why* she's horrible."

I sniffed. "Well, anyway, I only know because Annie stupidly wrote a letter to the advice column about it."

Ruby was looking very serious. "What should we do?"

I shifted awkwardly. I had just been calculating how much it would cost to make fifty photocopies. "It's none of our business," I muttered.

Ruby nodded and took a sip of juice. "I guess."

That afternoon, I saw Kitty in a fresh new light. Whereas before she had always seemed spoilt, irritating and obnoxious, now she seemed frustrated, angry and... sort of sad.

In Art, she ignored Miss Appleby's request to stop swinging on her chair. She didn't do any work, other than to paint Annie's hands blue. And then, in Ms Sorenson's lesson, she wouldn't stop pinging rubber bands across the circle during the start of *Tin Time*.

"Miss Warrington!" Ms Sorenson warned. "Stop that immediately."

Kitty slammed her chair against the wall and gave a loud yawn.

"Miss Warrington!"

"What?"

Ms Sorenson informed her that if she couldn't behave properly she would have to go outside. Kitty sniggered and said she didn't care. Ms Sorenson sent her out. Kitty waltzed out of the room, swearing as she went. Ms Sorenson called after her that she could also have a detention.

I felt uneasy as I watched the scene unfold. Of course, Kitty was wrong to be behaving so badly, but I couldn't help but feel a little sorry for her. I pushed Annie's note deeper into my pocket as I caught eyes with Ruby and shrugged.

She shrugged back and whispered, "Awkward."

I sighed and turned back to Ms Sorenson, determined to concentrate on today's exercise.

"Let's begin with something simple," our teacher said with a smile. "Tell us something you did at the weekend."

My stomach churned as she sent the tin on its way. The first thought that came to mind was my encounter with God at the end of *Bible Bash* but the idea of sharing it with my class was mortifying. I didn't want anybody to laugh, or judge me, or perhaps think I was crazy. As the tin went round the circle I wrung my hands in my lap and wondered what to say. Was there any way of wording it that wouldn't sound weird?

The tin reached Ruby. "We found a dog," she said shyly. "We think his name is Dennis and we're going to keep him if nobody claims him." She beamed and passed the tin to me.

I took it and held it in my lap, feeling my throat grow dry as I opened and closed my mouth. Eventually I said quietly, "I helped Ruby bath the dog."

I sent the tin on and looked down at the floor. I could have kicked myself. How could something so real and so amazing seem embarrassing in the cold light of day? Was I really so bothered about the opinions of my class that I would hide the most exciting thing that had ever happened to me?

The tin got back to Ms Sorenson. She just sent it round again.

I sucked in my breath and willed myself not to miss this second opportunity to share my grand encounter. But when the tin reached me I stalled and chickened out once more. "I... er..." I stared at my bag. My English folder was poking out. "I've written a poem about the tin," I said, hating myself for being so cowardly. Ms Sorenson was smiling so I pulled the poem out. "Should I read it?"

She nodded.

I cleared my throat and started to read. *"I am a tin—"*

I was interrupted by a light tapping and looked up to see Kitty's face squashed up against the small window in the classroom door. With her eyes crossed and her lips flattened out, she looked a lot like a fish sucking the glass.

The class laughed and Kitty smirked, although she looked rather angry.

Ms Sorenson shot her a fierce glare and stood up. Without a moment's pause, Kitty's head ducked out of sight and Ms Sorenson sat down again. "Let's all ignore Miss Warrington," she said sternly. She looked at me. "Carry on, please, Livi."

I nodded and finished my poem. Then I passed the tin on and glanced back at the door. I spent the rest of the lesson staring at the little window but Kitty's face did not reappear. I wondered whether she was still outside the classroom or whether she had gone off to cry. I found it hard to concentrate on anything else. As the lesson drew to an end, I came to a decision.

"I'll see you in Maths," I told Ruby.

She looked at me curiously but didn't say anything.

I lingered as the rest of the class ran for the door, not entirely sure if I was even doing the right thing. When everyone else had left, I shuffled over to Ms Sorenson's desk.

She smiled at me. "Hello Livi."

"Hello. Er… I think Kitty is having some problems at home."

Ms Sorenson raised her eyebrows.

"Annie posted this to my advice column." I handed her the letter.

She read it and exhaled slowly. "I see…" She thought for a moment before giving me a curious look. "You have an advice column?"

"Yeah," I said, shrugging stupidly. "For our class newspaper."

"Oh? It must be a challenge to advise your peers when you're only young yourself."

I wasn't sure if that was a compliment or an insult so I just shrugged again.

"Well, I have to say you've handled this very maturely." Ms Sorenson folded up the letter. "Leave it with me, Livi. And well done. I'm proud of you."

I felt a lump in my throat as I nodded dumbly. "Okay Miss." Ms Sorenson being proud of me ranked far higher than owning a dog.

Kitty was at least half an hour late to Maths. To begin with, I thought she wasn't going to come at all and wondered if she had run away, like her mother. But then there was a soft knock on the door and she appeared, looking rather small and close to tears.

Fester turned abruptly and seemed on the verge of telling her off, but he took one look at her face and thought better of it.

Kitty sniffed and handed him a note in the same mauve colour as one of Ms Sorenson's filofax pages.

Fester read it and said, "Thank you, Kitty. You can sit down."

She nodded and marched through the room, forcing a smile as she caught sight of her friends.

I looked away as she hurried past my desk. It didn't feel right to stare.

For the rest of the lesson I was aware of her presence behind me. I wanted to turn around and see whether she was alright but I wasn't sure how to do this in a way that wouldn't seem like I was gloating. I knew full well that the last thing she would want was any attention from me.

The lesson came to an end and I watched Kitty out of the corner of my eye as she snatched up her belongings and stormed out of the room. I quickly grabbed my things and indicated to Ruby to hurry up. She gave an anxious nod and joined me in running out of the room. We followed Kitty from a distance as she headed out of the building.

"What are you going to do?" Ruby whispered as we crossed the playground.

"I don't know," I whispered back.

We reached the school gates and it looked as though Kitty was about to scurry across the street. Without thinking, I tentatively reached over and tapped her on the arm.

She turned and snapped, "What?"

I gulped and took a step back.

Before I could say anything, we were interrupted by the tooting of a loud horn. Kitty's mother had pulled up in a bright blue convertible.

I saw Kitty's eyes widen as she ran towards her. "Mum!"

"Hi darling," her mother drawled. "I thought we could go shopping."

Kitty grinned and yanked the door open. Then she saw me staring. "I'm going shopping," she said smugly. "With my mum."

There were a thousand things I could've said but, in the end, I said simply, "Have fun."

Kitty just sneered. "I will."

~ 19 ~

I know exactly what I'm doing

I don't know about Ruby, but I felt mighty holy as we walked home from school. In a single day, I had achieved Jesus' great command to love my enemies. I hoped that God had taken note. I found myself grinning all the way home as I convinced myself that a grand reward was on its way— an opportunity to witness a miracle, perhaps, or another encounter with God himself. But, despite my earnest expectations and my constant glancing at the sky in search of angels, it seemed that God had other plans.

I let myself into the house and was greeted by the sight of Jill sitting on the stairs looking rather vacant.

"I did a good deed today!" I said.

She ignored me.

"Ms Sorenson even said she was proud of me. That's my Personal and Social Development teacher."

No reply.

I paused. "Can I have some chocolate as a reward?"

She didn't respond so I went into the kitchen and helped myself. When I came back, Jill still hadn't moved.

I waved a hand in front of her face. "Are you okay?"

Jill let out a long sigh and said quietly, "I've lost my job." She rubbed her head and looked away.

I wasn't sure what to say. "Do you want some chocolate?" I held out the rest of my bar.

Jill shook her head.

I sat beside her and gave her an awkward hug.

"I don't know what to do," she muttered.

"Get another one?" I suggested.

She gave me a withering look.

"I could help... What kind of job would you like?"

Jill sighed again.

I chewed my lip and wondered what to do. I sat with her for a while before saying, "Well... I'd better go and do some homework."

She didn't reply so I left her sitting on the stairs and ran up to my room. I stood for a moment before coming to a decision. My homework could wait. Jill needed me more.

Golden Opportunities Girl to the rescue!

I threw my school bag on the floor and pulled out some paper as I considered what kind of job Jill could do. She was rather bossy, so she'd probably enjoy a job where she could order people around. Something with lots of money would be good too; then she'd stop worrying about not having enough. I wrote down *'Bank manager'* and then stopped to think. Before we moved to Leeds, Jill had worked in a little farm shop where occasionally she would come home with a free stale cake. I stuck out my lip as I considered what other kinds of careers might involve free gifts. Then I chewed the lid of my pen as I realised I had no idea what sort of job Jill would even *like*. When she was at school she'd wanted to be a psychologist. However, I only know this because I read her old diary a few months ago. My snooping had led to a whole series of regrettable events, culminating in my father's departure. It probably wasn't the right time to remind her. Still, she might enjoy a job where she could help people... I sighed and tapped my pen against my teeth. There aren't many jobs designed for bossy, depressed people. It took me over an hour, but I finally drew up a list.

Five possible jobs for Jill
1. Bank manager
2. Assistant in a trendy clothes shop, preferably Tizzi Berry
3. Someone who helps people pick new glasses
4. Librarian
5. Taxi Driver

As I heard Jill calling me for dinner, I looked over my list and frowned. It didn't look very inspiring. I crossed out *'Taxi Driver'* and exchanged it for *'Flower delivery girl,'* then I shoved the list into my pocket and ran downstairs.

I entered the kitchen with a leap but Jill didn't even look up. She retrieved a couple of ready meals from the oven and put them down with a sigh.

"Mmm!" I said heartily. "Macaroni cheese."

She didn't reply.

I fiddled with the list in my pocket, hoping for an appropriate moment to share it.

We sat in silence for a while until, all of a sudden, Jill said, "I've spoken to Aunt Claudia. She suggested we move in with her for a while."

I dropped my cutlery. "What?"

Jill continued as though she was speaking about something as trivial as switching washing powder. "I can look for jobs down in Suffolk. You could even go back to your old school if I find a job close enough—"

"I don't want to move," I said loudly.

Jill looked disappointed. "I thought you'd be glad. You've not really settled in Leeds."

"I have!" I exclaimed. "I really, really have!"

She sniffed. "You've only made one friend and, although Ruby's nice, you could do a little better."

"I've made loads of friends!" I retorted.

"Violet and Oscar don't count."

"Not them! Grace, Nicole, Mark, Joey..."[50]

"Who?"

I rolled my eyes. "From Ruby's church." Then I added as an afterthought, "From *my* church."

Jill gave a careless shrug and started moving her food around with her fork.

I pushed my half-eaten plate aside. "I'm not moving."

"Please, Livi," Jill said tiredly. "I have to make the best possible decision for us and I need you to be reasonable."

"Me be reasonable?!" I shrieked. "I was happy in Little Milking and *you* made us move for a job that *you* wanted that was supposed to make everything better. And now that I am actually, *finally,* happy in Leeds, *you* want us to move again and go and live with Aunt Claudia the crazy cat lady!" I was going to keep ranting but then I noticed Jill had started to cry. I bit my lip, ever-so-slightly peeved that Jill was playing the 'crying' card. It's so much harder to fight for my rights when she cries.

---

[50] At this moment in time, I'm not sure I could legitimately call Joey my friend. Other than an awkward moment at the end of *Bible Bash* in which both tried to squeeze through a door at the same time, we haven't spoken since the incident with his surname. Come to think of it, I'm not sure the others like me anymore either. They'd had lunch with Joey immediately after my insult and one by one I had caught them glancing across at me in bemusement. I hadn't dared speak to any of them since. But there was no need for Jill to know this.

"I'm sorry, Livi. I've messed up."

"You haven't!" I said rashly.

"I can't do it," she continued with a sob. "I hated my job. I was rubbish at it and I have no idea how to get another one. I hate Leeds and I can't go anywhere without fearing I'll bump into your dad—"

"He's in Hull."

Jill looked at me in confusion.

"FriendWeb," I grunted.

She sighed and let out another sob.

"You don't need to give up so quickly," I insisted, pulling out my list. "There are loads of jobs you could do."

I slid the list across the table but she shook her head and turned away. I wondered if I should read it out for her although, looking over it once more, it suddenly seemed rather pathetic. As I watched Jill grab a tissue and blow her nose, I dug my nails into my hands and begged silently, *God, please make her change her mind...*

"I wouldn't want us to live with Aunt Claudia *forever*. Just until I sort myself out..."

"No!" I yelled. Why wasn't God *listening?* I tried another tactic. "Please, please, please, please, please, please—!"

"Livi, stop it!" Jill covered her face and moaned.

I gave a cry of frustration and ran to my room, heading straight for my phone.

"Ruby, it's me..."

"Hi Livi!"

I burst into tears. "Jill wants us to go and live with Aunt Claudia!"

"Oh no!"

"I don't know what to do," I blubbered.

There was silence.

I waited on the line, hoping that Ruby would come up with some grand plan or reveal some secret prayer or routine that would get God to make Jill change her mind.

"Me neither," she said finally.

I barely slept all night. I lay awake, still in my school uniform, with my light on and my curtains wide open as I fought desperately for a plan. Immediately after phoning Ruby I had spent an hour sifting through the Bible in search of wisdom but God did not come to my aid. As I slammed the book shut and tossed it onto the floor I wondered how life could turn so suddenly. Mere days ago, in the ecstasy of God's presence, I had felt as though nothing could touch me. Yet, less than a week later, my whole world was about to collapse and God was a million miles away once more.

The next morning Ruby met me on the pavement looking as miserable as I felt. "Are you really moving away?" she asked sadly.

I gave a heavy sigh. "That's what Jill said last night."

"What about this morning?"

I shrugged. "She's still in bed." I had debated doing something nice like making her breakfast in bed in the hopes of getting her to change her mind. But the last time I'd tried to carry a tray up the stairs I had dropped it. I didn't think it would help my cause if I woke Jill up by spilling a hot drink on her head.

Ruby stared at the ground. "Maybe you could come and live with me?"

I didn't need to answer. We both knew that wasn't an option.

After walking in silence for a while, I pulled the list of possible jobs out of my bag. "Can you think of a job Jill might like?"

Ruby looked over my list and bit her lip. "Does she like animals?"

"No."

"Oh. It's just that there are jobs going at the pet shop."

I scratched my chin. "I'll write it down anyway."

Ruby nodded. "What about babies? My mum used to work at a nursery. She might be able to help Jill make some contacts."

I wrinkled up my nose. "She doesn't like mess. And anything living generally involves mess."

Ruby thought for a moment. "She could see if there are jobs in the cemetery. Everything there is dead."

I blinked at her.

"They might need a warden or something."

I shook my head. "I don't think so."

"Well, I can't think of anything else."

I rolled my eyes and shoved the list into my pocket. "What do *you* want to do when you're older?" I asked indifferently.

Ruby perked up a little. "I'm going to go to Africa and build an orphanage."

I looked at her in surprise.

She shrugged before explaining, "When I was little I saw a film about missionaries in Mozambique and I decided that's what I'd like to do one day. And, once, I was at church and somebody said

God had given them a picture of me surrounded by lots of children in Africa. So that kind of confirmed it. How about you?"

I squirmed awkwardly. "A writer, I think. Although God hasn't confirmed it or anything."

She nodded. "You'd be an amazing writer, Livi."

"I hope God thinks so."

"He does. I think he made you good at writing."

As pleased as this made me feel, I couldn't help but ask sorely, "What about Jill? What did God make *her* good at?"

Ruby chewed her lip. "I don't know. But there must be something."

We didn't come up with anything all morning. So, during our lunch break, we logged onto the computers in the Careers suite and filled in a skills questionnaire on Jill's behalf. Based on our answers, the programme suggested that she become a carpet fitter or a window cleaner.

We stared at the results in disappointment.

"That's rubbish," I muttered.

One of the Careers advisors came over and asked if I wanted to print the results out. "It will tell you what grades you need in order to fulfil your career goal of..." She peered over my shoulder. "Carpet fitter or window cleaner."

I turned to her in dismay. "It's not for me! I'm going to be a writer."

"Would you like me to help you find out what grades you need to be a writer?"

I shook my head.

"Or what kind of back-up job you could do if that vocation fails?" she continued carelessly.

My stomach lurched at her words. For the briefest of moments, I felt afraid. What if I couldn't be a writer and had to be a carpet fitter instead? Or what if I couldn't get *any* job and ended up living on the streets? Or worse, with Aunt Claudia *forever?* I gave myself a shake and stood up. Now wasn't the time to grow uneasy about my own destiny. "No thank you," I said. "I know exactly what I'm doing. I was just here to help somebody else."

The Careers advisor watched as I gathered up my stuff and stormed out of the room.

"And *she's* going to Africa to work with orphans," I added as Ruby got up to follow me.

155

As we walked home that afternoon I considered the job options for Jill. Despite adding, *'Pet shop worker,'* *'Nursery nurse,'* *'Cemetery warden,'* *'Carpet fitter'* and *'Window cleaner'* to the list, it still didn't look strong enough to save us from having to leave Leeds. I scrunched it up and tossed it away.

"What should I do?" I pleaded with Ruby. "I don't want to move." I sighed as I tried to be a bit less selfish. "Plus, I want Jill to be happy and I want her to know that I care. It can't be easy not being good at anything."

Ruby thought for a moment. "You could offer to pray for her."

I screwed up my nose. "But she doesn't believe in God. It might just make her angry."

"Maybe."

"And anyway, why would God help her get a job if she doesn't believe in him?"

"He still loves her," Ruby insisted. "And it's important to you. So it's important to him."

I chewed my lip and mulled this over. "Do you think, if she lets me pray for her, she'll have an experience like I had at *Bible Bash?*"

Ruby cocked her head to one side. "Maybe..."

I gave a moan as we crossed a busy road. "Imagine if this is the last time we ever walk home together."

Ruby looked at me in horror. "Don't say that."

We walked in sombre silence for the rest of the journey. As we reached my house, I gave a mighty sigh. "Wish me luck." I blushed and corrected myself. "I mean, pray for me."

Ruby nodded.

I gave her an awkward hug and let myself into my house. I had half expected all our belongings to be packed up and ready to go so was more than a little surprised when I found Jill in the kitchen surrounded by vegetables. She was bent over an old cookbook looking perturbed.

"What's a sauté?" she muttered, poking through the vegetables. "I didn't put that on my list..."

I shrugged. "What are you doing?"

Jill forced a smile. "I'm learning to cook. We can't afford to keep buying takeaways and ready meals."

I raised my eyebrows. "Cool... What are we having?"

"Ratatouille." Jill's brow wrinkled as she tapped the recipe. "But I don't think I've got everything..." She rubbed her head.

I stood nervously in the doorway. "If you learn how to cook... Will that mean we won't have to move?"

Jill waved a hand. "Hold on a minute, Livi."

I followed her into the hallway and watched as she dialled the Ricos' number.

"Sorry to bother you, Belinda. It's Jill."

Belinda responded with some joyous squawking which made Jill screw up her nose.

"Yes, yes, I'm fine, thank you," my sister said quickly. She cleared her throat. "I'm just cooking ratatouille and I seem to have forgotten to buy any sauté. I wondered if you had any?" There was a pause and then Jill read from her cookery book, *"Add the aubergine and sauté."* She went bright red as Belinda replied. "Okay. Thank you, Belinda." Jill put the phone down and gave a cry of frustration. "Idiot, idiot, idiot!"

I watched as she burst into tears. "Won't she give you any sauté? I could ask Ruby—"

"Sauté isn't a food!" Jill bawled. "It's a way of cooking something. I'm so stupid." She flung the cookbook down the hall. "Let's just get a takeaway."

"Don't give up," I said. "You're so close."

Jill shook her head. "I can't be bothered." She reached for the phone again.

"I'll cook it!" I offered wildly. If it meant staying in Leeds, I would gladly leave school and become a chef.

"Don't be silly. You can't cook."

"Can't be any worse than you!"

Jill opened her mouth to respond and then laughed despite herself.

I grinned at her. "Let's cook it together."

She rolled her eyes and made some vague sounds.

"Oh come on!" I exclaimed. "It will be fun. And if we mess it up... we'll give it to Belinda as a gift and *then* get a takeaway."

Jill laughed again. "Fine."

I pulled her off the stairs and we headed back to the kitchen together.

"I'll be the head chef," I said, picking the cookery book up off the floor. "You can be my minion."

Jill gave me a playful shove but seemed relieved to let me lead.

"Okay..." I ran a finger across the page. "First, preheat the oven."

Jill nodded and went over to switch it on. "Done."

157

"Now... chop up the garlic." I rooted around for a knife while Jill located the garlic from her shopping. "See, this is easy!" I said eagerly.

Jill ignored me, although I saw her smile a little.

After frying the garlic we added some aubergine. Then we filled a dish with the aubergine and covered it with layers of other chopped vegetables and loads of cheese. It was really simple. Kind of like following an experiment in Science except we didn't even need safety goggles. And nothing disastrous happened apart from Jill stepping on a tomato and crying again. Before we knew it, our ratatouille was in the oven and we were wiping down the work surfaces and removing stray cheese from our hair.

"That wasn't too hard, was it?" I said.

"I guess not," Jill agreed.

When we took the dish out forty minutes later, Jill looked positively radiant. "It smells great," she said.

I grinned and grabbed two plates.

I don't know whether it was just because of the effort that had gone into the meal but it tasted delicious. I shoved the food into my mouth and made hearty yummy noises.

Jill ate hers in silence, scooping the food up very slowly. Eventually, she said, "Thanks, Livi."

I beamed. "See?" I said with my mouth full. "I'm quite responsible."

"You are," Jill agreed. She gave a sad smile and looked down.

I felt my chest tighten and wished I knew what to say to help her feel better. I recalled Ruby's suggestion about praying as I eyed Jill carefully over my food. I wondered what she would say if I asked to pray for her. Would she think I was being unrealistic? Childish? Thoughtless, even? What if I prayed for her and nothing happened? Or worse, what if I prayed and something *awful* happened instead? My hands grew clammy as I fiddled with the edge of the table and deliberated over what I could say. But, just as I had summoned up the courage to say tentatively, "Jill, can I—" the telephone rang.

Jill pushed her chair back and wandered into the hallway.

"Hello? Oh." She didn't even try to hide the annoyance in her voice and, as I listened to her growing more and more irritated, I hoped vainly that the caller was Aunt Claudia and that Jill had changed her mind about the value of our aunt's advice. "Not particularly," she said shortly. "Well, whatever makes you happy."

She ended the call with an angry retort, "If I need your help, I'll ask for it," and slammed the phone down.

I shifted in my seat as she came back into the kitchen.

"Just Belinda checking on the ratatouille," she said scathingly.

I forced a smile. "That's nice."

Jill gave a sneer. "Apparently, the *Good Lord* is watching over me."

I said nothing.

"And Belinda's praying for me. As if I'm going to care that she's talking to herself about me. Is that meant to make me feel better?"

I opened my mouth and closed it again. "I don't know," I said hoarsely.

Jill started to clear the empty plates away. "Do you want anything else?" she asked, switching on the kettle.

I shook my head. "No..."

"Do you have any homework to do?"

"Yeah," I whispered. I stood up and lingered awkwardly.

"Go and do it then."

I nodded and left the room, almost tripping over my heart as I went.

~ 20 ~

Nothing surprises him

For the rest of the week I approached each day as if it were my last. Ruby greeted me every morning with mild surprise, as though she had expected me and Jill to have moved away in the night. She asked me every day whether we were staying but all I could do was shrug and whisper, "Keep praying."

I didn't dare discuss the issue with Jill. My plan to get us to stay had stooped to the level of making the house as messy as possible in the hopes that the efforts needed to pack would be too overwhelming for her. By Thursday Jill was in a truly hideous mood and the state of the house had only added to her distress.

"For goodness sake, Livi!" she shouted after tripping over a pile of coat hangers in the living room.

"So that's where I left them!" I called carelessly before heading to the cupboard under the stairs in search of more junk to scatter about. I pulled out a box of old magazines, the bundle of dirty paintbrushes from the start of the year and a lone Christmas cracker. I shoved the brushes into a pair of Jill's boots and arranged the magazines haphazardly across the floor. Then I took the cracker to my room where I pulled it apart. It contained an eraser shaped like a dustbin and a rather poor joke.[51] I put the paper hat on and sat on my bed, feeling an odd combination of sorrow and recklessness.

A little while later I heard Jill crying on the phone downstairs. I paused for a moment before creeping into the hallway to listen.

"I'll never get it, Aunt Claudia!" Jill exclaimed. "They want someone with experience in PR." She coughed as our aunt asked a question. "No, I did sales. No, it's not the same... Next Thursday."

---

[51] *Why can't dogs dance? They have two left feet.*

I sat up straight in surprise. It sounded as though Jill had a job interview. I was a bit miffed that she hadn't told me, especially since I was working so hard to find her a job myself. I shuffled further along the hallway and carried on listening.

Jill paused as Aunt Claudia asked another question and then replied with a sob, "Three... No, two weeks."

I sucked in my breath. Two weeks until what?

"No," Jill continued. "I don't want you to lend us any money. If I don't have a job by the time the rent's due, then that's it."

I exhaled slowly and gripped the edge of the banister.

Without warning, Jill put the phone down and turned to come up the stairs. I tried to flee before she saw me but wasn't quick enough.

"Livi!"

I gave her a sheepish smile. "How's Aunt Claudia?"

She growled and came marching up.

"So..." I said as she pushed past me. "I hear you have a job interview?"

Jill sighed. "Yes I do. But I'm not going to get it. I'm completely under-qualified."

"No you're not!"

She gave me a withering look. "Do you know what a press officer is?"

I shrugged. "Like a police officer?"

She rolled her eyes. "No, Livi."

I blushed. "I don't know."

"Then believe me when I say I won't get it." She went into her room and closed the door, leaving me staring miserably after her.

By Friday I felt pretty desperate. I had prayed every day for God to do something but was yet to see any breakthrough. According to Belinda, prayer is as simple as picking up an imaginary phone and chatting to God. In my head I knew that God was available whenever I wanted to talk to him. But, in my heart, I felt like an unwanted caller, diverted to his answer phone every time.

By now, my prayers resembled a monotonous mantra devoid of any real hope: *Dear God, please let me stay in Leeds, please let me stay in Leeds, please let me stay in Leeds...* over and over.

It had occurred to me that perhaps God didn't *want* us to stay in Leeds. Maybe having us move back to Suffolk was part of his grand plan. If that was the case, then praying was surely futile. But how was I supposed to know what he wanted? And, if everything fell apart, how could that possibly be his plan? Many times that week I had asked to no avail, *God, don't you care? If you do care, give me a sign.* His silence was almost more than I could bear.

Initially, I had told Ruby that I wasn't interested in going to youth group that evening. I'd not seen Joey or the others since *Bible Bash* and wasn't sure I wanted to add an awkward social gathering to my list of ordeals. But, at the last minute,[52] I changed my mind.

As I climbed into the Ricos' car beside Ruby, Stanley looked round and said, "Hello Livi."

"Hello," I said politely.

"How are you?"

"Fine, thank you. How are you?"

"I'm very well, thanks." He looked like he wanted to say something else but, fortunately, he lacks the clumsy tactlessness of Belinda. Instead, he put on a worship CD and sang along. He got rather into the music and hearing him sing was almost as awkward as watching him dance.

After a while Violet joined in, followed soon after by Ruby.

I closed my eyes and pretended to be asleep.

We pulled up outside Eddie and Summer's house and I slipped out of the car as quickly as possible.

Stanley wound his window down and stuck his head out. "I hope my singing wasn't too hideous, Livi."

"It was fine," I replied, forcing a smile. "Thanks for the lift."

He beamed and added, "If I cannot fly like a bird, I have to make do with singing like one!"

I stifled a giggle and conceded privately that Stanley was really not so bad, as grown ups go.

As I joined Ruby and Violet in waving him goodbye my stomach lurched at the sight of Joey's mother's car pulling up a few metres away.

"There's Joey!" Ruby pointed.

"Can we just go in?" I said. "I'm a bit cold."

---

[52] Faced with the prospect of listening to Jill sobbing and sighing as she prepared for her impossible job interview.

She shrugged. "Okay." Then she yelled down the street to Joey, "We'll meet you inside!"

Joey looked across and nodded awkwardly.

I blinked and turned away, staying as close to Ruby as possible as we walked into Eddie and Summer's house and into the living room.

Grace Fletcher was showing off a pair of brightly sequinned shoes. "They're actually my mum's," she said as we gathered round to stare. "But we have the same sized feet so she let me borrow them."

"You're lucky," Violet said. "Our mum has tiny feet."

Ruby nodded in agreement which I found quite odd. Belinda tends to wear the kind of shoes that even a scarecrow wouldn't be seen dead in. Being unable to share her footwear was something of a lucky escape if you asked me.

Grace turned to me and giggled. I braced myself for the question of my mother's shoe size. But instead she asked, "How was your week, Livi?"

"Fine," I muttered, desperate for the meeting to begin so that I could avoid any uncomfortable small talk.

Grace went to say something else but I pretended not to notice and marched into the hallway under the guise of needing the toilet.

Unfortunately, I almost walked straight into Joey who was bent over, untying his shoelaces. He looked up and blushed.

I avoided his gaze and took off my own shoes, as if that had been my reason for coming into the hallway. Then I ran back into the living room and carefully positioned myself slightly behind Ruby, willing myself to project the right level of normal; content to be there but neither bubbly nor miserable enough to attract anybody's attention.

Finally, Summer and Eddie came in.

"I know you're all having a great time chatting," Summer said loudly. "And we hate to break that up. But we're going to start now!"

I breathed a huge sigh of relief. I had survived the small talk. Now I just had to get through the rest of the evening.

Eddie began handing out large sheets of paper as we shuffled onto spots on the carpet. He put some pens and a pot of crayons in the middle and said, "Now then, it doesn't matter whether you count yourself as good at art or not..."

A few people squirmed at his words. Violet gave a haughty cough and sat up straight.

"I want you to draw things that depict you and the things that are important to you. For example..." He held up a drawing that he'd done earlier. "My name, Edward, means *'Wealth protector,'* so I've drawn a guard holding onto a treasure chest. This sunny beach scene with children playing represents Summer and the boys. And the cross down the centre of the page represents Jesus because I want to keep him central to everything." Eddie put his drawing down and beamed. "There's no right or wrong way to do this. So grab some pens and make your own!"

I watched as everybody else got started. The smell of the crayons made me think painfully of my father. He hadn't written to me again and I wondered whether he'd got sick of waiting for my reply. I sighed and grabbed a handful. They had boring names, like *'Lemon yellow'* and *'Twig brown.'* I sucked in my cheeks and turned to my blank sheet of paper. It felt appropriate to begin my picture with something holy but my attempts to sketch Jesus kept failing miserably and I wasted several sheets of paper as I repeatedly drew him as a bearded lady. In the end, I just copied Eddie's example by drawing a cross down the centre of my page.

Ruby was drawing a giant red gem. She caught my eye and grinned.

I forced a smile back. I had no idea how to depict *'Livi'* since it's just a made up name that doesn't mean anything. Instead, I drew a bird for *'Starling.'* Then I stole a peek at Joey's drawing, curious as to how he might depict his own surname.

To my surprise he'd drawn a gigantic leopard. He glanced up and I quickly looked away, pretending to be absorbed in my own work.

I bit my lip as I considered how I could possibly represent the complicated web of relationships that had existed between my mother, my father and Jill. In the end, I drew three clouds around the bird's head with tiny question marks under each one. Then I worried that it looked a little too sombre so I coloured in the cross in rainbow colours and added another large cloud to depict God. I didn't know what to do after that so I just continued to add more and more layers of colour to the cross until Eddie called an end to the exercise.

I flung the crayons back into the pot and clutched my drawing anxiously as Eddie asked us to come into a circle. I hoped we weren't going to have to talk about what we'd drawn.

Thankfully, Eddie said, "You don't need to explain your drawings because I'm sure they're very personal. But, if you don't mind, I'd like you to hold them up for each other to see."

I looked around as everybody held their drawings up. To my relief, there were quite a few of poor artistic quality so I didn't feel too silly holding up my own vain offering.

Joey had added a series of stars to his drawing. He had also drawn a shiny gold coin inside the leopard's mouth. There was some writing round the edge of the coin but I wasn't close enough to be able to read it and I didn't want to stare too intently.

I was pleasantly surprised by Violet's work. She had drawn a purple flower, with each petal depicting the face of somebody special to her. In the middle she had written, *'Faith, hope and love.'* It was rather gentler than her usual aggressive artwork.

I also liked Grace Moore's, although I couldn't understand it in the slightest. She had drawn an enormous tree with fruit of different kinds growing from it. The roots went deep into the soil and formed the shape of many clasped hands. I wished I'd had the wisdom to draw something so profound. My own picture looked hopelessly simple in comparison.

After a few minutes Eddie thanked us and we put our drawings down. Then he asked, "Why are you alive?"

Violet shrugged and said simply, "Jesus."[53]

At the same time, Rory said, "Because our parents made us."

A few people sniggered at this but Ruby put her hand up and said, "No they didn't. God did. People can't make people."

Nicole put her hand up. "My parents thought they couldn't have a baby. Doctors had said it was impossible. But they prayed and prayed and then I was born. My dad used to call me his little miracle."

I bit my lip and looked at the floor as several people put their hands up and added to the discussion. The general consensus was that God had chosen every one of us with a unique plan and had carefully knitted us together in our mothers' wombs. I didn't see how this could possibly apply to me. My parents hadn't loved one another. They hadn't married. They hadn't planned me. They certainly hadn't prayed for many nights to conceive me. I looked on in envy as people shared stories about how their parents had met

---

[53] One thing I have learnt from Violet is that, when in doubt, most theological debates can be answered by simply saying, *"Jesus,"* and shrugging in a nonchalant manner.

or how God's hand in their family history could be clearly seen. When it came to God being known in my family I felt as though I was both the beginning and the end of the line. The thought crossed my mind that if Jill and I moved back to Suffolk my present faith adventure might prove to be an isolated chapter, never to be opened again.

As the discussion came to an end Summer said, "Well, we've almost run out of time. Before we finish, does anybody want prayer for anything?"

I felt my face burn as she looked at us all in turn. Up till now I had always avoided any offer of prayer. I didn't like the idea of people knowing my problems so I would say things like, *'No, I'm fine,'* or, *'Can't think of anything today,'* or I would choose that moment to go to the toilet. I also felt bad because I still wasn't very confident at praying out loud so it didn't feel fair to ask people to pray for me if I wasn't going to return the favour. But today I felt my heart pounding desperately and I knew that if there was ever a time to admit to weakness, this was it.

I put my hand up.

Summer smiled. "Livi?"

I shifted uncomfortably as I muttered, "I might have to leave Leeds."

The group stared at me in surprise.

I swallowed hard and fought to keep my voice steady as I explained, "My sister lost her job and if she doesn't get another one in the next two weeks then that's it..." I sniffed. "Just pray she gets a job."

Summer looked concerned. "Thanks for sharing that, Livi. Perhaps we could all gather round you and pray?"

I gave half a nod.

Without a moment's pause everybody came and huddled around me. Ruby and Nicole each put a hand on my shoulders. I kept my head down and stared at the floor. I could see Joey's green trainers out of the corner of my eye but didn't dare look up at his face.

Summer started by thanking God for everything he was doing in my life and asking him to bring me peace and hope in this *'difficult time.'*

Then Grace Moore began one of her eloquent prayers. She used phrases like, *'God our provider,'* and *'the God of the impossible,'* and I squeezed my eyes shut as I thought hopefully, *God HAS to listen now. Grace is praying!*

Violet prayed next, making a great show of the fact that she knew my sister's name and where we lived and how long I had been a Christian. "Lord, you know how far Livi has come since she moved to Leeds. You've saved her from a life of unbelief and foolishness. Now, come and break into the life of her sister, Jill, who is even more unbelieving and foolish..." I resisted the urge to take offence at that, not wanting anything to discourage God from coming to my rescue.

As the prayers came to an end, I looked up and said a shy, "Thank you."

Summer squeezed my arm and said, "Keep us updated, Livi."

I nodded, feeling like I might cry. "I will."

I got awkwardly to my feet and, as they started to leave, a few people gave me an extra tight hug, as if worried that they might never see me again. This made me want to cry even more.

Summer handed me my drawing. "This is really lovely, Livi."

I shrugged.

"What are the clouds about?"

I pointed to the three above the bird. "Those three are Jill and my parents. And the big one is sort of God."

"And the question marks?"

"It's complicated."

She gave me a thoughtful smile before saying, "You need to know that you were not a mistake."

My heart jolted. I blinked as I nodded and looked away.

"God created you on purpose," she continued. "He knows what he's doing with you. And nothing surprises him."

"Thanks," I muttered. I folded up my drawing and followed Ruby out of the room.

Joey was lingering at the front door, looking a little agitated. I wasn't sure whether to blank him or acknowledge him so I hurriedly pulled on my shoes, shooting him a hasty nod as I walked past.

"Hey, Livi!"

I glanced back. "Yeah?"

"I'll be praying for your sister."

"Thanks." I turned to go before adding, "Don't tell her. She doesn't like that."

He gave half a smile. "Alright."

I smiled back. "Bye. Oh and I liked your leopard drawing."

He blushed and said wryly, "Better than drawing a bottom full of cash."

~ 21 ~

Last-chance Thursday

It was the morning of Jill's job interview and I had a sinking feeling in my gut as I rolled out of bed. Outside it was rather gloomy and a few spots of rain splattered against the window as I got dressed. This is what Mrs Tilly would call *'pathetic fallacy,'* where the weather reflects the mood of the protagonist. I drifted across my room in slow motion, pretending I was in a movie with my own depressing soundtrack playing over the scene. Downstairs, Jill was bustling about like a madwoman. I could hear her tripping over chair legs and banging cups about in the kitchen. I closed my eyes and let out a long sigh. She had no other options lined up so this truly was do-or-die. Either we were staying in Leeds or we were moving back to Suffolk. It all came down to this one interview.

I rubbed my head and headed down to breakfast. On my way, the telephone rang. I grabbed it, stifling a groan as soon as I answered. It was Aunt Claudia.

"Good morning, love," she said shrilly. "How are you?"

"Fine. And you?"

"Can't complain. The daffodils are coming up nicely. I was going to take a photo but I realised you'll see them for yourselves soon enough!"

I fought to keep my voice steady as I said, "Not necessarily. Jill has a job interview today and she might get it."

My aunt chuckled. "Well, you never know."

I forced a cough. "Were you phoning for a reason?"

"Of course! I rang to tell Jill not to wear her plaid suit. It's not at all flattering."

I rolled my eyes. "I'll pass the message on."

"And tell her to smile. She doesn't smile enough, your sister."

I felt that was a bit rich coming from the woman who once labelled smiles *'a waste of muscles.'* "Hmmm," I murmured.

At that moment Jill came out of the kitchen wearing her plaid suit. "Is it for me?" she asked miserably.

I put the phone down, cutting our aunt off mid-sentence. "Just Aunt Claudia wishing you all the best for today," I told Jill.

She gave a grunt and went back into the kitchen.

I followed her in. "How are you feeling?"

Jill grunted again and mumbled something about being useless.

I tried to be kind as I said, "Just do your best."

She didn't reply so I made myself some toast and watched as she went over several pages of interview preparation.

"Do you feel ready?" I ventured.

She waved her notes at me. "Have to be."

I nodded and forced a smile, privately despairing over the fact that my future lay in the hands of an under-qualified depressive in a plaid suit.

As I watched Jill concentrating hard on her notes I couldn't help but feel sorry for her. I debated telling her not to worry because it really didn't matter and that, no matter what, I would appreciate how hard she was trying. But the honest truth was that it *did* matter and saying I was proud of her would prove to be hollow if we ended up having to move.

I had finished my toast and was making a face out of the crumbs when there was a knock at the door.

"That will be Ruby," I said.

Jill looked up from her notes. "Have fun at school," she said distantly.

I got up and went towards her. "You too... I mean, I hope it goes well."

"Thanks."

I wasn't sure what else to say so I just gave her a quick hug and left.

Jill's interview was at eleven fifteen, smack-bang in the middle of our Drama lesson. We were meant to be creating scenes in which a conflict arises between two characters but, instead, Ruby was consoling me in the corner of the room.

"I feel awful," I wailed. "I can't breathe."

"Yes you can," Ruby replied. "Just open your mouth."

I panted heavily as she held my hand. "My life is over!"

Ruby bit her lip. "Not yet. Jill might get the job."

"She's wearing a plaid suit. And she doesn't smile enough."

Ruby opened her mouth to protest but thought better of it.

We sat staring helplessly at one another until, without warning, Miss Waddle got our attention. "You've had enough time!" she barked at the class. "Come and sit down."

Ruby and I exchanged uneasy glances and headed to the back of the room. In an attempt to look inconspicuous, we tucked ourselves behind Rupert Crisp who has undergone a recent growth spurt.

Unfortunately, Rupert turned and beamed at me. "Greetings, Livi! And how's my editorially enlightened friend?"

I faked a smile and nodded apologetically towards Miss Waddle, as if to indicate that I would have loved to stop and chat if it wasn't for our teacher speaking.

"Got it!" Rupert shot me a knowing wink as he turned back to listen to Miss Waddle.

"Conflict!" she was exclaiming. "It is the heart of all good drama. I'm looking for passion and I hope I won't be disappointed. Now, who should go first?" My heart sunk as her beady eyes roamed across the room and finally came to rest on me. "Livi and Ruby."

As we got to our feet, I whispered quickly to Ruby, "Pretend you lost something of mine."

She clutched my arm. "Lost what?"

"Anything! It doesn't matter."

"Okay."

We stood in front of our classmates, their gaze a mixture of scorn (at our misfortune) and fear (for their own inevitable fate), and I felt the familiar rise in heart rate as we summoned up the courage to begin performing. I looked at Ruby and nodded.

She fiddled with her top and said clumsily, "I am sorry."

I coughed and tried to sound natural. "Why are you sorry?"

"I lost your pencil," she replied robotically.

"WHAT?" I shrieked, clutching my chest theatrically.

"Your pencil," Ruby repeated. "I lost it."

"How did you lose it?" I yelled.

"Er..." Ruby blushed as she improvised wildly, "It fell out of my pencil case."

I left a dramatic pause in which I took a deep breath and swayed a little. Then I turned suddenly and let out a roar. Ruby gaped at me as I shook her by the shoulders and screamed at the top of my lungs, "Why?! Why all this testing? I'm close to the edge here and I can't take any more!"

Ruby stumbled back as I let go of her. "I'm sorry..."

"It doesn't matter. It's too late now." I finished with a heavy sigh, my lips quivering slightly as a tear rolled down my cheek. I looked down and let out a long breath. I felt it was the rawest piece of acting I (or *anybody* for that matter) had ever achieved. I anticipated a standing ovation, a hushed gasp, or at the very least some polite applause.

But Miss Waddle just looked up from her desk with a half-hearted grunt and said, "Okay. Who's next?"

Kitty and Molly got up and began their scene as though nothing had happened.

I returned to my place at the back of the room and sunk to the floor, shaking as I wrapped my arms round myself.

"Wow," Ruby whispered as she sat beside me. "That was mental."

I looked at her in dismay. "You mean *good* mental?"

"Of course. Really good. Just kind of extreme."

Rupert turned and gawped at me. "I am stupefied!" he said breathily. His glasses looked a little steamed up.

I didn't ask him what he meant by this. I just closed my eyes and put my head in my lap. I muttered a silent prayer and willed myself not to cry as I wondered how Jill's interview was going.

As the rest of our classmates performed their scenes I slipped into a daydream in which a visiting film director burst suddenly into the Drama studio after spotting me through the window.

'You!' he would say. *'How would you like to be in a film?'*

'Who, me?' I would gasp.

'Yes, you! There's something mysterious about you. You have a depth in the eyes that can only come from a wounded heart. Have you ever felt abandoned?'

'Actually, yes,' I would reply. *'My mum died when I was a baby and my dad isn't really around.'*

'I knew it!' he would exclaim before offering me the lead role in a contemporary adaptation of *Bambi*.

I was brought back to reality by the sound of Miss Waddle scraping her chair against the floor. She got up and paced backwards and forwards as she harked on about the lack of energy in our scenes. "If I'd wanted wooden performances, I'd have gone to a puppet show!" She glared at us before demanding, "Did you all notice the passion that Kitty had in hers?" She pointed to Kitty as though she were a prized courgette at a vegetable-growing contest.

Kitty gave a smug beam and simpered, "I thought I'd messed it up. I wasn't really concentrating."

"Not at all!" Miss Waddle trilled. "You were exceptional today. I hope everybody learnt something."

I sniffed and looked away, feeling like an overlooked turnip. I decided that, if Jill and I did have to move away, I would leave Miss Waddle an anonymous note telling her that when I'm a famous writer I'll write a story about a terrible monster and name it after her.

As we broke for lunch, I sent Jill a quick text. *'Did you get it?'*

A short while later she replied, *'Don't know yet.'*

I bit my lip and wrote, *'Do you think you'll get it?'*

'Don't know.'

I growled and shoved my phone back in my bag.

"She probably won't know for a while," Ruby said. "They'll have to interview all the other people and then talk about who they liked."

"Maybe we could pray that nobody else turns up," I suggested. "Or that they're all rubbish."

Ruby nodded slowly. "Maybe."

I put my head in my hands.

Ruby gave me a gentle pat. "It will be okay."

"Says who?"

She shrugged. "God."

I stared at her. "Did God tell you Jill would get the job?"

"Well, no. But everything's always okay in the end. So, if things aren't okay... then it's not the end."

I groaned and put my head back down. "Not good enough," I muttered into the table.

I checked my phone all afternoon in case Jill had texted me. Twice I almost got my phone confiscated. I ended up excusing myself by saying I was waiting to hear news about a dying relative. My teachers cut me some slack after that[54] but, having recently got a

---

[54] Miss Dalton even said I could go outside and make a call if I needed to. I took the opportunity to go to the library and check Jill's FriendWeb status but she hadn't posted any updates.

lot better at telling the truth, the freedom soon gave way to a huge overload of guilt.

I felt like a simmering kettle as Ruby and I walked home from school. By this I mean that everything in me was boiling with rage and steam was pretty much coming out of my ears.

Ruby jumped as I performed a perfect *Ballistic Bull* impression under my breath.

"Jill must know by now!" I cried, almost walking into a puddle as I shook my phone in frustration. "She's probably already gone to Aunt Claudia's!"

"Shall we pray again?" Ruby whispered.

I let out a growl. "What's the point? It's done now, isn't it?"

Ruby blushed and said nothing.

I tried to call Jill but she didn't answer so I gave a moan and whacked my phone against a lamppost. "Oh rubbish!" I yelled. "I've cracked the screen." Ruby shot me a sympathetic smile but kept silent as I complained all the way home. "This is so annoying... Life sucks... I hope Jill realises how depressed I feel... I bet God doesn't even care..."

As we reached our street, Ruby asked, "Are you sure you don't want to pray one last time?"

I gave a heavy sigh and ushered her into my house.

Jill wasn't around so we went straight up to my room and closed the door firmly behind us.

"This is it," I said.

Ruby made a nest with my pillows as she curled up on my bed. I sat down and stared at her, hoping she would take the lead.

To my disappointment, she said, "You start."

"I don't know what to say!"

"Just tell God how you're feeling. Imagine Jesus is sat right there." Ruby pointed to the end of my bed.

I gazed at the empty space beside me. "Can I use something to pretend?"

"Like what?"

I grabbed Sausage-Legs and perched him on the end of the bed. "Him?"

"Er..." Ruby gave me a baffled look. "I don't think you should do that every time. It might be classed as idol worship..." She regarded my crestfallen face and added, "But just this once is probably fine..."

I turned to Sausage-Legs. "Okay, hi Jesus."

Ruby stifled a giggle. "Sorry," she whispered as I pouted at her. "Carry on."

"I don't want to leave Leeds," I continued to my teddy. "And you're the only one who can help."

Ruby let out a splutter. "Sorry!" She covered her mouth with her hands and started to shake.

I sighed. "Jesus, please help Jill get this job. I want us to stay in Leeds. I like it here. I don't want to leave."

I turned to Ruby. She stopped laughing and let out a sob instead.

"I don't want you to leave either!" she exclaimed. She leant across me and pleaded with Sausage-Legs, "Please, please, please, Jesus. Please let Livi stay. She's my best friend and I don't know what I'll do without her!"

We looked at one another and burst into tears.

"You're my best friend," she blubbered.

"You're my *only* friend," I whimpered back.

We clung to one another and sobbed.

Suddenly, Jill burst in with a huge grin on her face.

"Hey!" I hastily wiped my eyes. "We're having a private conversation."

Jill ignored me. "I got the job!"

I leapt up. "Seriously?"

"They just called and said I was brilliant. I start on Monday."

I let out a shriek. "So we're staying in Leeds?"

She grinned and nodded.

I threw myself onto her and hugged her.

Ruby giggled. "That's so cool. We were just praying for that."

I glanced quickly at Jill.

"God answered our prayer," Ruby added with a beam.

Jill laughed. "Or maybe I was just brilliant."

Ruby shrugged. "Maybe."

"No!" I gave Jill a firm look. "God did it. We prayed and he did it." I figured now was a good time to stop being scared of offending Jill. He'd helped her get a job, after all. Surely she'd believe in him now? I retrieved the flyer Mark had given me weeks ago and stood in front of Jill. Then I cleared my throat and began to read it aloud. *"Repent and be saved. Do you ever feel like you are lost? Do you ever feel like a sheep without a shepherd? Do you know that you cannot enter Heaven unless you are born again—?"*

"Er, Livi," Jill interrupted. "What are you doing?"

"I'm just reading this flyer. It gets better in a bit..."

She raised her eyebrows. "Well, maybe save it for another time?"

"It's really important."

"I came in to tell you about my job. If I ever want a preach, I'll ask for one."

"But you never do ask," I muttered.

Jill looked slightly irritated. "Anyway, back to *my job*. I thought we could go out for a meal to celebrate. You're welcome to come, Ruby." She smiled and left the room.

I turned to Ruby and let out a squeal.

She grabbed me by the arm and bounced up and down. "You're staying in Leeds!" she sang triumphantly. "I'm so happy!"

I gave a cry of delight. Then I swung Sausage-Legs round the room by his ear and closed my eyes. *Thank you, Jesus.*

~ 22 ~

God does not have favourites

Aunt Claudia phoned just as we were heading out of the door.

"Don't tell me," she drawled as soon as I answered. "They didn't like the suit."

I gave a scoff as I exclaimed, "Jill got the job!"

"Oh!" She didn't even try to hide the surprise in her voice. "Did the other candidates drop out?"

Jill and Ruby looked over from the doorway.

"Who is it?" Jill asked.

"It's Aunt Claudia," I whispered. "Do you want to speak to her?"

She shook her head. "Just tell her I got the job."

"I did. She asked whether the other candidates dropped out."

"Nice to know she had confidence in me," Jill muttered.

"We're going out for dinner," I told Aunt Claudia, interrupting just before she could begin a discourse on the dangers of accepting a job that nobody else wants. I hung up the phone and grabbed my coat, grinning from ear to ear as I skipped out of the house.

"She didn't think I would get it, did she?" Jill snapped as she fumbled for her car keys.

"It doesn't matter," I said cheerfully. "What matters is we're staying in Leeds."

Jill sighed.

"We're staying in Leeds!" I repeated. "That's great, isn't it?"

"Yes, it's great," Jill insisted, although she didn't look completely convinced.

I shot Ruby a baffled glance.

"Maybe you shouldn't have repeated what your aunt said," she whispered.

I gave a sheepish shrug as I considered Jill's crestfallen face. I tried to think of something helpful to say but all that came out was, "Don't worry... Aunt Claudia smells like a cat."

Jill rolled her eyes and said glumly, "Let's go and celebrate."

Before we could get into the car we heard a loud squeal from across the street. Belinda had emerged from her house and was waving like a maniac as she dashed towards us. It seemed Aunt Claudia's lack of enthusiasm was about to be countered by zeal on a giant scale.

"Jill," Belinda began gingerly. "I had to come over to ask... How did the interview go?"

Jill gave a timid nod. "I got the job."

Belinda gasped before letting out a shriek and taking Jill's face in her hands. "Oh Jill! I'm so pleased for you!" she exclaimed, plonking a huge kiss on the top of Jill's head. Jill broke free and forced a little smile as Belinda let out a long dramatic sigh. "I had every faith that you would get it. Every faith."

Jill blushed. "Thanks."

"We're going out for dinner," Ruby told her mother.

"Noodle Head!" I added.

Belinda looked at me in confusion.

"The new Chinese," Jill explained.

"What a lovely idea!" Belinda said. "I'll tell Stanley."

Before Jill could clarify that she had not intended to issue an invitation, Belinda scuttled off to gather the rest of her family.

I suppressed a giggle and said, "The more the merrier."

From the look on Jill's face I was fairly sure she wanted to swear. But she just shot Ruby a well-mannered smile and said, "Absolutely."

It turned out that the day was not only a momentous occasion for me and Jill. Violet's life had also been significantly altered by the acquisition of a pair of painful-looking orthodontic braces. Whilst it could be hoped that this would have encouraged her to feel self-conscious and withdrawn, it appeared to have had the opposite effect. She arrived at Jill's celebratory meal full of energy and grinning like a robot.

"That's right! I'm a Metal Mouth!" she said, invading Jill's personal space in case she wanted a closer look.

My sister nodded politely. "They look great."

Violet gave another dazzling grin and handed Jill a hastily wrapped bar of soap. "Congratulations on your job!"

"Thanks." Jill unwrapped the soap and gave it a little sniff before adding, "This smells very interesting."

"Gorgonzola," Violet said proudly.

Jill blinked at her and set it down beside the menu.[55]

I attempted to take a seat as far from Violet as possible. I also wanted to avoid Oscar who tends to throw his food when he gets excited but, in my haste to get a good seat, I tripped over and whacked my head against the wall.

"Goodness, Livi!" Belinda exclaimed.

"I'm fine," I muttered as everyone stared at me. I got to my feet and forced a smile.

"A suicide bid after I've worked so hard to keep us in Leeds! Well there's gratitude for you!" Jill chuckled as she helped me into a seat.

At this, Violet let out a loud roar of laughter and promptly sat down beside me.

I ignored her crazed grin by burying my head in the menu and murmuring, "Mmm, noodles."

Ruby took the seat on the other side of me and did her best to make me feel better by saying, "The floor is kind of slippery, isn't it?"

I let out a snort. "Kind of."

One of the waitresses came over to read us a list of specials. It took her ages because Violet interrupted after every dish to enquire loudly, "Will it hurt my teeth?"

Halfway through, Oscar started asking, "Does it have bananas in it?"

The waitress looked up from her list. "Bananas?"

"I'm allergic to bananas!" Oscar cried. "Start the list again."

"There won't be banana in any of the meals," Stanley told him.

Oscar gave the waitress a menacing stare. "Is that true?"

The waitress blushed as she said, "Well, there are bananas in the banana fritters…"

Oscar let out a squeal and turned to his father. "Bananas!"

"I'll start again," the waitress said quickly.

She turned back to her list but, before she could continue, Ruby put up her hand and said, "Excuse me? If you have any bananas in the kitchen, I'd like the stickers."

---

[55] It blended in with a yellow pot of toothpicks leading Jill to accidentally-on-purpose leave it there.

At this, Oscar went purple and started banging his head on the table. Belinda tried to calm him down but Oscar put his hands over his ears and shrieked, "I'm too young to die!"

The waitress stared at us all in shock. Eventually, she offered to take Oscar to discuss his concerns with the chef. Oscar gave a great sniff, got down from his chair, and followed Belinda and the waitress into the kitchen.

In the silence that followed, Violet and Ruby started laughing and Stanley said, "Oh dear!"

I stole a glance at Jill. She was wearing her 'peeved-but-pretending-to-be-fine' face. I hoped she wasn't debating turning her new job down.

Ten minutes later Oscar emerged from the kitchen with an approving nod and we were finally able to order.

"Everybody okay now?" the waitress asked nervously. She took down our order as quickly as possible and fled to the kitchen.

Belinda gave a contented sigh. "Well, isn't this lovely?"

Jill responded with an overly enthusiastic beam. "Lovely!"

I smiled to myself and took a moment to appreciate the great miracle of the day. *Jill got the job. We're staying in Leeds. God answered my prayers!*

Ruby was gazing at the ceiling. "The lampshades look like spring rolls!" she said. "Maybe we should do a review for the class newspaper."

"That's a good idea!"

Despite the fact that my own work already made up close to eighty percent of the newspaper, I grabbed the wrapping paper from Violet's soap and a pen from Stanley and started to write. We spent the next few minutes counting the number of chairs and tables and taking note of the restaurant's furnishings.

"Mention Oscar's visit to the kitchen," Ruby said keenly.

I grinned and jotted down, 'Guided tours on request.'

Down the table, Belinda had returned from a visit to the toilets and had begun a hearty critique of the facilities[56] to which Jill was nodding politely and throwing the odd glance in the direction of our waitress, clearly afraid that she might overhear and spit in our food.

For want of something better to do, Ruby and I went to explore the toilets for ourselves. They were rather plain, although there was

---

[56] Apparently not as sparkling as the ones at *Wok Over Here.*

a striking painting of a woman with noodles for brains. We took down some notes for our review before returning to our seats.

When our food arrived, the first thing Oscar did was dig through his noodles with his bare hands, possibly wary of a stray banana hiding underneath. I hoped Belinda would notice and tell him off. I was scared he might start throwing things.

But Belinda was busy grilling Jill on her new job. "What exactly does a press officer do?"

"I'll be dealing with press relations for the company," my sister explained.

"I see... And what's the company?"

Jill blushed. *"Colin's Tasty Chicken."*

"Ooh!" Belinda gave an animated nod. "The famous eatery?"

"No," Jill said awkwardly. "That's *Captain Barry's Chicken.*"

Belinda looked confused. "And which one's yours?"

"Colin's Tasty Chicken."

Belinda thought for a moment. "Oh, the one..." She stopped short of saying, *'The one who was on the local news for repeated outbreaks of food poisoning,'* and kept nodding instead.

Beside me, Violet was beginning to sound like her usual self as she sucked miserably on her noodles. "This is a plate full of woe!" she sobbed. "I feel like Job." Then, quite possibly for Jill's benefit, she added loudly, "Job lost everything good in his life but he remained faithful to God."

Fortunately Jill didn't hear. She was far too busy struggling through Belinda's interrogation.

Violet turned to me instead. "How straight are *your* teeth, Livi?"

I ignored her question but tried to be kind as I said, "I'm sorry your braces are hurting."

"Thanks." She gave me a quick smile. "I bet you're glad you're staying in Leeds?"

"Yeah, it's great!" I said. "We prayed and God answered! Jesus is amazing!"

Violet raised an eyebrow. "I hope you'll show that same level of devotion if, one day, God does not answer your prayers in the way you'd like." She gave me a pointed look, as if warning me not to get above my station.

I scowled at her. "Obviously."

Violet sniffed before enquiring, "How are you getting on with your Bible reading?"

"Fine."

"What are you reading at the moment?"

I frowned. "I like the Psalms, actually."

Violet nodded approvingly and sucked on another noodle. "Which ones in particular?"

I opened my mouth and then closed it again, feeling my cheeks grow hot. "I can't remember."

Violet sighed in disappointment and said nothing.

I looked down and spun my noodles angrily with my fork. Trust Violet to ruin my good mood by reminding me I was still so far from perfection.

Ruby gave me a little nudge. "Are you okay?"

"Have *you* read the Bible recently?" I muttered.

She gave a bashful shrug. "I try to read a bit each morning."

I rolled my eyes. "Well I'm just not good enough yet." Ruby went to say something but I went on, "Actually, Violet's right. If God hadn't answered my prayer I'd be really angry with him right now. I'd probably have lost my faith altogether. I'm a rubbish Christian."

"You're not a rubbish Christian!"

"Well I'm not a very *good* one. I haven't read the whole Bible and I still make mistakes."

"Everyone makes mistakes," Ruby insisted.

I shrugged and looked away.

Stanley, who it appeared had been listening all this time, leant across the table and whispered, "When Oscar was a baby, Violet and Ruby staged a protest and wouldn't look at him for days."

Ruby blushed and Violet looked up and hissed, "Dad!"

I looked at them in surprise. "Why?"

Ruby shifted uncomfortably. "One of Dad's uncles died and left us some money in his will. There was fifty pounds so Violet and I thought we would be getting twenty five each but, since Oscar had just been born, we had to split it with him."

"Even though he'd never met Uncle Bert," Violet snapped.

At this, Oscar looked up from across the table and said, "Who?"

Stanley chuckled. "You see, even though he'd done nothing to earn it, Oscar was immediately entitled to all the rights of the rest of the family." He gave me a wink but I just looked at him in bewilderment. I wasn't sure I understood. "A newborn baby is as much a member of the family as two fully-fledged adolescents," Stanley continued. And then, to spell it out for me, he added, "God does not have favourites."

My heart lurched and a cross between a sob and a giggle erupted inside me.

Violet looked from me to her father, as though unsure if she had just been slighted.

Before I could reply, Stanley put a hand up and said, "Just think about it."

I nodded and turned back to my food.

'A newborn baby is as much a member of the family as two fully-fledged adolescents... God does not have favourites.' I chewed this over before asking Stanley, "So it's alright that I don't read the Bible?"

"It doesn't change your worth," he assured me. "Or your place in God's family."

"You should do it though!" Violet insisted, an affronted look etched across her face. "You can't stay a baby forever!"

"It's alright, Violet," said Stanley. "You don't have to earn *your* place either."

She rolled her eyes. "I know!"

I gave her a smirk and looked back down. Just knowing I didn't *have* to read the Bible kind of made me want to start doing it more. I made a mental note to begin as soon as I got home.

At that moment, we were interrupted by a throng of waitresses coming over with a cake and singing, *'Happy Birthday.'* It transpired that Belinda had asked them for a little treat to mark the occasion but they had misunderstood. They had also misread Belinda's hasty scrawl and made their address to *'Jiff.'* Nevertheless, Jill accepted the sparkler-laden cake and bright yellow noodle-covered party hat with a good-natured smile and proceeded to wear the hat for the rest of the evening.

The meal was drawing to an end when Belinda suddenly tapped her glass with her fork and got to her feet. "I feel like I should say a few words," she said as she gave Jill a pat on the head. "Jill and Livi, ever since you arrived on our street, the Lord has given me a great love for you both. You are such beautiful and inspiring young ladies and I have loved every moment of getting to know you. I can't say how overjoyed I am that you're staying in Leeds!" She sat back down and shot Jill a beam.

Jill stared at her.

The whole family grinned expectantly, waiting to hear Jill's response.

To spare her any embarrassment, I jumped to my feet and said, "I want to thank everybody for a lovely evening. And I want to say

I'm very proud of Jill for getting this job and for being a wonderful sister."

Jill looked stunned. After a long pause, she arose and said, "Thank you, Livi. And thank you everyone else for sharing this meal with us... and for being such friendly and supportive neighbours."

"Oh Jill!" Belinda looked like she was about to cry. "What a kind thing to say!"

Jill gave her a quick smile and sat back down.

I decided to take advantage of Jill's good mood (and the fact that we had company) by asking casually, "Oh, by the way, can I get baptised?"

Jill exhaled slowly and for one dangerous moment I thought she was going to explode. Instead she shrugged and said, "If you want."

My jaw dropped open. "Really?"

She shrugged again. "Whatever makes you happy."

I let out a giggle and nudged at Ruby. She gave me a thumbs-up.

"How lovely!" Belinda said with a beam. "You'll enjoy it, Jill, I promise."

Jill looked at her in horror. It clearly hadn't occurred to her that she would be expected to come and watch. "Alright..." she said finally. She flicked the menu. "Does anybody want dessert?"

I took a deep breath before suggesting with a grin, "Banana fritters?"

Oscar looked up in dismay. "Livi Starling! Sometimes you're so silly!"

"Maybe," I replied. "Good job God doesn't have favourites."

~ 23 ~

And the winner is...

There are few things more exciting than a school trip; especially a non-uniform school trip centred on *me*— or at least a class newspaper edited by me.

It was a cool, crisp Wednesday afternoon and we were missing double Maths as we travelled to the awards ceremony in Hull. The school bus was being driven by Mr Bradley, the teaching assistant from Miss Appleby's Art class. I had been careful to give his clogs an approving grin when I got on the bus. Unfortunately, he had given me a rather terse smile in return and Ruby informed me afterwards that it had looked as though I was jeering.

Mrs Tilly was navigating in the passenger seat. Her map reading skills left much to be desired and we found ourselves passing the same petrol station at least three times. Initially, I was afraid that I would bump into my father and kept my eyes peeled for a crayon factory. But, as we drove through the centre of Hull, I realised it was a large place and it was quite unlikely that my father would randomly be attending the community hall where the awards ceremony was being held. Nonetheless, just thinking about him unearthed a familiar angry sensation in my chest and I had to fight hard to put him out of my mind.

In my lap were several copies of *The Traffic Light*. We had also sent one ahead to the judges and I spent most of the journey daydreaming about their enamoured response. I was very pleased with the end result, despite having to abandon the advice column due to a lack of response. Ruby had tried to make me feel better by sneaking in a handful of pretend letters[57] but I recognised her

---

[57] Including one from someone named *'Confused and desperate'* who had a problem tying their shoelaces.

handwriting. She had also stuck a banana sticker over a spelling mistake.

I kept an eye on the time as we drove round and round. Once or twice I debated calling down to Mrs Tilly just to make sure she knew what she was doing. But she and Mr Bradley sounded a little irate as they quibbled over whether 'first left' meant the *immediate left* or the more *prominent left* beyond it.

Most of our classmates seemed to think the whole thing was hilarious. I even heard Wayne Purdy say, "How funny would it be if we broke down?"

I scowled at him and looked helplessly at Ruby.

She shrugged and said, "It'll be fine."

I didn't care much for her casual optimism and whispered an anxious prayer under my breath, "Please help us get there, Jesus..." I shut my eyes and willed God to send an angel to bump Mr Bradley out of the way and take the wheel.

It wasn't quite what I had in mind but, at that moment, Rupert Crisp started calling out directions with the use of the satellite navigation system on his phone. "Take a sharp left, Sir. Proceed for five hundred yards with a speed limit of 30..."

Mrs Tilly threw her map down and the class groaned and called Rupert a geek.

"Oh, you may mock me," Rupert said. "But any man is a fool who does not know where he's going!"

"We know where we're going," Mr Bradley retorted. "We just don't know where we *are*."

I bit my lip and prayed that Rupert wouldn't withdraw his help as the class erupted in laughter.

Finally, and despite much distraction from our classmates, Rupert was able to direct Mr Bradley to the place we needed to be. We pulled into the car park just as the ceremony was due to begin. I let out a huge sigh of relief and jumped off the bus as quickly as possible, afraid that the award would go to somebody else if we were late. Without waiting for the rest of my classmates, I sprinted across the car park and entered the building.

I was greeted by a beaming middle-aged lady who welcomed me with the words, "Good afternoon! We have—"

"I'm here for the newspaper awards!" I said breathlessly, interrupting before she could waste time with whatever she was going to say.

She raised her eyebrows and said, "Great. What school are you from?"

"Hare Valley, Leeds. Has it started yet?" I tried to look beyond her into the hall but she was rather large.

"Not quite." She indicated a table laden with food. "Do you want some—?"

"There's no time," I insisted, pushing past her and running into the hall.

The room was pretty packed out and full of eager chatter. Schools were assembled in their separate tribes and I felt rather self-conscious as I wandered alone down the aisle in search of an empty row. Every now and then somebody gave me a quick look up and down before turning back to their classmates. I wished I'd dressed a little smarter, perhaps in Jill's plaid suit or with a badge marked 'Editor.' I found an empty block of seats near the front and sat down. A few girls from a nearby school turned to stare and I felt quite awkward sitting by myself so I pulled my phone out of my bag and pretended to be engrossed in a text message.

My classmates joined me several minutes later, having stopped to grab biscuits and cakes at the door.

Ruby sat beside me. "Thanks for saving everyone seats, Livi."

"No problem." I eyed her stack of chocolate biscuits.

On the other side of me, Annie Button was cramming a whole donut into her mouth. I watched out of the corner of my eye as jam dribbled down her chin.

"They had a bowl of bananas," Ruby said, grinning as she showed me a handful of banana stickers.

I gave an absentminded nod and checked the time on my phone. "When are they going to start?" I moaned. "I could have eaten a whole packet of biscuits by now!"

Ruby nodded before saying, "Oh! Do you want one?" She held out her stash.

I took a couple and muttered, "Thanks."

"You also missed the programmes." Ruby whipped a shiny brochure out of her pocket.

"Oh!" I grabbed it from her and thumbed through it.

I located our school's page where there was a photocopy of the front cover of our newspaper, accompanied by the words, 'The Traffic Light. Edited by Livid Starling.'

My jaw dropped open. "They spelled my name wrong!"

Ruby peered over to stare. "How?"

I stabbed my name furiously. "Look!"

Ruby looked again. "Oh yeah! Hey, that's weird, isn't it?"

I gave a growl and flung the programme onto the floor.

It seemed Kitty and her gang had also discovered the error because, at that moment, a loud shriek erupted a few seats away and I heard Molly cackle, "Ooh, look! Livi's livid!"

I grunted and made a mental note to correct the judges when I got onstage.

Finally, the large lady who had met us at the door made her way down the aisle and took to the stage. It turned out she was one of the judges. I bit my lip, grateful that voting was over and that my impatient greeting couldn't be counted against me.

"Good afternoon everybody!" she said, beaming as the last few snippets of conversation died down. "Welcome to the fifth annual *'Scribes of Yorkshire'* competition. I have to say it is simply marvellous to have so many schools taking part..." She introduced her fellow judges, who were sitting in a row at the side of the stage, before waffling on for several minutes about community spirit, the joys of learning and the difficult job they had had in choosing a winner.

I tried to nod and smile along but the anticipation was almost too much to bear.

After that, we had to watch a short film about the history of the written word and the hidden wonders behind the scenes of the publishing industry. It certainly whet my appetite for my future career as a writer but I wished they would just get on with the prize giving.

When the film finished, the large lady came back onto the stage and said, "Now it's time to announce this year's winners!"

I sat up straight and uttered a hasty prayer. *Please let me win, God...*

Ruby gripped my arm as the runners-up were announced. "Oh, we didn't come third," she said in disappointment. And then, "Oh, we didn't come second."

I rolled my eyes. "We don't want to be third or second. We want to win!"

"They're still getting a prize though," she replied as the school that had come second cheered and approached the stage.

I sniffed. "Second is first loser."

Ruby blushed. "Don't be disappointed if—"

"Shh!" I interrupted. "This is it!"

The runners-up had left the stage and the large lady was looking very excited.

She took a deep breath before exclaiming, "And the winner is..."

I perched on the edge of my seat, ready to gasp in surprise or perhaps even hug Mrs Tilly.

"...St Augustine's of York!"

A cheer erupted on the other side of the room. I sunk down in my seat. Of course, I had practised my gracious loser face but I hadn't expected to have to use it. I gave a careless sniff as the school trotted to the stage to accept their prize. Their paper was called 'Prep Talk' and their editor was a rather horsey-looking girl called Meredith. Unlike us, their school had not authorised a non-uniform day and they looked like a bunch of grapes as they lined up in their bright green blazers and fancy pleated skirts.

Meredith thanked the judges before taking the microphone from the large lady. "I am so thrilled to receive this award on behalf of our school," she said smoothly. "I want to give special commendation to our English teacher, Miss Merry. You have been such an inspiration to us all."

Her classmates nodded and, across the room, I saw Miss Merry sobbing and waving. The man beside her looked more like a royal chauffeur than a teacher. He wasn't wearing clogs, at any rate. I expected he had driven the class to the ceremony in a limousine.

"And, all of you," Meredith went on, giving her classmates a gushing smile. "We could not have done this without every single one of us. You are my life, seriously."

Her classmates applauded her and patted one another on the back.

I exhaled out of my nose as I admitted grudgingly that her acceptance speech was far more polished than mine.

They sat down and the large lady got up once more. "Well done, St Augustine's!" she said before giving the crowd another of her irritating beams. I folded my arms and debated getting up and walking out. But, before I could summon up the courage, she continued unexpectedly, "Before we end, we have one more prize to announce."

I sucked in my cheeks and tried not to look interested.

"I speak for all the judges when I say the standard of writing this year was truly phenomenal." The large lady looked over at her fellow judges and they nodded. "We read so many brilliant pieces of writing and I'm sure your teachers will agree that some of the country's finest future writers are sitting in this room today."

The audience applauded politely.

"We have decided, therefore, to introduce a prize for the student who, in our opinion, has shown great writing potential.

This year, the award goes to Livi Starling from Hare Valley High School in Leeds for her fascinating report on animal impersonations!"

My heart exploded with joy. Ruby nudged me and grinned.

The large lady peered into the crowd. "Come and get your prize, Livi!"

I pretty much sprinted to the stage, totally disregarding the little block of steps as I clambered clumsily onto the platform.

The large lady laughed as I came rolling on beside her. "You must be Livi!"

My cheeks throbbed as I stood to my feet and accepted my certificate and a shiny book of poetry. I gave a quick smile before turning towards the audience.

Ruby was grinning insanely. Some of our classmates looked mildly interested. Kitty and Molly were sneering. I gave them all a wave before grabbing the microphone and saying loudly, "I want to thank everyone who voted for me." I glanced at the judges who were looking a little bemused. I coughed and continued, "And I want to thank my English teacher, Mrs Tilly. She's a real inspiration to me." I squinted into the crowd but I couldn't tell if Mrs Tilly was crying or not. "And, erm, my class. I couldn't have done it without you... especially my best friend, Ruby." I pointed into the audience and Ruby stood up and gave a bashful wave. I paused and wondered what else I ought to say. I couldn't think of anything so I finished my speech with my *Ecstatic Bush Baby* impression and returned to my seat.

Ruby was jumping up and down. "Well done, Livi!"

"Was the *Bush Baby* impression alright?" I whispered. "I've only just perfected that one."

"Oh, is that what it was?" Ruby giggled. "I thought you were just really happy."

"I should probably have thanked Jesus too. But I didn't want to sound silly... I *am* grateful though." I peered at my name on my certificate which, this time, was spelled correctly. "Do you think this means I'll really be a writer one day? Is this God confirming it?"

Ruby grinned. "Could be."

I closed my eyes with a contented sigh as I considered all that God had done for me in the last week. *We were staying in Leeds, Jill had said I could get baptised, and I was pretty much the best young writer in Yorkshire.*

At the front, the large lady was calling the ceremony to an end as she thanked us all for taking part.

I joined in with a final round of applause as she and her fellow judges left the stage, then I got to my feet and said, "That was fun."

On the other side of me, Annie leant over and said, "I liked your bat impression, Livi."

I was about to respond when, beside her, Kitty let out a giggle. "Well done, *Livid*," she sneered. "I bet you're really *livid* about it."

I rolled my eyes. "That doesn't even make sense."

"You think you're so great," Molly chipped in. "Just because you won a stupid prize."

"Not particularly," I said. "I thought I was great already." Before they could reply, I turned on my heels and walked out.

As I entered the foyer, Mrs Tilly came over to congratulate me. "I can hardly believe it," she said dreamily. "To think a few months ago you didn't even know how to read! This really is a testimony to your hard work, Livi."

It didn't feel appropriate to remind her that I had always been able to read. So I just gave a humble nod and stayed silent.

As my classmates gathered at the door I helped myself to a couple of biscuits, making sure to keep myself accessible in case anybody wanted to congratulate me. I hoped that there might even be a publisher lurking about, keen to publish my autobiography. I decided I would call it *'And the Winner is Livi,'* or maybe, in keeping with the theme of animal impressions, *'The Zoo in My Head.'* Unfortunately, no such publisher appeared and, pretty soon, Mrs Tilly was hurrying us all out to the car park.

"If we leave now, we won't get home too late," she insisted.

"Unless it takes as long as it did to get here," Mr Bradley muttered under his breath.

I fanned myself with my certificate one last time before following my classmates out of the building. *Oh well,* I told myself. *I'm sure God will send me a publisher at just the right time.* I marvelled at how much easier life is with a God who knows who you are, where you are and exactly where you're going.

I was about to board the school bus when Rupert Crisp sidled up to me and said, "Livi, many congratulations on your prize. You must be thrilled!"

"Thanks," I replied.

I turned to go but he kept staring at me.

"Are you alright?" I asked, wondering if he wanted to look at my certificate.

Rupert gave a little cough. "We've known each other for many months now, Livi. I wondered whether it was time to take our friendship to the next level."

My stomach lurched. "Excuse me?"

"I'm talking about courtship." He beamed.

I felt myself blushing and quickly checked to make sure nobody was listening. "I'm very flattered," I said. "But I think we should just be friends."

Rupert looked deflated. "I see. *Alterius non sit qui suus esse potest*, hey?"

I raised my eyebrows. "What?"

"It's Latin. *Let no man be another's who can be his own.*"

I forced a smile but didn't reply. If there's one thing I've learnt recently it's that I don't want to be my own. I want to be God's.

~ 24 ~

Whatever makes you happy

It was early on Sunday morning and I was pacing the living room as I psyched myself up for a very public bath. Since the moment that Jill had said I could get baptised I was determined that this day would mark a clear point in my life. This was me saying, *"I really, truly want you, Jesus. No going back."*

As part of that, I had been praying that God would help me become braver about sharing my faith. It bothered me that I felt shy about mentioning Jesus in public or that it made me squirm when Ruby talked too loudly about youth group at school. To try and combat this, a few nights earlier I had created a quick invitation on FriendWeb.

Unfortunately, I hadn't seen Jill come up behind me and, just as I was about to send it to half of my classmates,[58] she started to read it out loud. *"Livi Starling is dead! To celebrate, I am getting baptised this Sunday. I hope you can make it. P.S. You don't need to wear black because I have come alive as a whole new creation! Wear something bright like yellow."*

I'd turned to give her a sheepish smile but she just stared at me.

"I'm being dramatic," I stuttered. "I don't mean that I'm actually dead or that I'm a new breed of animal or anything..."

Jill looked even more bewildered.

"I just mean this is important to me. I hope you understand, even a bit?" I gave her a beseeching stare.

After a moment, she shrugged and said, "Whatever makes you happy."

"It does!" I insisted. I wanted to add that, more than that, it made *God* happy too. But I was worried that if I was too pushy she

---

[58] The half I hoped would be least likely to mock me.

might decide I couldn't get baptised after all. "I was just joking with this," I added, deleting the invitation with a cheery grin in an attempt to prove that becoming a Christian hadn't turned me weird.

Jill had forced a smile and gone off to make a cup of tea.

We hadn't discussed the matter since and, now that the day had arrived, I wondered if I ought to go upstairs and make sure she was awake.

In my hands I held a short speech which Stanley had kindly laminated for me. Summer had said I would be asked to say a few words about why I wanted to get baptised. Since this was my chance to explain things to Jill without her cutting me off I had spent a long time planning what to say. I was shaking with nerves as I practised it over and over. I kept an eye on the time, afraid that Jill had forgotten to set her alarm. I was concerned that if she got up too late she would argue that she didn't have enough time to get ready. But, equally, I didn't want her to feel pestered by me hurrying her up. I supposed I could ask if she wanted a cup of tea under the guise of making breakfast.

I was about to shout up when, to my relief, Jill came down. She was wearing one of her work outfits and looking a little stiff. I gave her a smile.

She didn't return it. Instead she asked, "Do you need to bring anything?"

"Nope!" I said happily.

"You're just going like that?"

"Yup!"

"What about afterwards?"

"Nothing happens afterwards. I get baptised. Then I just sit down again."

"But you'll be soaking wet."

"Oh yeah! I should bring a change of clothes. I didn't think of that."

She rolled her eyes and handed me an empty bag from under the stairs.

At that moment, the phone rang. I tried to grab it before Jill, afraid that it might be Aunt Claudia and we would have to tell her where we were going. But Jill got there before me.

"Hello..." She sucked in her cheeks. "Oh, good morning, Belinda."

I breathed a sigh of relief and listened to Belinda's familiar squawk as she asked whether Jill and I wanted to have a lift in their car since it was big enough for us all to travel together. Jill tried to protest[59] but eventually had to concede that she was awful with directions and had no idea how to get to our church.

"Alright. Thank you, Belinda," she said, rubbing her head as she hung up the phone.

I ran upstairs to grab some clean clothes and a towel.

Ten minutes later we were squeezing into the Ricos' estate, greeted by Violet's metallic grin and her words, "Are you ready to be put to death, Livi?"

I gave her a withering look and glanced at Jill who was looking a little startled.

As we set off, Ruby handed me a card and a chocolate figure wrapped in foil. "It's Moses," she explained.

I looked at the chocolate man and gave an approving nod. "Cool." I put him on my lap and opened the card.

Ruby had drawn a tiny foetus suspended in space by many rainbow-coloured strands. I gulped as I turned to her message. 'Congratulations on your baptism, Livi! I couldn't think of the right words to say but I think the Bible says it better...' A lump formed in my throat as I read on, 'God knit you together in your mother's womb and you are fearfully and wonderfully made. He thinks about you all the time. Read Psalm 139!'

Out of fear that I might start crying, I shoved the card into my pocket and unwrapped the chocolate figure. "Who wants a piece of Moses?" I yelled. I smashed the chocolate man on my lap and handed it round.

Oscar took some and crammed it into his mouth. "Moses tastes nice!" he roared in my ear.

I giggled and offered some to Jill. She shook her head and glanced out of the window. She didn't even tell me off for eating chocolate so early in the morning.

As we drew near to church I started to feel anxious. What if Jill got angry at the frequent mention of Jesus? What if she changed her mind about me being baptised and dragged me out halfway through the service? I half wished she wasn't coming. It was much safer to keep it all to myself.

I absentmindedly flattened the chocolate wrapper in my hands, folding over the edges and twisting it between my fingers. I tilted it to one side. Crushed into a circle with Moses' face sticking out in a crooked manner, it looked a little like a turtle. I instantly thought

---

[59] I expect she wanted her own getaway car.

of Joey since turtles are his favourite animal. I felt a pang of anguish as I hoped our friendship wasn't ruined forever.

We pulled into the car park and Belinda turned in her seat and sang, "We're here!"

Jill looked in confusion at the school building in front of us so I said quickly, "Church is the people, not the building. Don't worry, it's not a cult."

She nodded slowly.

We piled out of the car and headed across the playground. I could see members of the welcome team beaming as we approached the door and I prayed nobody would say anything strange to Jill.

As it happened, they barely had time to greet her because, as soon as we got through the door, Jill grabbed my arm and asked, "Where are the toilets?"

Knowing Jill, I was aware that she probably didn't actually need the toilet. I expected she just wanted to avoid having to talk to anybody. I led her down the corridor towards the toilets and, once there, she took her time in front of the mirror, brushing her hair and blowing her nose.

Eventually she ran out of things to do so I asked, "Are you ready?"

"Yup." She gave me her best *'I'm-totally-in-control-and-not-remotely-intimidated'* face.

We came out of the toilets and almost walked smack bang into Joey.

He caught my eye. "I hear you're getting baptised today?"

"Yeah," I replied. And then, to fill the awkward silence, I added, "I brought a change of clothes."

He nodded.

I couldn't think of anything else to say so I just smiled. He smiled back and turned to walk away.

I took a deep breath and called after him, "Hey, Joey!"

"What?"

"I've got something for you." I retrieved the foil turtle from my pocket.

He looked at me as I held it out.

"It used to have chocolate inside," I said quickly. "So don't lick it. But I made this from the wrapper."

Joey raised an eyebrow as I put the turtle in his hand. It had got rather misshapen in my pocket and he turned it round as he tried to figure out which way up it was meant to be.

"It's a Moses turtle," I explained.

"Thanks," he said.

I gave an uncomfortable shrug.

Neither of us spoke for a moment and, in the silence, my brain began to sing, *'Cashbottom! Cashbottom! You're talking to Joey Cashbottom!'*

I almost started to hum along. Instead, I coughed and said clumsily, "So... do you still want to hang out some time?"

He grinned. "Maybe in the Easter holidays?"

My stomach squirmed. "Sounds fun." I beamed as he walked away and then turned to Jill, who had been lingering beside me the whole time. I expected her to comment on the fact that I had just been talking to a *boy* but she looked rather distracted. "Want to sit down?" I asked.

She nodded and forced a smile.

We entered the main hall where, to my delight and Jill's dismay, Ruby had saved us seats on the front row. I saw my sister grimace as Ruby waved and yelled, "Livi! Jill! We're over here!"

We joined Ruby and her family at the front where Jill sat down as quickly as possible.

I hung my coat over my chair and looked around. To the left of us was the baptismal pool. It was a large wooden bath that had been specially brought it for the occasion. A hose, stretching all the way down the hall, was slowly filling it up with water. I wandered over and dipped my finger in. Out of the corner of my eye I could see Jill watching me and was suddenly struck by how odd it must all seem. For a fleeting moment, I feared that I was making a foolish mistake. *No!* I told myself. *This is what I want.*

I sauntered back to my seat. "The water's a bit cold," I announced. "But I'll endure it for Jesus!"

Ruby giggled but Jill just blinked at me.

As the hall filled up around us I kept turning in my seat to see who else had walked in. I caught eyes with several people from youth group and waved. I wanted to shout, *'I'm getting baptised today!'* but I figured they would find out soon enough.

A short time later Jim, who was leading the meeting, got up to welcome everybody and I took one last look around and grinned.

"Livi, sit still," Jill hissed. "You're in church!"

"It's alright," I whispered. "God doesn't mind."

She gave me a funny look but said nothing.

"...A special welcome if you're here for the first time," Jim was saying. "We hope you enjoy the service. We're going to start with some singing but, if this isn't normal for you, please don't feel any pressure to join in."

The worship band came to the stage and I jumped to my feet. I was determined to sing at the top of my lungs so that Jill would know how much fun church was. She stood up with me and then immediately sat back down.

Belinda leant over and whispered something to her and she nodded quickly in return.

It was a little distracting having her beside me so I closed my eyes in an attempt to concentrate on worshipping God.

During the third song, Stanley got up to dance and I cast Jill a sideways glance, afraid that she might start laughing. But she didn't. She just stared straight ahead.

The worship drew to an end and Eddie came to the front. "We're doing something a bit special today," he said. "It involves a funeral, a birthday and a bath..."

The congregation chuckled, apart from Jill who was eyeing Eddie with the same trepidation usually reserved for the dentist.

Eddie invited me and three others to join him at the front.[60] He went on to explain that baptism represented the washing away of all our sins as we put to death our old selves in return for new life in Jesus. "Being baptised today won't make any of these people a Christian," he added. "They've chosen that already. This is a public way of showing they belong to Jesus."

"Like a wedding," I offered timidly.

"Indeed!" Eddie laughed. "Right then, so this is a funeral, a birthday, a bath *and* a wedding! Talk about multitasking!"

The congregation laughed again.

I stole a glance at Jill. Her *'visiting-the-dentist'* face had been upgraded to *'facing-an-armed-robber-at-midnight.'*

Eddie talked a bit more about baptism before saying, "Let's get on with it! We'll start with Livi."

I felt like jelly as I went to stand beside him.

Eddie smiled at me. "So, Livi, can you tell us a bit about why you want to be baptised today?" He held the microphone towards me.

I coughed and turned to my speech. *"I never really used to think about God,"* I read nervously. *"He didn't seem that important. I was kind of scared of dying because I didn't know what would happen next. But I'm not so scared any more. I'm not*

---

[60] They were Bill, a student called Jasmine and a middle-aged lady.

so scared of life either because, since I started following Jesus, things just kind of make sense..." There was a bit more that I'd planned to say, such as appealing to those who were yet to find Jesus and asking if anybody wanted to make that commitment there and then. But I'd started to choke up so I put my notes down and gave Eddie a helpless shrug.

"Thank you, Livi," he said. "That was great."

The congregation applauded as I got into the baptismal pool. I tried not to shiver as I wobbled into the middle of the tub, feeling really heavy as my clothes filled with water. It was all rather surreal. I didn't want to look at anybody so I just stared at the water as it rippled in front of me.

Eddie held up a little card for me to read before I got dunked.

I took a deep breath and declared, *"I have accepted Jesus Christ as my Lord and Saviour and I have resisted the devil and all his ways!"*

Eddie grinned. "Then it gives us great pleasure to baptise you in the name of the Father, the Son and the Holy Spirit!"

At this, he and Summer held me by the shoulders and submerged me backwards into the pool. The noise from the room was suddenly drowned out by the rush of water hitting my senses. I tried to pray or think of something holy but it all happened so fast and suddenly my head was out of the water again and everybody was cheering.

I climbed out of the pool with a grin and Ruby handed me my towel. I took my change of clothes from Jill and plodded down the hall towards the toilets, feeling a rush of emotion as people applauded and patted me on the shoulder.

I trotted down the corridor and locked myself in the disabled toilet where I peeled my soaking clothes off and dried myself quickly with my towel. I paraded up and down, wearing my towel like a turban as I performed the rest of my speech. *"The choice to follow Jesus is the most important choice you will ever make! If you think it doesn't matter, then that in itself is a choice to reject him. Is there anybody here who wants Jesus? Put your hand up if you want to be saved today!"* I caught sight of my reflection in the mirror and stopped.

Outside, I could hear somebody shuffling about, possibly waiting to use the toilet. So I hurriedly pulled my dry clothes on and kept my imaginary address to a whisper.

When I returned to the main hall the rest of the baptisms were over and Jim had begun preaching. He was talking about God as a perfect Father, a common theme for Jim's preaches. For a brief moment I wondered what my dad was doing. I felt the familiar rush of anger and quickly pushed the thought away. I didn't want to think about anything that would ruin the holiness of this day. I tiptoed down the aisle and took my seat.

Jill gave me a bemused look, as if she couldn't work out whether she was supposed to be proud of me or not. Eventually she whispered, "Well done."

I grinned and turned to listen to Jim but I couldn't take much in. I was far too excited about my baptism. Instead, I entertained myself with wild daydreams about telling thousands of people about Jesus and dunking them in a line like dominoes.

When the service came to an end, Jim blessed us with the words, "May you all spend quality time with your Father this week."

The word 'Father' jarred awfully inside me. I bit my lip and looked at the floor.

As people broke into conversation Jill glanced around the room, looking a little lost. Belinda had hurried off to fulfil her duty on the tea and coffee rota and, for the first time ever, Jill seemed rather alarmed by her absence.

"Do you want a drink?" I asked.

"No." She looked like she wanted to go home. She had already done up her coat and held her bag on her lap as though it were a guard dog.

"Well, wait here for me. There's something I need to do."

I left Jill looking scared as I ran to find Summer. Something was bugging me. I located her by the bookstall and dragged her into a corner. "Summer, I need your help."

"What's up?"

I took a deep breath. "I need to forgive my dad..."

She started to smile.

"But I still don't want to," I confessed.

She took my hand. "That's okay, Livi. Just ask Jesus to help you."

A small tear trickled down my cheek. I wiped it away and whispered, "How?"

"Ask Jesus how he sees your father."

I wrinkled up my nose. I didn't particularly want to think about how Jesus saw my father. I wanted Jesus to hate him, like I did. I felt sick as I said, "Okay." I squeezed my eyes shut and prayed, *God, how do you see my dad?*

199

Almost immediately, an image formed in my mind. I wondered if I was just making it up, but I couldn't shake it away. I looked at Summer in confusion.

"What happened?" she asked.

"I kind of saw a picture in my head." She kept looking at me so I explained, "My dad was on a desert island all alone and looking sort of sad. Jesus was waiting in a rescue boat but he couldn't see him."

Summer nodded. "How do you feel about your dad?"

I took a deep breath. "I want him to get on the boat." I frowned before adding, "I don't want to talk to him though. I don't want to pretend everything's fine!"

"You don't have to," Summer insisted. "A relationship requires two people and maybe you'll never have that with him. Forgiveness is about you and your heart."

"Stepping out of a cage?" I ventured.

"Exactly!" She gave me a gentle smile. "Are you ready to forgive him?"

I nodded. "How do I do it?"

"Do you want to repeat after me?"

I nodded again.

Summer took my hand and whispered, *"Dear God, I choose to forgive my dad. I'm sorry for hating him."*

A lump formed in my throat as I muttered, "Dear God... I choose to forgive my dad... I'm sorry for hating him."

"I can't do it by myself. Please release your forgiveness from your Spirit within me."

"I can't do it by myself. Please release your forgiveness from your Spirit within me."

"Heavenly Father, I reject the lie that you are far away or uninterested in me."

I gulped and repeated Summer's words, squeezing my eyes shut so that I wouldn't cry.

"I accept the truth that you will never leave me or hurt me."

I took a deep breath. "I accept the truth that you will never leave me or hurt me."

"I am lovely and I'm the apple of your eye."

I opened my eyes and shook my head. "I'm not saying that!"

Summer gave me a hug. "You've done really well, Livi. And you *are* lovely."

I pulled away and sniffed. "Okay. Thanks."

Ruby came over. "Are you alright, Livi?"

I wiped my eyes. "Yeah."

"Do you want to talk about anything?"

"Maybe later." I gave Summer a small smile as she walked away. Then I looked across the hall to see what Jill was doing.

She was attempting small talk with Mark who was jabbering wildly as he handed her a flyer.

I grinned at Ruby.

She nodded and said shrewdly. "One bite at a time."

I glanced back, just in time to see Jill frown and walk off. I gave Ruby a timid shrug. "I guess that was more like a nibble."

~ 25 ~

And that is what I am

I'd had no idea how horrible the cage of unforgiveness was until I finally left it. As we walked out of church that morning I felt as though a great weight had been lifted off me. I still felt kind of sad that things weren't as they should have been and Summer was right that my dad and I might never have a proper relationship, but I didn't feel anywhere near as bitter about it. According to Summer, forgiveness often happens in stages. Choosing to make the first step is really important.

I tested myself when I got home by listening to one of the worship CDs Ruby had given me, cranking up the volume on the ones that had previously caused me pain. To my delight, I didn't feel any rising rage at the mention of the word *'Father.'* If anything, I felt sort of free.

After that, I flicked through the Bible in search of as many references to God as my Father as possible.

One verse in particular made my heart leap: *'How great is the love the Father has lavished on us, that we should be called children of God! And that is what we are!'*

I'd heard it before but, for some reason, it seemed to spring to life this time, almost like the words were radiating off the page. I couldn't take my eyes off it. I circled it with a bright red pen and marked it with the date of my baptism. Then I flung myself on my bed and grinned. Everything was falling into place. *How had I ever lived without Jesus? I must have been crazy.*

That evening, I logged onto FriendWeb and re-read the messages my dad had sent me. I thought for a moment before finally replying.

'Dear Dad,

I'm sorry that it's taken me a while to reply to you— I wasn't sure what to say. Recently I have learnt that honesty is really important. So I am going to be honest with you.

1. I've been very angry with you and, whenever I think about you, I feel sad.

2. I don't think you understand me at all.

3. A few months ago I became a Christian and everything is getting better now.

4. I have decided to forgive you.

5. Jesus loves you.

Love from Livi.

P.S. If you still have those crayons, I would like them.'

~*~

I woke up on Monday morning feeling joyful. There were two days of school left until we broke up for Easter and I was looking forward to two weeks of freedom, not to mention the prospect of hanging out with Joey.

I rolled out of bed and landed on my Bible which was still open on the verse I had circled the day before. I straightened out the pages and held it in my lap, determining to start the day with some Bible reading. As I thumbed through it I bit my lip and wondered where to begin. Perhaps I should start from the beginning again. Or maybe I ought to skip all the Old Testament stuff and go straight to the stories about Jesus. Or... I flicked to Revelation... I could see how everything ends. After some serious deliberation, I just jammed my fingers halfway into the book and read one of the Psalms. There was mention of a place called Zion and I felt a pang of shame as I realised I had no idea what it meant.

But, before I could give up in despair, I sensed God's peace as he whispered with a smile, *One bite at a time.*

I grinned and read a bit more. Then I put the Bible down and plonked Sausage-Legs over it. "Guard this with your life!" I told him.

After getting dressed, I danced my way down the stairs and grabbed a handful of toast before heading across the street to Ruby's.

Violet, still in her pyjamas, opened the door with a yawn and said, "You're early."

"Oh! Are you just getting up?" I asked nonchalantly. "I've already done my morning's Bible reading."

Violet sniffed. "I was halfway through mine when you knocked." She gave a terse smile before turning on her heels and running upstairs.

Ruby appeared from the kitchen. "Hi Livi!"

"Hi," I said cheerily.

"How come you're so early?"

"Don't know. I just feel all peaceful since yesterday."

"Since being baptised?"

"Yeah. And, also, I kind of did that stepping out of the cage thing."

"What?"

I shrugged and explained, "I decided to forgive my dad. And it's like he popped right out of here..." I patted my heart. "And God popped straight in!"

Ruby grinned. "Cool!"

I munched on my toast and watched as she hunted for her school bag. On the side table was an Easter card from some people named 'Nooni and Pops.' It had a picture of an empty tomb on the front, emblazoned with the words, 'He is risen!'

Ruby saw me looking at it and said, "That's from our grandparents. We're seeing them on Good Friday."

I nodded politely. Other than Aunt Claudia, I don't really know any older people. I resisted the urge to be envious of Ruby's large and perfect family and asked instead, "Why is it called *Good* Friday if that's when Jesus *died?*"

Ruby sucked in her cheeks. "I don't know."

I thought for a moment as I traced a finger around the picture of the empty tomb. "Oh, I know!" I put the card down. "Because of what happened next."

Ruby's eyes widened. "Oh yeah! Just when everyone thought it was all over, God was waiting to play his trump card."

I nodded and made a mental note: *God has really big sleeves. He knows what he's doing.*

It's an unspoken rule that teachers shouldn't set work on the last week of term. So, when Mrs Tilly announced a surprise composition challenge, the entire class erupted in outrage, several people even breaking down in tears as they exclaimed they'd left their pencil cases at home. After spending ten minutes reminding her how hard we had worked on the class newspaper, she conceded and said we could play hangman instead. The class cheered and Kitty ran to the front to go first.

"It has to be Easter themed," she declared. She proceeded to choose the word 'Tadpoll.'

It took a long time for us to guess it and, when we did, nobody dared tell her that she'd spelled it wrong or that it wasn't quite an Easter word.

Molly went next and did 'Chocolate.'

Then Annie had a go and did 'Egg.'

We played steadfastly for the whole morning and, with it being a double English lesson, we ended up having many turns each. Whenever it was my turn I debated choosing a holy word such as 'Resurrection' or even 'Jesus' but, every time, I chickened out at the last second and did something normal like 'Holidays' or 'Chick' instead. However, I ended up kicking myself for not being braver after Georgina Harris did 'Palm Sunday' and nobody batted an eyelid.

As we broke for lunch I whispered to Ruby, "There are a lot of Easter words that are nothing to do with Jesus, aren't there?"

She frowned. "Yeah. I wanted to do 'Resurrection' or 'Jesus' but I got too scared."

"Me too!" I sighed. "How do we tell people about Jesus without sounding weird?"

"I don't know. I suppose it will always sound a little bit weird."

I wrinkled up my nose. "I wish I was braver."

Ruby nodded and bit into her sandwich. I waited for her to say, 'One bite at a time,' but she didn't. She just shrugged and said, "Me too."

We began the afternoon with Art where Miss Appleby was waiting for us with a cheery smile.

Once we'd taken our seats she declared, "Since you've all worked so hard this term, I have a treat for you!" She shook several huge bags of sweets. "Hangman!"

The class looked at her in bemusement. I think it's fair to say that our enthusiasm for hangman had diminished about halfway into Mrs Tilly's double English lesson, but the bags of sweets were so big that nobody dared protest.

"I'll go first!" Kitty declared, leaping out of her seat and running to the front, her eyes fixed on the sweets the whole time.

She did *'Egg,'* which had featured about five times that day already. In fact, we chanted it in unison before anybody had even guessed a letter.

"Well done!" our teacher said in surprise. "That certainly deserves some sweets."

We grinned at one another as she opened a bag and passed it round.

Melody went next and did *'Chocolate,'* another recurring choice. In one voice we yelled the answer out and, once again, Miss Appleby praised us and opened another bag of sweets.

With every word that was guessed correctly Miss Appleby sent round a new bag of sweets. As exciting as this was to begin with, after the fifteenth bag I found myself unable to concentrate. We had now been playing hangman for three hours straight and the novelty had well and truly worn off.

I willed myself to be brave when it reached my turn and stood with my hand poised over the white board as I tried to figure out how to spell *'Resurrection,'* but then Molly yelled, "Hurry up!" and I shuddered at the idea of ruining the game by picking a word that my classmates might not guess. I bit my lip and opted for the safe option: *'Egg.'*

I was extremely pleased when the lesson came to an end.

"I feel sick," I muttered to Ruby as we followed our classmates down the corridor. "Why did she keep giving us sweets?"

"You didn't have to keep eating them!" she said with a giggle.

"Yes I did! We never get sweets at school!"

Ruby laughed and opened the door to Ms Sorenson's classroom.

I followed her in and saw to my relief that the chairs were arranged in the usual circle.

"Oh good," I whispered. "No more hangman."

The rest of the class seemed equally relieved and, slightly wired from Miss Appleby's sweets, we took our seats and looked expectantly at our teacher.

Ms Sorenson held her famous tin up in the air and said, "This is the last time we will do this."

I wasn't sure whether I was relieved or disappointed. Ms Sorenson's lessons had been fraught with danger but I had grown quite used to communicating to my class via a tin of beans.

"You can say anything you like," Ms Sorenson said as she passed the tin to Connie.

Connie grinned and said, "I'll miss the tin."

Rupert went next and said, "At times it has been tedious. But, overall, a winning formula for social integration. I too will miss the tin."

He passed it to Fran who declared, "I won't miss the tin. It's been annoying." He shot a daring glance at our teacher but she just smiled and said nothing.

Next was Ritchie. "Leeds United are the best."

Some of the boys gave a silent cheer.

He passed it to Wayne who said, "Boobies." Wayne smirked as the class laughed. Then he passed the tin to me.

I clasped the cold tin in my hands and considered what to say. I felt like it needed to be something really good since it would be the very last time. I knew what I *wanted* to say but I wasn't sure I had the nerve. I looked up at Ms Sorenson and she smiled.

I closed my eyes and uttered a quick prayer for boldness. Then I cleared my throat and declared, "I got baptised at the weekend."

My classmates stared at me.

"It's er..." I chewed my lip and looked at the floor. "It's because I'm a Christian and it's sort of a symbol of having new life in Jesus." I went to pass the tin to Ruby and then took it back again. "Oh and, by the way, I should never have said my dad was an actor. I made that up because I wanted to make my life sound more exciting. I'm sorry." I avoided everybody's gaze and handed Ruby the tin.

She blushed as she said, "I'm a Christian too." Then she passed the tin to Annie.

Annie opened her mouth and closed it again. Eventually, she said, "I'm not a Christian but I sometimes go to church with my grandma. I don't understand what it's all about but I like the singing." She shot us a triumphant beam and passed the tin to Kitty.

Kitty looked at her in bewilderment before saying, "I went to a horse show with my mum at the weekend." She attempted a pompous sneer as she passed the tin to Molly.

As the tin made its way round the circle I looked to see if anybody was laughing at me. They weren't. In fact, nobody was paying me any attention at all apart from Annie who was grinning at me. I gave her a small smile in return.

The tin reached Ms Sorenson who took it with a nod and said, "Thank you very much." We tried to look proud of ourselves as she praised us for the growing initiative and confidence we had shown over the last few months. "I hope you've all learnt more about yourselves this term."

We nodded.

"And I hope you've grown in appreciation for one another."

We nodded again.

"Great. Now then, if you can put the chairs back nicely you can have some free time for the rest of the lesson."

We cheered and picked up our chairs.

I followed Ruby to a desk at the side of the room.

"I can't believe I told everyone that I'm a Christian!" I whispered as we sat down.

"I know!" she whispered back. "Me too!"

"Do you think they thought we were silly?"

"Maybe. But it felt good."

"Yeah! What do you think Ms Sorenson thought?"

Ruby shrugged and glanced at our teacher.

I followed her gaze and watched as Ms Sorenson put the tin of beans into her bag. I wondered if she would eat them for her dinner.

"I wish we could tell her about Jesus," I said quietly.

Ruby nodded. "Me too..."

A little while later, the bell rang and Ms Sorenson told us we could go.

"What should we say to her?" I whispered as Ruby and I got to our feet.

Ruby gaped at me. "You mean *now?*"

I paused. "Yeah."

"I don't know!" Ruby spluttered, turning bright red. "I'm scared."

"Okay. Come with me," I said, heading towards the front of the room before I could lose my nerve.

Ruby followed shakily behind me.

As we approached Ms Sorenson's desk, she looked up at us and smiled.

I took a deep breath and blurted out, "Miss, do you believe in God?"

Ms Sorenson raised her eyebrows. "I'm not sure. I think there's probably something out there."

"Yes, there is. Have you ever met Jesus?" Before she could answer, I began to babble, "You need Jesus. He's the only way. You should ask him into your life, Miss."

She gave a bemused chuckle. "Thanks, Livi."

I shrugged and ran out of the room, cheeks burning with shame.

Ruby found me cowering in the toilets.

"That was really brave," she said, sitting down beside me under the paper towels.

"I'm such a loser," I moaned. "She *laughed* at me!"

"She didn't laugh," Ruby insisted. "She just didn't know what to say."

I put my head in my hands. "I just want her to know. I want her to meet Jesus."

Ruby grinned. "You're an evangelist, Livi!" she said with glee.

"No I'm not!" I shot back. I paused. "What's an evangelist?"

"Somebody who tells people about Jesus."

"Oh... That's good, isn't it?"

"It's very good."

I gave a smug smile. "Then, yes," I said. "I am."

~*~

Stop Press!

Father makes appeal for his lost children to come home!

All over the world, children are growing old with no idea that their heavenly Father is looking for them. As a consequence, vast numbers are oblivious to the rich inheritance available to them, some believing that the Father has abandoned them and many others doubting his existence altogether. But the Father declared long ago, "My love for my children is perfect and complete. I know they have many flaws, but I see the glory that I put within them. I would do anything to show them who they truly are."

To demonstrate his love further, he even made the unprecedented decision to send his own Son into the mess to forever pay the price for sin. This, it is said, is the ultimate display of self-sacrifice. No longer is perfection a requirement. A simple 'Yes' will suffice. The implications of such a sacrifice are yet to be fully understood but the Son himself is keen to emphasise that he had YOU on his mind when he did it.

With tears streaming down his face, the Father has made his appeal loud and clear: "I am not angry. I love you. All is forgiven. Come home."

This divine call is for all who are yet to be reconciled with the Father. If this is you, receive the invitation today and come to Jesus exactly as you are. Tell him 'YES!' He will do the rest.

Over and out,

Roving Reporter, Ruby Rico